CW00515935

The Repulse Chronicles
Book Three

The Battle for Europe

by
Chris James

www.chrisjamesauthor.com

Also by Chris James

Science fiction novels:
Repulse: Europe at War 2062–2064
Time Is the Only God
Dystopia Descending
The Repulse Chronicles, Book One: Onslaught
The Repulse Chronicles, Book Two: Invasion
The Repulse Chronicles, Book Four: The Endgame
The Repulse Chronicles, Book Five: The Race against Time

Available as Kindle e-books and paperbacks from Amazon

ISBN: 9798663892810

Chapter 1

General Sir Terry Tidbury stared in growing confusion at the screens on the walls around the War Room. Operators sat beneath large digital maps that glowed with shifting lines of colour. Thousands of silent curves and streaks described the oncoming battle. Muttered queries and explanations darted on the air, but the operators' professionalism did little to ease Terry's disquiet.

"Rescan the diagnostics," he ordered, wishing he had not been so hasty giving his adjutant, Simms, twenty-fours hours' compassionate leave. "There must be some kind of fault. The enemy cannot have made such an obvious tactical error."

A flaxen-haired operator with a tight, nervous voice said: "Sir, the diagnostics show no inaccuracies. The screens are displaying what is actually happening."

Terry shook his head and put his fists on his hips. Fluctuating digital greens and reds hued the operators' hair and faces as the images changed to take account of new data. He spoke, addressing no one in particular: "This is not how you

1

crush your enemy when you have overwhelming superiority in numbers. Something is wrong somewhere. We trust these damn computers too m—"

"Sir?" the operator broke in. "SACEUR is requesting urgent contact."

"In my office," Terry replied. He strode through the open doorway into his small, private room and shut the door behind him. "On the wall-screen," he instructed.

The broad, African-American face of General Joseph E. Jones, Supreme Allied Commander Europe, enlarged over the map of Europe on the furthest wall, his wide jaw set in a grimace. "Are your civil defences ready for what's about to hit them, general?" he asked.

Terry ignored his superior's question and replied: "SACEUR, the enemy is making a fundamental tactical error, and he should be—"

"I don't think so. He's in total control of the battlespace, so he can do whatever he goddamn pleases. Even if that means breaking all the rules. The computers are telling us that we got a real stark choice right now. But I guess it depends on the politicians."

"We cannot reallocate what limited defences our militaries have to civilian concerns, general," Terry insisted.

"I agree. But the politicians have the—"

Jones's face shrank to a thumbnail in the lower righthand corner to be replaced with the red-eyed expression of the English Prime Minister, Dahra Napier. Her drawn face showed how much the stress of the war had inflicted over the preceding four months. "Terry?" she said in apparent distress. "I'm told hundreds of the enemy's flying bombs are about to destroy London and there's nothing we can do. Is that right?"

Terry felt like pointing out that similar waves of the enemy's machines also approached other major European cities, but instead said: "I recommend making no changes to

2

our current deployments. We must let the armies keep the support they have. If we reallocate—"

"But London could be levelled by sunrise," Napier exclaimed, her voice rising further.

"That is very unlikely, PM," he replied with care, fighting to keep the frustration from his own voice. "But yes, London is about to experience something similar to that which the rest of Europe has been enduring since February. I believe it won't be so severe, however."

"Can't you do something?"

"We are ready. But any reallocation would leave our military forces even more exposed. We have to trust the civil defences we have in place." Increased concern honed Terry's senses. He wondered if Napier would order him to reassign his sparse resources and stared into her eyes, willing her not to. He added: "PM, our civil defence units have been training hard for this. I know they are ready and they can and will do their duty."

Her left eyelid flickered and her voice wavered: "What? Yes. All right. Yes, if you think so, Terry. Very well."

Before she could say anything else, Terry leaned forward and dabbed a square of light on the surface of the wall-screen. Napier's face shrank back to a thumbnail. He exhaled with a hiss of relief. The map of Europe that re-emerged on the screen showed the extent of the Caliphate's developing attack. Terry waited for SACEUR to become available, noting comms updates from civil defence units stationed around London.

On the European mainland, regiments of the British Army in southern France and northern Italy stood ready, subordinated to their NATO formations. As he viewed the screen, all of them came under attack. He scanned their regimental designations at each location, recalling the names of the colonels in charge and silently wishing them and their troops luck.

Jones's face enlarged to cover the screen. The American frowned and said: "We've run diagnostics here and everything's working fine—"

"But look," Terry said, "all of the major cities in northern Europe are moments away from material destruction while our military forces are facing far fewer enemy forma—"

"They're facing plenty, general," Jones cautioned. "They're still gonna have to pull back, just as they had to in February and March."

"Only now it's June," Terry said.

"I think I can guess why the enemy waited so long."

"Apart from raping the territory he'd gained up until March?" Terry noted with a raised eyebrow.

Jones replied: "The summer heat. Now his army's gonna be fighting in similar conditions in which they trained."

Terry frowned: "If they're obliged to fight at all. With this volume of autonomous combat aircraft, his warriors can follow behind a screen of hardware and simply enjoy the spoils of conquest."

"One thing at a time, general. His lines have to weaken somewhere, depending on terrain and other conditions. He's not advancing over a goddamn football field, all flat and straight and easy. Somewhere, sometime, we gotta get our troops to kick his warriors' asses."

Terry nodded in agreement and said: "If we could capture just one of those brutes alive, we'd have a potential goldmine of intel."

"That is what we need to aim for. We have to seek unorthodox advantages in this most unorthodox of wars."

"I think we should do this a little surreptitiously, sir," Terry said with caution, aware that Jones was the superior general. "Let's get through this attack first and then we can

4

have quiet words with the other generals and colonels in the NATO high command in a way that won't draw too much political attention."

Jones replied: "Agreed. Good luck over there, general. Looks like it's gonna be a long morning for all of us."

"Long and disagreeable," Terry replied. Jones's face disappeared. Terry turned and left his private office, needing to escape an abrupt sense of claustrophobia. However, when he emerged into the more spacious main War Room, the sense of concern among the operators felt palpable. "What is it?" he asked, glancing at the same flaxen-haired female operator who had spoken earlier.

"Er, sir," she stammered. She nodded towards a large map of London and said: "We are tracking two wings each consisting of two-hundred-and-sixty Blackswans approaching in a pincer—"

"Yes, I can see," Terry broke in, watching the screen as the two formations of enemy ACAs unified their altitudes on final approach to their target. The two pincers began to envelop London. Terry forced his lungs to take in and expel air as he fought to breathe against an overwhelming sense of inevitability.

The operator said: "Five-hundred-and-twenty Blackswans will be carrying twenty-six thousand Spiders, sir. Squonk says that's more than enough to reduce all of London to rubb—"

"That will not happen," Terry broke in. "Squonk? When will civil defence units engage the approaching enemy formations?"

"Eleven, ten, nine, eight—"

"Stop. Estimate percentage of attacking force that will be destroyed."

"The battlespace is currently too dynamic to sustain a resp—"

"Damn you," Terry hissed, punching his right fist into his left palm. "Speculate—at once." A voice inside urged him to control his temper in front of his subordinates, but now it was no longer only mainland Europe that suffered. On this bright morning, England would bleed.

Squonk's gender-neutral voice did not waver in reaction to Terry's outburst. "Enemy forces have been engaged. The only noteworthy variables concern atmospheric conditions and how they will affect ACA flight characteristics. Current atmospheric variables favour the attacking forces. It is unlikely more than thirty-five percent of enemy forces will be destroyed during the attack."

Terry smothered a curse as he fought to bear the crushing weight of frustration.

Chapter 2

Medical Orderly Maria Phillips stared in shock at the burning building in front of her. The heat from the inferno stung her face but she could not think, could not concentrate, could not believe the shrieks of people burning to death that drifted with the intense, repeated whoosh of flames.

She tried to retreat but one of her legs gave way and she stumbled backwards, tumbling down a gentle escarpment away from the pyre. The cooler air accentuated the burning sensation on her face.

Her friend Nabou Faye appeared from nowhere and said: "Maz? Maz? Come on, mate. We've got to help people."

Maria squinted at her.

"Don't worry," Nabou reassured her. "Your eyebrows will grow back, sweetie-pie. Can you get up?"

"Yeah, I think so." Maria said. She pushed her legs up as Nabou pulled. Maria said: "My Squitch's priority filter is all over the place."

"Follow me," Nabou replied. "There's nothing wrong with the tech. We're getting swamped with casualties."

As Maria stumbled over the thick grass away from the burning building, her Squitch overlaid in her vision location dots denoting victims. The colour of each dot varied depending on how badly injured the Squitch estimated the casualty to be: yellow for non-life threatening injuries, orange for injuries that would prove terminal without assistance, and red for the most serious victims. White dots denoted the locations of fatalities.

Nabou said: "We need to get to those blocks of flats on the other side of the green."

"But we've got casualties everywhere."

"Orders. Come on."

"I know." Maria concentrated on following the equipment pack on Nabou's back as its owner jogged over the grass. She touched the straps of her own equipment pack and asked herself when she would be able to use the GenoFluid packs inside and actually help the injured.

"Not much further," Nabou called out.

Maria's chest ached with exhaustion and the tendons in her legs strained to keep her upright and moving at sufficient speed to stay close to Nabou. A pang of envy rippled through her at her friend's lithe body which seemed to have so much greater flexibility than her own. Above her, the growing light of the morning gave the clear sky a hazy, liquid blueness. Black dots dived and climbed and pitched and rolled and yawed while little puffs of grey smoke belied the power of the explosions they concealed.

A masculine voice spoke in her ear: "Defences are being overwhelmed, teams. We're going to have more casualties than we can treat. Squitches will prioritise for all teams."

Maria heard Nabou shout: "Sarge, why were we ordered away from the emergency response centre when it was h—"

Suddenly, the air split in a deafening crack and the ground seemed to drop half a metre before coming back up and hitting Maria hard on her knees. She fell headlong. Time stopped. She grasped the damp turf with her hands and the chilled wetness on her fingers brought her senses back in a sudden rush. Time began again and seemed to accelerate a fraction. "Shit," she hissed. "What happened? Are you all right, mate?"

Two metres ahead, Nabou lay motionless on her front, her head obscured by the equipment pack on her back.

"Mate?" Maria asked, concern rising to mingle with the physical pain of the impact. As she crawled forward, over the growing agony she became aware of new sources of flames pushing heat onto her.

Her Squitch spoke: "You are injured and require medical assistance. Remain still until assistance arrives."

"Diagnosis of Private Faye, now," she instructed.

"Severe impact bruising to the upper thoracic cavity. Private Faye has priority for medical assistance."

Maria lay on the grass and put her hands on her head, a feeling of motion sickness causing sparks to wink and flash in her vision. A sticky moistness she recognised as blood seeped out around the rim of her helmet, and she surmised that shrapnel must have found a path between it and her uniform. She asked the Squitch: "How long until assistance gets here?"

"Uncertain at this time."

"Clarify." Maria wished the Squitch would talk like it had during her medical orderly training. Then, when they were pretending to respond to an enemy attack, the Squitch had given her clear instructions on nearby dangers and casualties, and what she needed to do. Now, it sounded like it didn't know what was happening.

The Squitch said: "The battlespace is too fluid to provide accurate estimates of when assistance will be available."

Maria forced herself up on her hands and knees. She grimaced when a wave of nausea rolled over her, but the sparks in her vision abated. "Overlay casualties now," she demanded, concluding that her injuries made the Squitch deactivate that feature.

The Squitch said: "Confirmed. However, you are injured and should wait for—"

"No!" Maria yelled when in her vision a red indicator blinked over Nabou's inert body, and a countdown resolved giving her friend less than three minutes to live. "Get help for Private Faye, now."

The Squitch's voice didn't waver: "Private Faye's priority will shortly be superseded by the urgency of other casualties."

"Excuse me?" Maria asked at the same instant as she realised what the super AI meant.

"The most effective use of available resources will decide which casualties are ascribed priority."

Maria shouted in frustration. She grasped clumps of cold, damp grass in her hands and pulled herself forward, closer to Nabou. The ground underneath her shifted from left to right, as though she were drunk. When she pushed with her legs, she fell on her front again and new pain in her face burned. The bright summer morning air carried foul and polluted odours, but the chilled dew on the grass helped Maria concentrate through the pain.

"You are injured and should wait for assistance," the Squitch repeated.

"State my injuries."

"Fragments of shrapnel have penetrated several areas of your upper body—"

"Are my injuries mortal?" Maria demanded, struggling to control her breathing from the exertion.

"Negative, provided they are treated within four hours."

"So shut the fuck up now, please."

"Excessive profanity may be reported to your superior officer."

Maria ignored the Squitch's admonition. She strained to hook her right thumb under the strap of her equipment pack. A painful tingling made her grimace. The material of her uniform felt saturated with blood. She leaned to her left, using gravity to make the pack fall onto the grass. In her lens, the countdown above Nabou's inert body dropped below two minutes as the swelling from her friend's tracheobronchial injury increased slowly to block Nabou's throat and subsequently cause suffocation.

Maria called out: "Sarge? Sarge? Golf zero-five in the shit, over?"

But the Squitch answered: "Your squad commander is injured and unable to respond."

"Relay me to an officer then," Maria instructed.

But the Squitch demurred: "Private Phillips, you and Private Faye are scheduled to be assisted as soon as is practical—"

"But Private Faye is going to die before help gets here, isn't she?"

"Affirmative."

"But why?" Maria asked, her voice cracking, her mind questioning how this enemy attack on England could have turned into such a living nightmare.

"Due to the overwhelming number of ca—"

"You are artificial intelligence. You don't know what it is to feel—"

"Irrational human emotions would undoubtedly lead to more deaths, not fewer, as has been proven on numerous occasions in actual battle conditions."

"Please stop talking, then," Maria said. The equipment pack hung on her left arm. She unclipped the clasp and ripped the Velcro flap open. She lay back and paused from the effort, heaving in breath after breath. She wished that the agony would lessen enough for her to be able to try to save her friend.

The Squitch advised her: "Remain still until assistance arrives."

"I told you to shut up."

"You have been hit by numerous shrapnel fragments. Movement risks exacerbating your injuries. Refusal to obey instructions designed to assist you may lead to a court martial."

Maria pulled a GenoFluid pack out of the rucksack. Deadening pain shot along her left arm followed by a numbness that almost paralysed the entire limb. Like forked lightning, more tingling spread out from her spine and down her legs. She craned her head to look towards Nabou and lost the remaining feeling in her left arm.

"Further movement will continue to exacerbate your injuries so that you may die before assistance can arrive," the Squitch clarified. "Remain still until assistance arrives," it repeated.

Maria swore and kicked with her legs to drive her body level with Nabou's. The battle in the bright blue sky above went on: black dots zipping and flashing past at unknown altitudes. Screeches of rent air and the thuds of damaged ACAs hitting the ground came to her ears. The soft grass underneath her vibrated with deadening impacts both near and far.

She pushed again with her legs and called Nabou's name. She reached her friend and tugged Nabou's equipment pack. The Squitch repeated its warning. Maria used a leg to push herself onto her side and laid the GenoFluid pack on Nabou's neck. She cried out. Her skull burned in pain as she fought to force the small battlefield GenoFluid pack around to the front of Nabou's throat.

The countdown dropped to less than thirty seconds.

Numbness spread down Maria's left arm. She felt the warmth of new blood seep out on the back of her neck. The Squitch repeated its instruction for her not to move.

She replied: "Activate the GenoFluid pack on Private Faye's neck. Instruct the bots to—"

The Squitch broke in: "The GenoFluid pack is active. Appropriately configured nanobots are in transit to the injury site."

Maria flopped back flat on the grass and stared at the sky above her, filled with contrails. Paralysis encroached through her limbs like an invading army until she could feel nothing except the warm summer sun on her face. Consciousness fading, she asked: "Will Private Faye live?"

"Affirmative," the Squitch replied.

"Will I?" she asked, but passed out before she could hear the Squitch's response.

Chapter 3

Journalist Geoffrey Kenneth Morrow ran through the streets of London, chest aching and heart pounding with an overwhelming desire to reach his partner Lisa before she gave birth to their child. The lens in his eye gave him only intermittent directions towards St. Bartholomew's hospital. These flashed and shimmered in his vision, passing like bubbles in a glass of champagne, because the local authority's super AI had declined to recognise his journalistic credentials.

There came another explosion from above. The people on both sides of the street all seemed to stop momentarily and stagger as a single entity. He glanced a lump of falling debris before it crashed into the roof of a building on the other side of the street.

"This is a load of bollocks," he muttered aloud.

The morning light grew as ACAs and missiles streaked in every direction, either attempting to cause devastation or to prevent it. Of all the destruction Geoff had witnessed in the four months since the Caliphate invaded Europe, this hurt him the most. As an Englishman, he'd felt concern for those on

15

the mainland, but also a sense of reassurance that such wholesale obliteration could never befall the British Isles. And now, it did. He ran past chunks of rubble and damaged vehicles, his feet crunching on smashed glass. He coughed on the wafts of smoke the wind blew over him.

He rounded a corner and entered the narrow thoroughfare of Giltspur Street. Repeated blinking did not improve the feed in his lens. Frustration burned inside him, madness at the authorities for restricting civilian communications at this hour of highest drama. His inability to contact Lisa or link to the AI managing the bots inside his partner's womb, which should be overseeing and advising the midwife, caused him as much concern as the supersonic battle of ACAs in the sky over London.

The glass from a hundred windows blew out and cascaded down to the road with a whoosh like a powerful wave. Geoff stopped and gripped the nearest palings when the ground shuddered. The people underneath the deluge of falling shards collapsed and did not move. The closest victim lay no more than five metres from Geoff.

"Christ," he muttered, noting half a dozen lines of blood emerging from pieces of glass embedded in his hands. "If I'd been three seconds sooner."

He fought to control his breathing and stared at the bodies that littered the street, people who had been living, breathing individuals mere seconds earlier. One of them twitched, making dust rise from their torn clothes and causing slivers of glass to slide off them. Dismay swept over Geoff because he had no way of helping the person. The victim shook, every fibre in her body tensing as if to explode, and then she became limp. Geoff exhaled in relief at realising it was a death throe.

He let go of the palings and lurched across the road to get away from the building whose windows had been blown out. A series of explosions made loud cracking noises that echoed. Geoff judged these to be in the next street on his left. He gathered his arms close to his chest as the burning sensation from his hands worsened. A sudden breeze carrying the heat of a nearby fire rolled over him and made him grit his teeth. For a moment, he wondered if his clothes would combust, but then just as suddenly the gust passed and the temperature dropped.

He staggered forwards. His lens flashed back into life for an instant and relayed a mass of localised alerts and warnings. His journalistic credentials were supposed to count for something in crises and the local authority should've allowed his and other journalists' lenses to access real-time data. The information fractured and vanished. But the last data he'd received announced that St. Bart's had been targeted.

"No. Please God, no," he muttered.

High in the air, over a tall building on his right, a continuous cascade of black dots descended in a sweeping geometric orderliness. From his left came the hiss of missiles as a handful of contrails streaked towards the enemy machines. Geoff stopped and stared, almost losing his balance when he slipped on some debris. The defending missiles vanished in puffs of murky grey tinged with a green flash, and the attacking machines raced on towards the hospital.

The last thing Lisa had said to him echoed in his ears as a sense of inevitability settled like a blanket thrown over his life. She'd said: "Please, Geoff. You understand, don't you?" in that special tone she had. And he recalled his reply: he'd promised to protect them—both of them.

He broke into a run, overwhelmed by a sudden, irresistible urge to be with them at the end. He darted right into an alleyway that led to the south side of the square around which abutted the three wings of the hospital. Lisa and the baby were on the second floor in the west wing. His mind recoiled in horror when he saw that which he'd seen so many times on the continent: Caliphate Spiders smashed into the roof of the north wing, directly in front of him.

He stopped dead, a deeper sense of self-preservation overriding his burning desire to reach Lisa and their child. An ominous clicking came to his ears. The Spiders crawled over the parapet and descended the façade of the north wing. Some Spiders smashed through the windows and clattered away inside the building. Faint screams emanated through the broken glass.

Geoff stepped backwards, the impassive journalistic observer in him noting that there had to be many more Spiders than required to level the building and that he should retreat.

He felt a wrenching inside him. Then, he turned and fled.

"Please, Geoff. You understand, don't you?" echoed in his memory.

All emotion transferred to energy in his legs as he ran with the longest possible strides. The Spiders detonated and the tarmac in the alleyway juddered. He stumbled and fell. He scuffed his hands and forearms, pushing the chips of broken glass deeper into his flesh, but he rose almost at once and continued running.

Lisa's voice spoke again: "You're a bastard, Geoff Morrow."

He emerged from the alleyway and turned left. Dust billowed out and over him. The whole world shook as though in an earthquake. He crouched and prayed for the violence to stop. When it did, he went back into the alleyway and advanced through the choking dust at a cautious pace. He pulled the breast of his cotton shirt over his mouth in an attempt to filter the dust. The battle overhead seemed more distant, as though the punishment meted out to London's oldest hospital afforded the immediate vicinity a temporary reprieve from further assault.

In his mind's eye, Lisa sneered and repeated: "You're a bastard, Geoff Morrow."

He reached the square. A breeze blew the dust in his face, making him squint. He had to cough a few times to clear his airway. Finer pieces of brick and mortar slid among heavier masonry, glass tinkled as it settled, smashed wooden frames continued to split under pressure, and distant cries and moans floated out from the three pulverised wings of St. Bart's hospital.

Visibility improved and Geoff nodded, recognising the damage. It didn't matter if the buildings were constructed from outdated materials like brick, wood and plaster, or from more modern replicated materials that utilised 3-D ultra-Graphene, the Spiders' explosive power always killed the occupants; if not at once, then before help could reach them. He recalled every mountain of rubble he'd climbed over since that fateful day in February when Alan at *The Guardian* had put Geoff on the payroll and sent him to continental Europe. How many bodies had he witnessed pulled from under glass and dust and splinter? How many more had he helped dig out? And now he had to dig for his own family.

He advanced to what had been the west wing of the hospital. He clambered over large, misshapen chunks of masonry. With a spirit-deadening familiarity, he listened as the debris continued to settle. A newly demolished building was not a static thing. The initial collapse left a mass of lesser motion, of voids that filled, of beams and lintels that, obliged to support weights for which they were not designed, gave way seconds or minutes afterwards.

Geoff stood still, fresh tears running through the dust on his face. Broken glass clinked, heavier dust and fragments of crushed masonry slid in rivulets deeper into the ruins. Metal scraped and screeched and wood split and larger pieces of debris thumped and slid. It seemed the whole mass urged to settle, to rest finally after the violence visited on it. From within came sounds of whimpering and mewling. He leaned forward, grabbed a chunk of half a dozen bricks still covered in render on one side and plaster on the other, and with a mighty heave, threw it towards the bottom of the hill of debris. The energy it cost him and the vastness of the mountain of rubble gave him a feeling of overwhelming inadequacy. It would require the largest and most modern construction replicators to clear this. And they'd require a ridiculous amount of time; Geoff estimated up to several hours.

The noise of a person stumbling behind him came to his ears. He turned around to see a female nurse, looking injured and disorientated. Her foot slid and she lost her balance. Geoff slithered down, stepped gingerly over the debris, and helped her up.

Blood ran from the nurse's head and stained her white jacket. She looked at him with shocked eyes. "What happened?"

"Were you in the east wing?" he asked in disbelief.

"No," she said, casting her eyes downwards, "I... I, we—I was going. My shift had just ended."

"We?"

"My friend. She—" the woman broke off when a piercing shriek sped overhead and a building in the next street exploded and collapsed, sending a deep shudder through the rubble around them. This made the debris on which they stood ripple and they staggered. The woman said: "We should take cover. There's a shelter over th—"

"No," Geoff said.

"Are you quite mad?" she asked, appearing to regain more faculty. "We can't stay here."

20

Geoff nodded his head at what remained of the west wing of the hospital and said: "My partner and our child are in there. I was too late. But I don't want to leave them. Not yet."

"What was the mother's name?"

"Doesn't matter. I'm certain they're dead."

"My lens doesn't work anyway. We should go, truly. This attack isn't over yet."

"It is for this location."

"Oh? You sound so sure."

"I have spent some time on the continent and I know how these attacks pan out."

The woman raised an eyebrow and asked: "And how is that, exactly?"

Geoff replied: "Their super-AI has a kind of sliding scale of priorities. Now this hospital is destroyed and only us two are left, we've dropped way down the list. Most of London would have to be flattened before they'd start targeting individuals like us."

"Most of it already has," the woman said with sourness.

There came a pause. Geoff tilted his head to better locate the hisses and sears while missiles and ACAs continued fighting overhead. He turned in concentration. The conflict moved southwards. He climbed the rubble.

"What are you—?" the woman began, but then stopped and blinked. She said: "My lens is back."

Geoff turned towards her. "And?"

The woman asked: "Her name?"

"Lisa O'Connell."

The woman looked at the rubble on which Geoff stood. Her face creased in pain and she let out a sob.

"I told you," Geoff said without rancour, knowing that the nurse had access to his own personal data as well as Lisa's details.

"They're dying," she said, her voice cracking. "All of them."

Journalistic curiosity rose inside Geoff. He wondered what the display in the woman's medical lens must look like.

"I'm sorry," she said in a flatter tone, "but yes, your partner and child have gone."

Despite all that had happened and his hitherto certainty, the news still stunned Geoff. In a strange shift of focus, he felt the nurse become more assured as his own spirit weakened on confirmation of the loss of his family. She stood, seeming to gain—or regain—her confidence. She appraised their surroundings, climbed the rubble to him and continued upwards. "Bastards," she muttered.

Geoff didn't respond. He stared at the debris, blinking and wondering why her medical lens worked but his own remained blank. A disembodied voice inside him questioned if it mattered; the nurse had confirmed what he'd instinctively known anyway.

"Absolute bastards," the woman said. Rubble crunched under her feet as she climbed.

The nurse's vitriolic tone finally caused a sliver of Geoff's attention to disengage from analysing the abyss of his grief. He stopped staring at the debris and mentally smothered the images of Lisa as she protected their baby from the dust and pressure of tons of masonry bearing down on them until the phenomenal weight forced the air from her lungs—

"Look," the nurse said. "Come and look."

Geoff struggled higher up, gripping exposed metal beams and pushing off twisted doorframes. He reached the woman after stumbling when some shattered roof tiles gave way under his weight.

"See?" she said.

"The attack seems to be ending," he replied, noting fewer machines in the sky. He scanned the blueness, seeking any hint of danger. The violence continued to the south and east, but wafting columns of grey and black smoke hid the details.

"No," she said. "Look, St. Paul's is still standing."

Geoff turned to the south where, a few hundred metres away, the dome of St. Paul's Cathedral protruded high and blue in the bright morning light, its prominence increased with the sudden removal of many of the buildings around it. "Good," he said in a reflexive response.

"What?" she rounded on him, her face creased in anger. "Did you just say 'good'?"

Non-plussed, Geoff said: "I don't really care. I want to see my partner and child. The first and last time." He cast his gaze back down the rubble, wondering how he could reach and retrieve them. His lens remained blank, a digital vacuity to match the emptiness in his spirit. Through so much of this war, he had remained untouched, a mere chronicler. Now his life had suffered a brutal corrective similar to that which millions of other Europeans also endured.

"You may not care," the nurse said, "but I do. You're a journalist, Mr Morrow. I understand you feel intense loss now, but does your reporter's mind not question how this venerable hospital, nearly a thousand years old, has been blasted to ruins while a cathedral half the hospital's age—but many times more famous—has been spared?"

An instinct deep inside Geoff flashed acknowledgement of the nurse's observation. His foot slipped suddenly and he fell. His shoulder hit a ragged chunk of concrete. He pushed himself away from a void that opened abruptly beneath him. He peered into it but perceived only blackness.

"Are you all right?" the woman called from above.

He mumbled affirmation as he pulled himself out of danger.

She called to him: "How is it possible? Who decided that my patients must die, while a crusty old church should come through unscathed?"

"No one 'decided'," Geoff answered, climbing back up to her.

"Well, someone must have," she insisted.

"It is really very simple," Geoff said, not caring if he sounded patronising, her tone of obduracy irking him. "Super artificial intelligence governed the entire battle. It allocated the resources which it had available to defend London to the best of its…" his words trailed off as he realised where his explanation had to lead.

"So our computers decided who lived and who died, yes?" the nurse asked rhetorically.

Geoff reached her and pulled himself level by grasping her proffered forearm. "It's not that simple—"

She scoffed and said: "It never is."

"We had limited defences—"

"But look," she repeated, "the computers made the decision. They decided that the empty St. Paul's Cathedral should be saved while the three hundred and forty-seven people in St. Bart's should die, yes?"

"No, that can't be right," Geoff muttered. His spirit wilted under the impact of this anonymous nurse's logical, irrefutable conclusion.

"It doesn't matter what you think is right, Mr Morrow. I can assess the view objectively with my own eyes. Tell me, what do you see, Mr Morrow?"

Geoff felt an overwhelming surge of unfairness. His lens remained blank, like his future without Lisa and their child. "I see what you see," he mumbled.

"So, can you answer the question? Why did these people die, and instead of defending them, the computers preferred to save St. Paul's?"

The unjustness within Geoff morphed into dark despair. He could not breathe. The inside of his chest felt as though a ton of concrete were pulling his throat down into his lungs. He sobbed—a deep, shuddering yelp that threatened to break his ribcage in half. He bawled and cried out in his pain and anguish and his knuckles bled afresh as he punched the side of a bent air-conditioning duct that jutted out from the rubble. He pounded the side of the aluminium until it crumpled, until the bits of glass in his hand could not be driven inwards any further.

"You shouldn't do that," the nurse admonished. "I shan't be able to help you if you injure yourself intentionally."

"Someone must have," he hissed through a deep breath, "must have decided, must have changed priorities—"

"Perhaps not? I can see the Shard has gone, and so have the Houses of Parliament."

As the notion took on a stronger outline in his mind, Geoff forced himself to gain control of his body. He asked the nurse: "Can you reach any of the other hospitals?"

She frowned and shook her head. "No, there's some kind of..."

"What?"

She sighed and said: "Yes, other hospitals must have been damaged, judging by the current range and number of urgent demands."

"Can you be sure?" Geoff asked. "London has just had the shit kicked out of it. There must be tens of thousands of ongoing emergencies." He watched as her eye blinked and twitched.

"Emergency centres in residential blocks have been activated. Triage looks bad. As soon as the jamming clears fully, we'll be able to—"

"Jesus," Geoff hissed abruptly as his own lens came back to life. With rapid twitches of his eye muscles, an

25

overview of the destruction wrought on the city splayed out in his view.

"What is it?" the nurse asked.

"Give me a second while I link to the governmental feeds."

"You journalists can do that?" the nurse asked in shock.

"Sometimes," Geoff replied.

He sensed her confident demeanour wilt. She said: "Please find out why, Mr Morrow. I should like to know the why."

"I told you: someone decided, someone changed the super AI's priorities."

"But who?"

"There are only a handful of people in the country who could instruct government-controlled super AI to vary to what it should devote the most resources to protect."

Geoff spoke while data flooded his lens. The abrupt activity and return to digital normality poured water on the flames of his loss, and through the thinning mist of rage, a new urge grew in definition. He said: "No, someone must have instructed the super AI to favour defending historical monuments. It wouldn't have taken much, just enough to allow—"

"But who? And why?"

Geoff shook his head and replied: "I think they'd do everything to hide their actions, and anyway, it's not so cut and dry. Enough history has been smashed as it is. It's just about equally possible all of the victims in your hospital could have died due to a military miscalculation lasting a billionth of a second." There, he told himself, he'd said it out loud: his partner and child were dead.

"But I can see how many hospitals have been hit—"

"Aggregating the attack data shows that too much infrastructure has also been destroyed when compared to the other European cities under attack."

The nurse flopped back and sat on a flat piece of rubble. Her tone descended to one of absolute misery: "We're finished," she said.

"Probably," Geoff conceded.

"And so many of us will die, will be lost, with no record that we had ever existed."

"That's impossible," Geoff answered.

"No, it isn't," she replied. "When they win, they might kill us all, and they certainly will kill those who have no use to them as slaves. But in any case, they shall absolutely destroy our culture, our monuments, and our history."

There came a brief silence between them. The rumbles of battle died down. Goff felt the heat of the morning grow in tiny increments; the day coming on immutably, oblivious to the carnage taking place on the surface.

The nurse asked: "Don't you agree? They will destroy all our heritage and history along with us."

Geoff didn't know how to answer. He only understood that someone had to construct some kind of record. He understood, now the violence had touched him personally, that each life snuffed out in this war deserved to be recorded for posterity, whatever shape that future might take.

The nurse stared into the mid-distance. Her eyelid twitched and she muttered: "They're dying. All of them."

"What?"

"The injured. Cardiac arrest, bleeding out, shock."

"My lens is out again," Geoff said.

"Let me link to you?"

"What's your name?"

"Tara Arnold."

"Thank you."

Data from the nurse's lens filled Geoff's view at the same time as his own lens re-established contact. He realised that emergency rescue support would not be assigned to St. Bart's for several hours because the few remaining life signs under the rubble would not survive long enough, therefore the limited resources had been directed to locations where they could save lives. Geoff scoffed aloud and said: "Just like on the mainland. Local defences totally overwhelmed and wiped out. You want to rescue anyone, you better dig them out yourself."

"Nothing's going to stop these beastly machines," the nurse said with finality.

Geoff stood and clambered down the rubble, certain that the nurse was right and equally sure that someone had to make a record of these victims' lives. Perhaps such a record would transpire to be as futile as his efforts to protect Lisa and their child, but as he left the nurse behind, he knew he had to try.

Chapter 4

Vitality surged through Major Kate Fus. Along with her superiors and her subordinates in the rest of NATO, she knew the invasion had to resume if the Caliphate were to overrun and subdue the entire European landmass. Finally, she would witness the most violent and powerful enemy the continent had faced in over four hundred years resume its overwhelming surge across the countries of democracy and liberty. And General Pakla, *her* general, had charged her with managing the fighting retreat from Zagreb to Pécs, a front of over two hundred-and-thirty-kilometres.

"Here they come," she muttered to herself, scanning the screens inside her command vehicle. "Bolek, why did you increase the retreat time-error margin to three-point-six seconds? I don't want to lose a single soldier if I don't have to."

The Polish super AI answered: "All constants and variables considered, that is the optimum."

Kate sighed in strained patience and said: "I know that, but it has put the likelihood of comms problems up at over twenty percent. And that is too high."

"To reduce this probability would require an unjustifiable lowering of other estimates."

"Hmm," Kate considered. "No chance of an electrical storm cracking off within the next thirty minutes, I assume?"

"Negative," the Polish super AI replied, continuing: "Flesh-and-blood troops are positioned as low as possible in the order of battle."

"Yes, but our ACAs, pulsars and tanks are not up to protecting them for more than a few minutes, are they?"

Bolek replied: "It is a question of numbers. If NATO forces could deploy sufficient—"

"Oh no, are those Lapwing signatures among the Blackswans?"

"Affirmative."

"Damn."

"All in-theatre troops have been advised. Retreat time-error margin lowered to counteract."

Kate watched the numbers that described the probabilities of casualties fluctuate as the battle of logic between Bolek and the enemy's super AI went on. From high above the battlespace, cones of NATO PeaceMakers spun and fanned out, descending to meet the Caliphate machines. Those PeaceMakers armed with Equaliser bomblets yawed in and zipped beneath those armed with Suletto missiles. The sense came to Kate that this could be just another war game, one more simulation. She shivered; real refugees fled headlong desperate not to be blasted or burned to a cinder, and real flesh-and-blood NATO troops could be blown out of existence.

The enemy's Blackswans and Lapwings approached the confrontation in straight lines varying in their altitude: pitching and angling to converge on their designated targets. Kate stared at the display, consternation and anger boiling inside her. With the Caliphate's overwhelming number of machines, its super AI could strut its superiority and use tactics to first terrify those whom it would then destroy. A bitterness scored the back of her throat. With all of the ACAs the Caliphate had thrown at northern Europe at the dawn of this dreadful day, it should not still have so many available to attack the defenders.

A comms indicator flashed. Kate blinked her eyelid and said: "Yes, Captain Boruc?"

A determined female voice answered: "Major, we've got Lapwings heading towards Varaždin. I believe they may be going after the refugees on the road next to the canal, but Bolek says we cannot divert resources to protect them. Please advise."

Kate froze. This was not an exercise—she had to decide who lived and who died. She barked: "Bolek, is there any way you can save those refugees and maintain the integrity of the line around Hills 113 and 213?"

"Negative," came the taut reply.

On her right, the screen that displayed immediate probabilities offered her a dozen scenarios of reassigning the limited resources in that locality, and how many of her troops would likely die, and how many refugees would be obliged to perish instead.

Kate ran her index finger back and forth along the lip above her cleft palate. If she didn't decide, Bolek would. A voice inside told her to leave it to Bolek. Officers should trust the super artificial intelligence; that's what she'd been trained to do. That's what all of the NATO manuals said and it's what everyone said. Except the general, *her general*. "Okay, Bolek," she hissed. "We need to save those refugees and maintain the line of the fighting retreat from Hill 213—"

"This tactic shall only gain approx—"

31

"Signal all autonomous ground vehicles to advance forwards from Hill 113."

The super AI replied: "To advance towards the enemy at this time will not—"

Kate barked: "Captain Boruc, accelerate your speed of retreat. Change your heading thirty degrees north to converge with those refugees."

"Roger," came the reply. "You want us to dogleg around that valley and at the same time provide some cover for the refugees."

Kate's eyebrows rose and she nodded in appreciation of Boruc's tactical nous. "Affirmative," she replied. "Thank you." The connection ended and Kate said: "And there you are, Bolek," with a note of satisfaction in her voice.

Bolek stated: "The enemy has adjusted its tactics. It is prioritising the advancing tanks and battlefield support lasers over the refugees. However, in five to seven minutes an approaching wing of enemy ACAs will be within—"

"So you need to deal with that at the strategic level, okay?"

"Confirmed."

"Well?" she demanded two seconds later.

"The strategic conditions are within previous forecast ranges."

"Good." Despite the unorthodox tactic to draw some of the Caliphate's ACAs away from the refugees, the satisfaction Kate felt soon dissipated. She thought aloud. "That will give them only moments. Those damn tanks—" and broke off when a secure transmission flashed for her attention.

"What?" she asked keeping all of her attention on the battle.

"Major? This is General Pakla."

Kate's spirit clamped down on her emotional reflex at hearing the general's voice—feelings of affection and memories of intimacy had no place in battle. "Yes, sir?"

"I have an important mission for our corps."

Kate said nothing as her command vehicle rocked and bumped along the road in retreat. In the display, she noted how well the American Abrahams tanks seemed to be performing in the line of small towns close to the canal, drawing the Spiders on, dodging, feigning movement, using selective attacks.

Her general's voice sounded strained: "It would be greatly appreciated if you could secure a living Caliphate warrior, preferably injured—although not too badly, obviously—and subdued, ready for transportation westwards. Please acknowledge, over?"

The order piqued Kate's curiosity, but she simply replied: "Of course, sir. I will forward your request to the troops in theatre."

"Thank you, major," came the terse reply. "Please assign it highest priority and contact me regularly with updates, understood?"

"Yes," she said, and the connection ended. "You heard him, Bolek. Give me options. Now."

Highlights flashed over the digital display in front of Kate. Something thumped on the outside of her command vehicle. "What was that?"

"Local fauna."

"Okay." Her eyes roved the screen, scanning the terrain as units and formations along the front withdrew in sections. She felt her heart rock inside her ribcage. What could her general want with a live Caliphate warrior?

Brighter light winked over natural features such as hills, ridges, valleys and escarpments. "That looks good," she said abruptly, stabbing her finger on the screen at the south-eastern edge of her section of the front. "Open comms to the company commander."

"Done."

"Captain Nowak?"

"Yes, ma'am," came the strained response.

"In a few moments, your Squitches will instruct you and the rest of black company to withdraw. Some squads will be told to go through a disused railway tunnel at the grid reference you see now."

"Roger. With respect, major, I've got incoming here, which you should be able to see. So if you could get to the p—"

"Delay in the railway tunnel. Ambush advancing enemy warriors and capture a live one. Select your best troops for this. We need to send a Caliphate warrior behind the lines."

Silence greeted her order.

"Captain?"

"Affirmative," she heard Nowak croak. "Although I think we would all prefer to kill any warriors if we get the chance, major."

"I understand, but we only need one alive. Questions?"

"Negative."

"Good. Give this order the highest priority," Kate said, echoing the general. "You will bring substantial credit on your company and the brigade if you can succeed. Fus out." She sat back and heaved a sigh, wondering if she were better off in her metal container on wheels, or if she'd rather be in Captain Nowak's position, leading his troops into an engagement.

The graphics in the screen changed. Caliphate machines attacked and destroyed the defending tanks and battlefield support lasers on Hill 113 and the line fell back.

Some refugees were saved, some not. Kate's gaze returned inexorably to the southeast. She asked herself the same questions but, at length, doubted if Captain Nowak and his troops would even survive any engagement.

Then, just as her mobile command slowed in its own retreat, Bolek reported that Nowak and his team had engaged enemy warriors inside the tunnel.

Chapter 5

Crispin Webb entered the air-conditioned comfort of Ten Downing Street, ignored the police officer inside, and hurried on along the corridor that gave off magnolia hues of indescribable blandness. He kept half an eye on the approaching staircase and half on the sneering face in a thumbnail in his lens.

"What? What did you threaten me with, you little shit?" he spat as he leapt up the stairs two at a time. The strength and regularity of his heartbeats reassured him a second heart attack would not happen within the next few minutes, and that was as much as he could care about on this atrocious morning. He continued speaking before his interlocuter could respond: "God knows how many thousands of Londoners have been killed, the Houses of Parliament, the very essence of England's great democracy, have been blasted to a pile of fucking ruins, and you are telling me you're going to focus your coverage on the fact that a disproportionate number of hospitals have been hit?"

Andy MacSawley, editor of *The Mail*, the most powerful media outlet in England, retorted: "Yeah, that's right. Because that's the issue my readers—"

"Why can't you just stick to the human-interest angle? You must be able to find thousands of heroes in that wreckage this morning."

"Because there's a shit-sight more to it than that, and, Cris, I'm willing to bet you know what went on behind the scenes to make sure—"

Crispin terminated the connection with a blink of his eye. MacSawley would hate that and there would be more trouble. Tough shit.

The door to the spacious meeting room opened and another aide to the PM, Monica, warned him with fearful eyes. She sat with the boss. The large screen on the east wall showed half a dozen feeds from key sites around the city that also ran counters of casualties whose tallies kept increasing. Crispin acknowledged his own growing indifference as one pile of smoking rubble appeared similar to any other.

He strode towards his prime minister. She looked weak and forlorn, as though the battering England had taken had also hit her personally. He said: "Boss, perhaps it would be better if we went to the War Rooms?"

"The attack has been over for a while now, Crispin. Terry said we're not in danger."

Crispin glanced at the screen on which the largest image showed the dirty brown River Thames in front of the destroyed Houses of Parliament. Crispin noted how little of the buildings could be recognised, for only one of the four giant clockfaces that had housed Big Ben lay fractured on top of a mound of rubble that formed a slope into the water.

The PM's eyelid flickered as she added: "The computers say that fifty-three people died in there."

Crispin ascribed the distant look in her eyes to fatigue and worry, but his sympathy had long been exhausted. And besides, she might merely be watching other feeds in her own lens. He said: "We need to put something out. You know, standing resolute with our allies, unbowed by this outrageous and illegal attack on us. That kind of thing." He saw the vague confusion on her face and so he continued: "One media outlet claims to have found a pattern of destruction that favoured the preservation of historical buildings over things like hospit—"

"Aiden's going to resign," she broke in.

"What? Boss, I smell a rat," he said.

Napier looked at him and said: "Does it matter?"

Crispin searched with his lens. As soon as the information he sought scrolled up in his vision, he replied: "London's defence was overseen by the mayor."

"Jack with the out-of-control penis?"

"Yes, which means Hicks had nothing to do with—"

"I don't care," Napier hissed.

"Hicks has never forgiven you for beating him in the race for the leadership nine years ago."

"Stop the party politics, Crispin. What is Hicks going to do, hmm? Whine to the world that I am a less-than—"

"Respectfully, boss, we do not need a loose cannon with things—"

"Oh, for God's sake. Hicks will either resign and be crushed or will burn to death with the rest of us in a couple of weeks."

"Yes, boss," Crispin said, trying to focus. "Sorry," he fumbled. "But I have to keep doing my job."

She stared at the screen. The digital counters of dead and injured increased with banal inevitability. She said: "I only wish there was something we could have done; some way to have prevented or delayed this awfulness."

With as much diplomacy as Crispin could muster, he said: "Boss, the media storm is already breaking. Each passing moment, outlets around the country have got their lenses and screens telling them that here in London, the decision was made—by a human being—to allow citizens to die to protect historical monuments."

She shook her head: "It doesn't matter. We're all going to d—"

"Yes, it does matter. We've got comparisons with Paris, Berlin, Brussels, Frankfurt and Warsaw which are showing that they all defended their people with more success, and lost more historical monuments as a result."

Napier put her hand to her forehead and frowned. She said: "It does not matter. Disregard it."

"What?" Crispin said for the second time in as many minutes. "But what am I going to tell the press?"

Napier eyes widened. "You are not helping, Crispin. Leave me."

Crispin felt his mouth fall open at the boss's instruction. He continued to stare.

Napier addressed the image of London's police commissioner in a thumbnail in the screen that expanded as she said: "Tom, the priority now is civil disobedience. Make sure your teams use minimum force with looters. How thinly are you spread?"

The police commissioner spoke with a fatigue familiar to Crispin: "Attendance from higher ranks is holding up pretty well, but a lot of constables and almost all of my specials have thrown the towel in."

"Liaise with the military where possible if you need support, then," Napier instructed.

"Very well, ma'am. Currently all areas are focused on rescue ops, so the general population are occupied, especially given the scarcity of construction replicators. But things might worsen once all the injured have been got out and we're only recovering bodies."

"Understood, thanks. We'll have a COBRA this afternoon at four and you can update all of us then. And good luck with the crisis management teams in the meantime."

"Thank you, ma'am."

Tom's face withdrew and there came a brief pause during which Crispin caught a flash of impatience from Napier.

The bald, pugnacious head of General Sir Terry Tidbury expanded to cover the screen. "Yes, PM?"

"Update, please."

Crispin perceived the curtness increase in Terry's voice. "The political leaders' instructions are being implemented, but we have a complication."

"Which is?"

"The enemy has reintroduced the Lapwing autonomous combat aircraft to the battlefield, and it is proving as devasting as it was previously."

Napier let out a sigh.

Terry went on: "The computers are continually updating their forecasts as new data becomes available, but my personal feeling is that the enemy has got a lot more in reserve which we don't know about, and I anticipate a further downturn in NATO's fortunes in the near future."

"I understand," Napier replied.

"If you don't mind, PM, the situation here is dynamic."

"Of course," Napier said. "Sorry to interrupt you. See you at the COBRA this afternoon. Good luck."

Terry's face withdrew and Crispin wondered how long they all had left—how long before the last ever COBRA meeting took place?

Napier rounded on him and spoke in the tone of a school mistress admonishing a wayward child. "Well, Crispin?

Why are you still here? Do you not have to go and play games with the press?"

"Er, yes. Er—"

"Well, go on, then. The rest of us have got more important things to deal with. Run along."

Chapter 6

Newly promoted Sergeant Rory Moore of 21 Engineer
Regiment, Royal Engineers, gritted his teeth as the
ageing Boeing 818 autonomous air transport lifted
off. His stomach fell and he stretched his jaw to counteract
the changing air pressure in his ears. He wondered again about
his promotion, about the two green platoons under his
command, the four other platoons on board, and exactly how
long they would last after deployment somewhere along the
Franco-Spanish border. They sat in one of a squadron of
twelve Boeings, part of a wing of six squadrons. Brass had
known the enemy would resume the invasion eventually, and
now the bastards had, he and his soldiers had to go to work
and slow them down for as long as they could.

The troops sat lining the fuselage. The glances that
flitted among them as the AAT climbed and banked reassured
Rory only to a slight degree. He'd chatted to many of them,
utilising the familiarisation methods he'd learned on his
sergeant-training course. Most of the recruits had only passed
out a week earlier, and now they were about to face the enemy.

Doubts still coursed through his mind: about his leadership skills, and about how these men and women would react if and when a Spider came hurtling towards them.

However, he could and did rely on his notoriety. As only one of a handful of NATO troops to have faced a Caliphate Spider and lived to tell the tale, some of these raw recruits treated him with a respect that bordered on awe. He had lost count of the times he'd given his presentation that summarised the night the invasion began, when he and his squad were deployed in the Sierra Nevada mountains in Spain, and he had destroyed a Spider. And Pratty had been killed on the transport. And Pip and Crimble had survived somehow, until Crimble's arm went gangrenous and Pip had left him with the locals in an abandoned mine.

A closed comms channel icon flashed in his lens. Rory smiled to see his fellow sergeant, Barry Smith, who said: "It's not too late to make your will."

"How do you know I haven't already?"

"I overheard you talking to the colonel."

"Nosy little toad, aren't you? Besides, if I did it wouldn't be needed. Not today, mate."

"Yeah? So what can you see from your end of this bloody aircraft that I can't see from mine, eh?"

"A positive attitude?"

"Oh, that's nice."

Rory chuckled and said: "Let's talk about this later, when we've held the line for as long as we can then retreated in an orderly fashion."

"Yeah, we live in hope," Barry concluded.

The pressure inside Rory's ears increased again as the autonomous air transport gained height. He stretched his jaw and swallowed until the feeling passed. His thoughts returned to Officer Cadet Pip Clarke, still in England awaiting deployment. He needed to use these few minutes' respite to remember and recall: struggling to fix the failing flood defences around northern England before the war—a lifetime ago now; losing her in the opening battle and finding her again in Spain after fearing she'd been killed; the weeks they'd spent trapped in the vast metal coffin called *HMS Spiteful* that returned them, finally, to England. But on their promotion, she'd requested a commission that would see them parted again. And as her commanding officer, he'd approved it.

With his regret duly acknowledged and allowed attention, he shunted it to the back of his mind and refocused on leading his troops. He shook his head at the contradiction of advancing towards the enemy merely to assist in a fighting retreat.

"Everything all right, sarge?" asked Private Antonia Savage with a confident smile.

Rory shrugged and said: "Apart from our complete destruction being assured? Yeah, great. It's all fine and dandy, thanks."

Some of the others sitting on Savage's side of the fuselage smiled. The corporal in charge of that squad rolled her eyes. Rory waited for Savage to retort, but the young private said nothing more. Good. Rory glanced down at his worn boots and watched the localised part of the battle progress through the digital representation the British Army's super AI, Squonk, gave him in his lens. As a sergeant, he had access to more data than a corporal did, but not as much as the captain.

Their autonomous air transport wing was part of a modest relief force already preassigned for reinforcement when the Caliphate resumed its advance across the European mainland. In formation with the rest of the squadron, their aircraft accelerated south over the English Channel. A mass of enemy jamming crackled and hid the bulk of the attack. Military-grade materials ensured comms among NATO units, unlike civilian kit, which, if it didn't burn out during the enemy's initial microwave burst, could not see into their jamming at all.

The captain's voice spoke in Rory's ear: "Attention, all teams. Squonk's detecting changes in enemy tactics. The probability's on the up that some of us might be reassigned."

One of the sergeants on another AAT said: "CV–125 requesting higher altitude."

Rory smiled because this would place the requesting AAT in a position from which Squonk would be more likely reassign it than the others.

Rory could hear the smile in the captain's response: "Easy does it, Vic. Squonk has control and will decide."

"Roger."

A long pause followed. The squadron passed through fifteen thousand metres and accelerated to Mach 6. An ache began inside Rory's head, like nails dragged across the inside of his skull. His eyes focused on the data Squonk relayed in the lens. It told him nothing of the thousands of Caliphate Blackswans and Lapwings that, in an apparent tactical misjudgement, had wrought extensive destruction over the cities of Northern Europe earlier that morning, and he felt another stab of guilt at the relief that these weapons were no longer available to attack NATO forces. He glanced up at his troops. Blinks, gulps and other twitches betrayed their fears.

The pain in his head vanished abruptly when a red light flashed in his vision. At the same time, a vast, unseen force pushed him back against the fuselage while the limbs of the troops opposite him flung out in response to the change in G-forces as the aircraft changed course.

A dry, super-AI voice spoke in his ear: "New heading applied."

"Explain," Rory ordered, his joints cracking as the compression of his limbs eased.

"Transports C–127 and C–129 have been reassigned to the Eastern Fr—"

"Okay."

The captain's voice spoke in Rory's ear: "Sergeants Moore, Smith and Heaton. You are to reinforce the First Polish Armoured."

"Roger," Rory said. The map in his vision deepened with new data. Their destination changed from the Franco-Spanish border to Hungary.

A small burst of relief comforted Rory because Barry Smith had been on the same training course as him, while Sergeant Heaton, a tough, plain-speaking Yorkshireman, was a career soldier who'd been in the British Army for fifteen years. Rory suspected that the northerner did not regard the new arrivals with particular affection.

Rory exhaled as the seriousness of the danger all around them became apparent. How could he lead his troops when he himself fought a familiar sense of futility? Whatever Heaton might think of him and Smith, he hoped the presence of the older man would lend a steadying influence to all of the troops.

Minutes passed in tense silence as the AAT sped over southern Germany and Austria. Rory watched in grim curiosity as the graphic display of the terrain below their aircraft showed flashes of anonymous destruction denoting the Caliphate's advance.

When they crossed the Hungarian border and approached their designated sector of the front, Rory appraised his troops: "Ladies and gents, as you might have guessed, we've taken a little detour, to Hungary. There is a chance we may be obliged to disembark under fire."

He saw faces drop and Private Savage said in a neutral tone: "I volunteer to exit first, sarge."

Rory sensed the young woman's turmoil underneath her level voice. But he shook his head and replied: "We exit the craft in the established order."

"Then I request permission to swap places with Private Hawkins."

Rory looked at Hawkins, a fit young man given to impetuousness. His hard stare remained impassive.

"Denied." Rory returned to the data in his lens.

The familiar voice of his Squitch replaced the British Army's super AI, although any comfort he might have felt vanished with its message: "Escorts have been engaged in the defence of this aircraft. Their destruction is estimated in seventy-seven seconds."

Rory shivered. The changing air pressure flashed and passed in his ears as the AAT descended. He twitched his eye muscles to bring up the relevant graphic. The four PeaceMakers assigned to protect their AAT ducked and dived and spun and released their bomblets, which had little effect against the enemy's shielding, before the Blackswans released enough Spiders to send the PeaceMakers tumbling from the sky a moment later.

"ETA?" Rory demanded, struggling to keep his voice level.

"Ninety seconds."

His heart stopped. Spiders were in the air and closing. Memories of Pratty getting blown to pieces in the transport in Spain resurfaced in his mind. He decided to hope it would be over quickly.

The Squitch said: "Diverting support from NATO ground units."

The display highlighted the remains of their escorting PeaceMakers falling away, but from below NATO missiles streaked to the aircraft's defence. Rory breathed in relief when Pulsar battlefield support vehicles on the ground also trained their cannons to assist the arriving reinforcements. The autonomous aircraft shuddered when something outside exploded. The frontline lay two kilometres to the east of their landing point.

"Stand by to disembark," Rory barked. "Twenty seconds to touchdown." From the corner of his eye, he glimpsed the recruits snap helmet-locks shut and shift in their seats. Each of them took their Pickups from the secure-supports next to their seats, and held the rifles vertically. From now on, every soldier would rely on their Squitch to direct them. Rory and Sergeants Smith and Heaton would only intercede if situations developed that required them to confirm their Squitches' instructions.

Rory looked through the windows and saw brownish-green terrain rise up to meet the AAT. He muttered: "Listen to me, you bloody super AI. Do not complain if I swear, okay? Do not tell me you will report me to a superior officer for excessive profanity, got that?"

The Squitch replied: "If you wish to change British Army regulations, you should apply to—"

He hissed: "I do not wish to change British Army regs, I want you to understand that we are in a fucking live shooting war and people are actually fucking dying."

The Squitch's answer was lost when a loud klaxon suddenly blared inside the fuselage and red lights hued the metal surfaces. The rear exit ramp clunked and yawned open. The transport rocked as it touched down and the ramp thumped into sandy ground. A twinge of pride flashed inside Rory as the Royal Engineers disembarked in an orderly fashion. He followed them out into thick, warm air heated by the intense morning sunlight. Large shrubs and small trees whose leaves hung dry and wilting ringed the expansive landing zone. When he jumped off the AAT's exit ramp, his boots sank into dusty earth that could not have seen rain in many months.

Over their devoted comms link, Sergeant Smith muttered, "Christ, we're going to roast in this heat," and Rory smiled. Little needed to be said and no orders had to be issued because each soldier's Squitch guided its owner in maintaining defensive arcs and proceeding to the forming-up point. The hiss of the Boeings' engines died down and the more distant sounds of battle became audible.

As though on a beach, Rory forced his boots through the dirty sand. His Squitch guided him to his platoons. He addressed his fellow sergeants: "I've got the front moving towards us. Are you guys getting that?"

They mumbled their confirmations through heaving breaths.

A burst of frustration angered Rory. They all knew the temporary nature of their objective to reinforce the line, lasting only until the super AI decided they had to pull back, but he didn't understand why they'd been brought in so close to the front. He asked: "Why did we land on top of a line that's about to retreat?"

His Squitch answered: "Polish units are in close combat with enemy forces."

"Blackswans or Lapwings?" Rory asked as he made his way to the head of the body of troops.

"Negative. The Polish squads have engaged the enemy's advancing warriors."

Rory heard the shock in his voice: "The Poles are fighting real, live Caliphate warriors?"

"Affirmative."

"Display distance and location, now." He blinked and opened communications with his subordinates. "Attention, all troops. We have Caliphate warriors within less than two klicks to the southeast."

The realisation that he might take his troops into combat with the enemy filled him with an excitement that overrode his doubts. Suddenly, an angry metallic shriek squealed high above them. Squinting skywards, Rory observed distant black dots zipping across his vision as ACAs exchanged fire. The graphics in his sight abruptly lit up with warnings and the Squitch advised: "Sixty-one Spiders have targeted this LZ. ETA ten seconds. Take defensive action immediately."

"Fuck," he hissed. He crouched on one knee and raised his Pickup to point it at the sky, noting every other soldier in the landing zone take the same stance. "Reinforcements?" he asked as the automated targeting on his rifle made its selection of shell and Spider.

The Squitch ignored his question and instructed: "Open fire now."

Rory did so, his weapon's noise lost in the pattering cacophony of tens of Pickups firing simultaneously. The shells exploded far above them, the flashes of their detonations hued a familiar green. Some of the Caliphate Spiders disintegrated and he realised that this debris alone would lead to casualties when it came down. The black dots grew larger. Dread crystallised in the back of his throat. He ejected the empty magazine and snapped a new one in without conscious thought. He resumed firing. The remaining Spiders descended with their appendages already deployed.

He sensed rather than saw a sudden flurry of shapes from the west invade the battlespace. New and more powerful explosions erupted barely a hundred metres above the landing zone. A massive, unseen force pushed him over and pinned him to the sandy dirt for an instant before vanishing as abruptly as it had arrived. On instinct, he pulled his arms up to protect his head and clenched his eyes and mouth shut in anticipation.

Deadening thumps reverberated through the ground. Rory waited in agonised tenseness for the life to be squashed out of him. Something heavy thudded into the ground close to his head; small pieces of debris hit his legs and back with the force of hard punches. The rain of destruction stopped. He opened his eyes to see a new field of carnage.

"Help, help. Please," called a distant voice in weak politeness.

Rory got to his hands and knees and then stood, feeling nothing unusual and silently thanking the adrenalin that he knew would mute the pain from any scratches. Some of his troops also rose. Across the broad expanse of the landing zone, he could guess that many others would never rise again. The fuselages of the Boeing 818s burned fiercely. Rory decided he hated this war. He hated the swiftness of the action, of how a distant black dot in a cobalt sky could, in mere seconds, blow his troops into bloody pieces.

His Squitch spoke: "You have sustained minor injuries."

"No shit."

"You have been reassigned to assist with a priority objective."

"What?" he queried, vaguely recalling a rule somewhere that the super artificial intelligence could take decisions like this.

"Follow the route indicated in your display. This is now your primary objective."

A wave of dizziness made him stagger but then it passed. Around him, the wounded moved and struggled. Among them, Private Savage stared at Rory with imploring eyes, but when she tried to drag herself over the sand, Rory saw that her legs had gone. Rory exhaled slowly, and in the time that took, Private Savage lost consciousness.

A new voice spoke in his ear, urgent and demanding: "Sergeant Moore? Are you fit? Respond, please."

Rory shook his head to dispel his disorientation and answered the captain: "Yes, sir."

"Please follow the directions your Squitch is giving you. You need to assist a unit of Poles. This has the very highest priority. Acknowledged?"

"Yes, sir. But we've taken a slight pounding here. We have quite a number of woun—"

"Not your concern, sergeant. The medical teams on site will deal with your casualties. And I've got more medics on the way."

Rory looked at the burning Boeing 818s and choked down an expletive-laden observation that the medical teams had nothing left with which to tend the wounded, assuming the medics had not themselves all been killed or incapacitated. "On my way," he said, turning from the chaotic landing zone at the fastest trot the fine sand would allow. His display showed that two others must have been given the same instructions.

"Right behind you, fella," called Sergeant Smith.

"Yeah, I can see, Barry."

"Know what this is about?"

"Nope. Only that there are real, live warriors ahead."

"Those Poles are lucky bastards to be able to have a go at them."

"You reckon?" Rory replied as he jogged around wilting junipers and other shrubs. He contrasted the desertification of this part of Hungary with his previous life, as a mere corporal, of shoring up flood defences around the coast of northern England.

His Squitch broke into his thoughts: "Caution. You are entering an active-fire zone."

Barry Smith remarked: "Where are their ACAs? I can't believe we're not getting fried now."

The older Sergeant Heaton admonished in his thick Yorkshire accent, "Be careful what you wish for."

Rory said: "They're going to be inbound. Why are we running towards a tunnel entrance?"

His Squitch answered: "You are assisting the evacuation of a wounded Caliphate warrior. Stand by to engage the enemy."

Epithets of shock and frustration echoed in his ears but Rory concentrated on the approaching fight. The terrain changed. Dried and brittle, low shrubs increased in frequency and Rory had to extend his gait to keep the same speed. If his foot came down on a plant, he might twist his ankle; when it came down on sand, half of his boot sank into it. His chest heaved in exertion and he swore as the pack on his back seemed to become heavier. Straps rubbed through his uniform and itched the skin on his shoulders and chest. Holding his Pickup clear of the larger bushes made his arms ache.

He heard Barry complain through heaving breaths, "I cannot believe… We are legging it towards… the enemy like this… When we are—"

The Squitch broke in: "You must increase your pace. Enemy ACAs are approaching from the east. NATO ACAs are three seco—"

And was itself interrupted by a stern female voice, identified in Rory's vision as Major Kate Fus. She said: "Attention, support troops. We have two AATs inbound from the south. A Polish fireteam will come out of the tunnel in front you with a wounded enemy. It is vitally important the wounded enemy is successfully evacuated."

Rory couldn't stop himself: "What the fu—?"

His Squitch broke in: "Danger: enemy contact, twelve degrees northeast. Distance five-fifty metres. Take evasive action immediately."

Amid shouts from the others to take cover, Rory stopped galloping and crouched close to a dried shrub that towered over him. Sweat prickled his scalp and ran down his face. He gasped for breath and every nerve tingled in anticipation. The display projected into his vision showed the tunnel entrance a hundred metres in front and to the right of his position. Further away in that direction, the pair of NATO autonomous air transports flew in towards the tunnel mouth, slowing on their approach. On his left, from the opposite direction, Caliphate warriors ran to converge. Beyond the immediate battlespace, both Caliphate and friendly ACAs streaked through the sky towards their position.

"We're going to be right in the middle of the party," Rory muttered.

"The ragheads are not interested in us," Sergeant Heaton said.

"They might not be, but their fucking ACAs will," Barry observed.

Rory raised his Pickup and aimed. "Let's nail these bastards now." He fired three shots in the general direction of the Caliphate warriors, knowing that the super AI would shift each shell's trajectory onto its intended target. The others around him also fired. He frowned in grim anticipation of savouring a taste of revenge. But when the enemy warriors were hit and fell down, their bodies gave off a green flash.

"Did you see that?" Barry asked rhetorically.

"Aye. Now we're in the shit and no mistake," Heaton said.

"That, that's not possible," Rory stammered. "They can't do that."

Barry said: "Look, the fuckers are getting back up."

"Oh no," Rory muttered, appalled at the implications of Caliphate warriors having personal shielding.

Barry said: "I think we should knock 'em back down," and recommenced firing.

Rory joined in, letting off several more short bursts. Their shots knocked the eight Caliphate warriors down again, and this time they did not reappear.

"Have we killed them?" Barry asked.

"I don't think so," Heaton said. "I reckon they've backed off into dead ground below the crest. Come on," he urged. "They might use that to get to the tunnel."

Rory rose to a crouch and began moving again, cursing the fineness of the sandy dirt as his boots sank into it. "Look sharp if the enemy comes into view," he cautioned the others, noting the distance to their objective drop to less than seventy-five metres. Beyond that, the AATs shimmered in the heat haze as they slowed to a stop above their arrival point and then set down vertically on the ground. The empty black semicircle of the tunnel mouth contrasted starkly with the hot, bright surroundings and azure sky.

Rory followed the indicators in his vision as the two sergeants running with him swapped opinions: "I heard personal shielding was impossible—"

"It don't seem like it now, do it, eh?"

"So how the fuck are they doing that? What about the headaches and the disorientation? How can they trot about li—"

Their Squitches broke in simultaneously: "Enemy contact twenty-one degrees east, distance two-fifty—"

"Take cover."

Rory fell straight down, training taking over his limbs. Lines of light flashed a fraction over his head and a fireball erupted on his left. He swore aloud and turned away. A wave of heat washed past and he wondered if Caliphate Spiders wouldn't be easier to deal with than these warriors.

The digital enhancements in his vision fractured, splayed out in a thousand directions, and then reassembled. His Squitch instructed: "Aim at the horizon where indicated and fire now."

He let off several more three-shot bursts. He dropped another empty magazine and inserted a new one. He became absorbed in the business at hand, a part of his mind wondering how on earth soldiers in earlier wars ever survived a firefight without the support of super artificial intelligence. Every time a tiny dot tried to move, he shot at it. The green flashes stopped. Two figures fell and did not rise again.

"Move south to the tunnel entrance," the Squitch ordered.

He checked the dots in his vision that represented the other members of the support party. He noticed one was missing. "Barry? Where are you?"

His Squitch answered: "Sergeant Smith is deceased."

Rory swore, turned and ran towards the tunnel entrance. The autonomous air transports sat close by, squat and unattractive and indifferent to the plight of those whom the super AI had brought the craft here to rescue. Next to the aircraft stood a small land transport vehicle whose markings denoted ownership of the Polish Army. There must have been some kind of problem because a young soldier clambered down from the front, as though he'd actually been driving the machine.

Breathing hard, Heaton said: "The good news is what's left of our forces are pulling back. The bad news is we are about to get proper fucked."

Rory gasped, "Twenty-one seconds can last ages."

His Squitch ordered: "Turn to the east and fire at the approaching targets indicated in your displ—"

"There's no time," Rory spat, aware that in a few seconds, fleets of ACAs would collide above them and rain down destruction.

He Squitch said: "You are disobeying an order from a superior—"

"Shit," Rory cursed, stopping and raising his Pickup. Heaton did the same. Flashes in the sky announced the arrival of the opposing wings of ACAs, while in front of them the remaining members of the advance troop of Caliphate warriors dropped down. Rory realised they would fire. He stole a glance at the tunnel entrance to see the vehicles there lit up by sparks and explosions as the enemy's ACAs dived in for the kill and the NATO machines fought to save the people there. He turned to face the enemy again, wondering how reliable the shells from their weapons might be. Something blew up at the tunnel entrance and he understood the Caliphate warriors were trying to stop that escape.

"Pull back," a voice shouted in Rory's ear. He kept firing short bursts, becoming aware of the growing violence in the sky but still wanting to protect the NATO troops.

His Squitch ordered: "Evacuate now. You have fifteen seconds to board an AAT, otherwise you will be left behind."

"Come on, Heaton," he yelled out. Now heedless of the Caliphate warriors approaching the tunnel entrance, he ran with the longest, most urgent strides. The sand seemed to become finer, sucking his boots in deeper. He shouted aloud in shock when the fiery remains of an ACA thudded into the ground a few metres on his left. He reached the nearest AAT, an Airbus C440, smaller than the Boeing 818 but more dexterous in the air.

Rory paused at the ramp and turned to assist Heaton. In the top-left of his view, a large, blinking '5' flashed for a second, changing to '4' and then '3'. He deactivated and threw his Pickup into the AAT. He swung around, grabbed Heaton's waist and heaved, dumping his colleague on the ramp.

Rory pulled with all of his remaining energy to drag himself into the aircraft as an alarm sounded and the ramp rose to seal the AAT shut. He brought his legs up with no time to spare. The ramp clunked closed and at once the aircraft lifted into the air. Rory stared fixated at the metal ramp, the images of the battle and destruction burned into his retinas, replaying repeatedly as though he were drunk on the intensity of the experience. He started to shiver.

His Squitch said: "You are beginning to hyperventilate. Please control your breathing."

Rory felt someone grab him under his armpits and drag him back from the ramp. The AAT staggered and shuddered under the impact of Caliphate ACAs, which must have surely defeated the meagre resources NATO would have been able to deploy. Rory turned over and clambered to his feet. He paused and brought his breathing under control.

His Squitch instructed: "Please sit and secure yourself. The journey will involve mild turbulence."

"I want to know what Sergeant Smith died for."

Heaton shouted above the noise: "You better secure yourself, Sergeant Moore. We're not out of this yet." Heaton shrugged his pack from his back and collapsed in one of the fold-down seats bolted onto the side of the fuselage. He strapped himself in and then secured his pack.

Rory took his own backpack off and clipped it to the fuselage. He steadied himself when the aircraft banked. His Squitch warned: "You must secure yourself. Evasive action must be taken that will result in serious injury and may cause your death."

Rory's strength deserted him. He pulled down a seat opposite Heaton and sat. The instant he clipped closed the straps to secure himself, the AAT pitched up and yawed hard over to starboard before rolling back to port. Rory ignored new pain in his chest from the G-forces of these acrobatics and demanded: "Show me the forward compartment."

A view resolved in his lens of the next compartment in the aircraft. A battlefield stretcher lay on the deck, it and its burden strapped down. The Caliphate warrior on it was covered in blood and Rory doubted he could still be alive. He noted the similarity in the design of his boots with the enemy's, but could make out little of the warrior's battledress or support tech. He shook his head in confusion—why had he been obliged to risk his life and to lose comrades to save this piece of shit?

Three figures were slumped along the other side of the fuselage next to Heaton, battle-weary troops like him. On the left sat a female private with long, straight black hair draped over a GenoFluid pack wrapped around her head. A deep crimson stained her torso, turning a dirty ochre at the edges as the blood dried. The other two were young men, eyes downcast and also injured. They had clearly not had a good day out.

Rory clenched his eyes and teeth shut suddenly when the AAT made more urgent evasive manoeuvres, as though they were all unwilling guests on an especially draining fairground ride. At length, the aircraft settled on a straighter heading. Rory asked: "Advise probability of successful evac from this op."

The Squitch answered: "Eighty-three percent and rising. This aircraft is not currently targeted by enemy forces."

Rory let out a long breath in relief. His memory threw up one particular episode from his sergeant-training course: *The Parable of the Lucky Frog.* This concerned a Frenchman called Marbot, who lived in the nineteenth century and who fought alongside Napoleon throughout all of the French emperor's campaigns. Marbot took part in numerous battles—any one of which might have killed him—and suffered many serious injuries in his forty-year military career. His story featured on the training course to help prepare new sergeants to accept the vagaries of chance on the battlefield. As Rory recalled Marbot's exploits and longevity in the face of staggering odds that should have seen the Frenchman killed long before he could retire, he wondered if he himself were destined to emulate the French colonel. He added up the engagements he had already survived. He saw again the faces of the comrades he had lost.

But he was no Marbot, facing mere cannonball, sabre and shot. Perhaps, he conceded, chance could still play a role in deciding who lived and died on the battlefield, but the technology deployed today by this new enemy minimised infantry's ability to survive in such an outrageously hostile environment.

As the AAT carried them away from danger towards temporary safety, Sergeant Rory Moore wondered when it would be his turn to be left behind, blown to pieces on the battlefield like Sergeant Smith.

Chapter 7

Polish General Pakla shrugged his shoulders and said in accented English: "Is there even any point to this discussion? With respect, General Jones and General Tidbury, tens of thousands are dead on this morning. The enemy has resumed pushing us back on all fronts. What is the life of one despicable Caliphate warrior? I would rather we discuss the retreat, yes?"

Terry Tidbury felt the weight of a thousand problems bearing down on them now that the battle for Europe would be concluded, but there were higher ideals at stake. He looked at the images of the Polish general and SACEUR on the screen in front of him and said: "This will go up to the politicians and they'll have the final say. Their conference call is due to start in seven min—"

"I suggest," SACEUR broke in, "that since he's in our possession, we proceed with sending him to the facility. The intel in his head is worth way more than his life."

"Are we sure he will live?" the Polish general asked. "If he dies, the intel dies with him."

Terry stuck out a placating hand at the screen and said: "Gentlemen, each of us has many more pressing issues. The injured warrior is stable and will arrive at the facility in due course. I will attend the meeting and see how the land lies—"

Pakla broke in: "Sorry, general, but how can 'land lie' exactly? Does not land always tell the truth?"

Terry shook his head and bit down frustration. "It's an idiom, that's all. It means we'll see how things are. I'll be in touch."

Pakla's face creased in thoughtfulness but he said nothing.

Terry noted the amused look on Jones's face in the instant before both of them disappeared to be replaced by a map of Europe. This brought Terry back to his—and NATO's—most pressing concern. He barked: "Sitrep, Squonk."

The British Army's super AI summarised: "NATO forces are retreating on all fronts at the tactically slowest rate."

"For Pete's sake, give me some details," Terry said testily.

"Please specify depth of summary, from level one up to t—"

"Two," Terry yelled as he recollected the ranges of Squonk's assistance.

Squonk went on: "Army Group East is following its projected retreat pattern in all sectors. Army Groups South and West are reversing at the fastest rate, despite localised attempts to frustrate the enemy, including increased deployment of FT–23/D anti-personnel smart-mines…"

Terry listened and stared at the map of Europe on the screen in front of him. A voice in his head kept asking why, why today and not any other day in the last three months? Arrows showed military movements over land as the enemy attacked and then overwhelmed town, city, forest and farm. A wave of guilt rippled through him. It forced him to consider if NATO should or could have done anything differently.

Terry blinked when Squonk's tone changed and the super AI questioned him. "What?" he asked.

"The emergency meeting is about to start. Do you wish to attend via VR or screen only?"

"Screen."

"Confirmed."

Terry's eyes stung as he rubbed them. The screen came alive with the lined face of German Chancellor Peter Mitsch. Terry estimated the man to be in his late sixties, but the previous months must have added to the German's gaunt appearance. Thumbnails of the other attendees resolved in a row along the bottom of the screen.

Mitsch spoke: "Thank you, everyone. The military made a request. They captured an enemy warrior, who is still alive. I am advised that he is en route to the *Institut Neuropsi* in Saclay, in the southwest of Paris. The proposal is to use the institute's scanning machines to remove all of his memories. These will be analysed to discover more about the people who are responsible for the disaster that has fallen upon us. However, in result of this, the warrior will die."

Terry saw beyond the elderly German's imperfect English and sensed what might happen. Before anyone else could voice an opinion, he spoke: "We are being destroyed by an enemy about which we know next to nothing. The institute can give us vital, invaluable intelligence concerning the enemy and how he functions and is organised. Whatever moral qualms might be involved, we absolutely cannot forego this opportunity—"

The French president broke in, an intense, penetrating frown narrowing his eyes: "We have no right to condemn this man to death without first convict—"

And was himself interrupted by Dahra Napier: "I'm not sure we can afford the luxury of holding the moral high ground here. I agree with you, but if the general says we need what is in that warrior's m—"

"Then we are no better than them!" the French president shouted. "If we kill without mercy, if we shrug our shoulders in such arrogant indifference to life, why should history regard our efforts to survive as any more worthy than those of our enemy's efforts to obliterate us, *non*?"

A few heads in the thumbnails shook in bemusement. Terry said: "Sir, that warrior's brain holds information which would certainly help us a great deal. The history of the Caliphate's isolation, the strength of its jamming abilities, and the complete supr—"

"And what?" the president's frown transformed into a sneer. "You think we can go back? You think we should, we should return to the politics we endured thirty or forty years ago?"

"No, sir. That's not what I meant. I realise—"

"Yes, it is," the French president insisted. "You would have us go back to those awful days when we killed at our leisure, when we executed our enemies without due process or a proper legal conviction, because their atrocities had enraged our own bloodlust. We knew then, we found out, we had to rise above them. We had to be better if we wanted to finally prevail."

Terry did not have time for history lessons. The West's moral collapse earlier in the century concerned him not at all compared with the military objectives with which his political masters had entrusted him since the start of this war. And the very last thing he could afford now was a morality that— however justified—could cost them a critical advantage in the face of certain defeat.

Terry sensed that fatigue and fear had ground each of them down to a desperate sadness that had upended all they had hitherto believed in. After a tense pause, he said: "Mr president, other members, please understand that I share your concerns regarding the morality of what the military is asking you to approve. However, I must stress a very salient point: there will be no history to judge the rightness of your decisions. In a few short weeks, the New Persian Caliphate will overwhelm our defences and crush us absolutely, militarily, physically, and culturally. When its forces have destroyed or immobilised a sufficient amount of NATO forces, and when its warriors have stamped on and eliminated any possible defence—even the meanest individual with his hunting gun—then the enemy will subsume the remaining civilians and Europe's destruction will be complete.

"Perhaps the knowledge inside the head of this anonymous warrior will not assist us in the final defence of all that we value in our lives and cultures. But, even if there is a tiny piece of intelligence, a single sliver of data that could provide a clue to how we might defend ourselves—even if it is only to delay the inevitable—I believe we owe it to the citizens who, even now, are counting the cost of this war, who are digging their dead out from under the rubble."

Terry understood he was no orator, but every face on the screen looked at him and the skin around the back of his neck prickled with the realisation that they waited for him to say more. An urge to conclude, to achieve what he needed to achieve, asserted itself. He said: "With your permission, I will advise SACEUR that we can ask the institute to proceed to scan the warrior."

The German chancellor heaved a sigh, pinched the bridge of his nose, and said: "I think that is how we must proceed."

Silence followed, as though everyone acceded but no one wished to voice it.

Without waiting a fraction longer than diplomacy required, Terry left the meeting. He barked: "Squonk? Get Jones, now."

"Confirmed."

Jones's face resolved on the screen a second later. "Yeah, what?" he asked.

"I persuaded the politicians to agree."

"Good work, general," SACEUR said.

"Thank you, sir, but we'll see about that."

"I'll contact the institute and give them the green light."

"What about his implant? If there's one thing we do know about the enemy, it's that every Caliphate subject has an implant that kills them if they stray too far beyond the Third Caliph's realm."

Jones clucked his tongue and said dismissively: "Super AI's got it covered. It's already disabled. The warrior's cut off. He's ours now."

Chapter 8

Duncan Seekings stirred the teabag in his mug, the metal teaspoon clinking on the porcelain as, in another part of his vision, he followed a dozen lines of vivid light that curved and wended and meandered in different directions. The colour of the hot, amber liquid deepened to a burnt oak. His lens notified him of an incoming contact from his friend, Graham English.

"Hullo, old chap," Duncan said airily, pausing the display of lights in his vision with a twitch of an eye muscle. "Have you got over losing last night's snooker?"

Thick, bushy eyebrows came together as Graham sighed and replied: "I didn't lose; I merely allowed you the pleasure of winning."

"Really, Mr English, sometimes you can be too self-effacing."

"What are you up to?"

"Making a cup of tea," Duncan replied, "for as long as I can still get teabags, at any rate." He used the teaspoon to squeeze the teabag against the side of the mug, then lifted the bag out and flicked it into the sink. "And I have also been delving into the finer points of Fermi-Dirac statistics."

"The issue of the muon power source?"

"Of course."

"And how, may I ask, is it coming along?"

Duncan sipped his tea and replied: "Like looking for a needle in a field of haystacks."

"Shouldn't the computers be able to solve that, and with relative ease, I would've thought?"

Duncan sat on his worn couch and rested the hot mug on the low coffee table in front of him. He said: "If we overlook the current fashion to distrust the bloody things, it is a little more boring than simply getting the super AI to perform quantum calculations."

"How so?"

"Because of the snags," Duncan replied as though the answer were obvious. "I've told you before: it's all about the snags."

Graham tutted and sat back, his thick-set chest coming into Duncan's view. He said: "Step away from the snags, Mr Seekings."

Duncan answered: "You provoke me, sir. As I suspect you may know, somehow the New Persian Caliphate has found a way to overcome the fact that a muon particle only has a one percent chance of sticking to an alpha particle. Not only that, but they have also managed to surmount the critical-mass issue regarding muon-based power sources in gen—"

"Yes, quite. But that is what we have super artificial intelligence for. Has it not given Reyer and his team the answers?"

"Snags, Mr English," Duncan repeated. "Despite quantum computing's undoubtedly impressive raw capabilities, it cannot predict a muon's relationship in the grand canonical ensemble so that it agrees with the extended Pauli exclusion principle."

"Ah, I read something about that a couple of years ago. The discovery of the extended Pauli was thought to be in some doubt."

"Oh, it exists all right. And no one expected it to exist. Snags, you see? They're always there, Mr English, ready to pop up."

"But the computers can at least give you an idea of when they will resolve the muon issue, surely?"

Duncan flopped back in the soft couch and replied: "It's offered Reyer what it calls a 'window of resolution' of thirty to sixty days—an appalling amount of time. I was looking to see if there might be a way to shorten that time when you called."

"Hmm," Graham murmured. "I do hope you will find something sooner than that. So are you officially on Reyer's team now?"

"Not officially, no. But we're all in this together and we can't have too many eyes on this problem."

"Agreed."

Duncan changed the subject: "How did the meeting go this morning? You seemed bothered by the prospect last night. Frankly speaking, I thought that's what put you off your game."

Graham scoffed and admonished: "I've warned you before not to keep speaking so frankly."

Duncan chuckled.

Graham went on: "It was the least-boring meeting I have ever attended."

"Really?"

"I presented our plans for the super-high frequency beams we're going to use to burn through the Caliphate's damnable jamming."

"Were the military people happy with it?"

"Quite, despite the fact that we will need a couple of weeks to test and maximise their effectiveness. The military types will probably hang on to surprise the enemy at some key juncture—"

Duncan's hearing perked up at his friend's abrupt curtailment. "What is it?" he asked.

Graham paused and then asked: "You haven't heard, have you?"

"Heard what? There are more than a few things going on at the moment, old chap. Is it more bad news?"

"Not at all... We both have the same level of clearance, I suppose."

"Spit it out, then."

"The Poles have captured an injured Caliphate warrior."

"Good Lord. Alive?"

"Yes."

Duncan sat forward and picked up his mug of tea. "What about the implant they all have? Surely that should have done for him, no?"

Graham shook his head and replied: "The super AI reprogrammed the medical bots in a GenoFluid pack to disable it."

Duncan sniffed and said: "So what are they going to do, interrogate him?"

"No need."

"Meaning?"

Graham's bushy eyebrows rose as he asked: "Don't tell me you haven't heard of the *Institut Neuropsi* in Paris?"

"Of course," Duncan said, putting the mug back on the coffee table. "But that's for people who have already died... Hang on a mo, if they scan him, they'll kill him."

Graham shrugged and replied: "The politicians have, quite rightly I think, decided that the benefits outweigh the costs."

Duncan nodded in consideration before answering, "Good show. His brain could answer more than a few questions. How long will it take?"

Graham frowned, "Several days, unfortunately."

"Everything connected with this damn war seems to be taking so long."

"Only for us. Not for them."

Duncan pushed back against the overwhelming sense of gloom. Futility encroached all around him, but he would not let his concern show, because that would not be British. He spoke in a tone of airy indifference: "That is rather boring, don't you think?"

The look on his friend's face told Duncan more than either man's words ever would. "Quite," Graham said in a flat tone.

"In that case I suggest another game of snooker, at your earliest convenience."

Graham smiled and replied: "Splendid idea."

Chapter 9

The Englishman had never known pain like it. Every cell on his skin screamed in electrified anguish. Wave followed wave in a methodical pattern of rise and fall to allow him just enough relief to gasp some air into his lungs before the next wave surged to bring ever-increasing agony. Beyond the physical pain lay the complete psychological disorientation. Time no longer meant anything, measured only in the waves that gave him just enough pause to steal a breath. He felt the agony destroy his memories, his experiences, the essence of who he was, extracted from him like a tooth that had shattered under the dentist's pliers so that each shard's removal took with it an irreplaceable portion of his soul.

The next wave withdrew. He stole another meagre lungful of air. The pause continued. Extreme exhaustion tore at his body. He breathed again, not understanding where the pain might have gone. He took another breath, irrational fear increasing once more. They only wanted him to experience as much agony as possible before they killed him. What had he revealed during this torture? Had he mentioned Marshal

Zhou? Had the pain been so bad he'd admitted to anything just to get it to stop?

He opened his eyes. Blue light illuminated grey ceiling tiles above him, the kind that hid air-conditioning ducts. He forced himself to control his breathing. He began to shake, a trembling deep in his limbs. Clamps held him fast on some kind of table, or perhaps in a horizontal dentist's chair. They pressed down and pinned him around his neck, chest, wrists, waist, thighs and ankles. His limbs vibrated against them as the shaking intensified.

Suddenly a figure appeared above him. A woman with a perfectly oval face, narrow eyes, and pursed, deep-red lips. He reflected that she might be the most beautiful Chinese woman he had ever seen. Her expression softened and she nodded. She spoke with a heavy oriental accent: "Now, you talk."

Through his disorientation and seared memories of overwhelming pain, the Englishman chose his words carefully: "Fuck off, you slit-eyed cunt."

As he expected, the agony slammed into him again like a concrete wall. Time passed. Every muscle tensed until he thought one or more might tear. The pain dissipated and he gasped for breath again. He waited for the next wave, but it didn't come.

The woman admonished: "You forget your manners, yeah?"

The Englishman said nothing. They were going to kill him, and he'd had enough of suffering.

"In your body you have bots, yeah?"

With the absence of the pain, the deep trembling of absolute exhaustion resumed in his limbs.

"I can make these bots hurt you very much. Bots tell me how much they hurt you. Bots tell me how much you can take. Bots hurt you to the max, yeah?"

As each cell in his body cried out for relief, the Englishman decided he would never willingly help them. He resigned from the circus. He'd had his fun. He'd enjoyed more highs and physical excitement than he could have imagined when he was just a teen confused by all of the conflicting signals and desires his body sent him. He'd been lucky: his wildest dreams had been fulfilled; his deepest, most intense physical desires sated. He'd played a tiny role defending his beloved England while its pathetic lack of true influence in global affairs made its leaders embarrass themselves further than their predecessors ever did. He had used his body to pleasure those who might help his country, but now that body wilted under the hours of near-constant pain. A distant voice in his head reminded him of the golden rule: that pain was so very close to pleasure. Marshal Zhou had understood that, but the Marshal must undoubtedly be dead by now.

The Englishman waited only for the end, to be finally free, to sleep the sleep of those who had fulfilled their obligations. He looked up at his tormentor and uttered: "I thought I told you to fuck off, you slit-eyed cunt?"

The beautiful woman's eyes narrowed in curiosity. She whispered: "You wanna escape, yeah? You wanna the pain stop. You fink you upset me and you die?"

The Englishman drew in a breath, ready to issue another foul-mouthed curse.

The woman smiled and said: "You no talk, no problem. I have not so much time for big nobody like you anyway. I tell you wha': I let bots do the work for me, yeah?"

"Fuck."

"Bots will fix you. You go back to your old job. But we will see and hear and know everything. Bots good, yeah? Bots make sure you work for us now. And if you tell, then maybe bots kill you." She gave him a sneer of contempt and added: "You just English dumbass."

Chapter 10

Turkish engineering student Berat Kartal watched the other refugees suffer in the heat. Forlorn figures trudged and limped to join lines waiting at the food and water replicators. He wondered why Europeans suffered from the heat so much when they'd had decades to get used to it. People queued under awnings to protect them from the worst of the sun, but the closeness and humidity made the air almost too heavy to breathe. He did sympathise a little: until the war began, all of these people would have enjoyed air-conditioned surroundings most of the time.

Berat rested by a wire fence that marked the enclosure of the refugee transit camp set up on farmland just outside the Austrian town of Krems. He'd used the pause afforded by the Tense Spring to gain as much ground in front of the Caliphate as he could. After walking north for several weeks, joining the thronging exodus only long enough to obtain food and water, he reached the Danube at Bratislava and turned west. He made this choice for two reasons: he wanted to get into Germany because he believed Teutonic resilience would better manage the chaos, and he could follow the Danube to Munich, from where he had an idea to head north to the Nordic countries. Secondly, following the river would involve less climbing and offer more opportunities to gain food.

Berat had learned to survive on almost nothing. At some deeper level, he even blessed the *lanet olası* Caliphate for invading when it had. Through the months of his endless flight, Berat had scrounged enough to keep his undernourished body pushing forward through the fear, deprivation, and desolation this war caused. The urgency in February and March had abated when news swept the columns of refugees that the Caliphate had paused its forces. However, as the Tense Spring evolved into summer, Berat sensed time running out on all of them once again.

Now, as he looked around at so many victims in the camp, he considered those utterances that he heard among the German and Czech and Slovak and Slovenian and Hungarian and Romanian languages invoke urgency of movement. News of the resumption of the Caliphate's advance across Europe had flashed and passed through languages and people with the speed of one of the enemy's flying bomb-carriers.

Berat shut his eyes and tensed his muscles. Memories of all the faces, of all the walking dead he had overtaken and left behind, rose up in his mind's eye, pointing accusing fingers at him, demanding to know what right he had to live when they had died. Berat interlinked his fingers and tightened his hands behind his head. The ever-present stench of stale sweat in his armpits invaded his nose and made the images in his mind's eye grimace.

He forced his eyes open, knowing that the faces of the dead would only fade into the background temporarily. Thirty metres across the open space crisscrossed by weary figures, a dishevelled woman pulled the arm of a young girl probably not more than six years old. The girl whined and refused to move by grasping the shirt of a prone male lying flat on the dusty ground. Berat recognised the stiffness in the man's limbs but had seen such events so many times, he no longer wondered nor cared what precisely might have killed the man. He only deduced that the young girl must be suffering grievously with hunger and perhaps thirst as well, given that her cries consisted of a weak mewling rather than the full-throated howls of anguish one might have expected from a healthy child. Her father—Berat chose to assume it was her father—had likely succumbed to the heat due to his obesity. Berat thought he could see the dead man's hillock of a stomach already begin to expand with the pressure of gases caused by putrefaction. The hot afternoon sun did its work on dead flesh with grim predictability.

He clenched his eyes shut to allow the ghosts to flutter and hiss and exercise themselves in his exhausted mind. Once again, they grimaced and then smiled at him, smiles to tell him to ready himself, for he was the next in line. He shook his head to expel them. He stretched and decided to leave the camp, find a quiet place in the surrounding forest, and make an entry in his paper journal. As the days and weeks passed, the journal became so much more than a mere record. He noted in it as many details as he could remember, and he often considered that those walking dead who invaded his mind from time to time would drive him completely mad if he did not record in the journal that they had lived before they were—

Sudden screams and shrieks broke out on the other side of the camp. As one, the mass of people lurched away from whatever threat had arrived. Berat knew instant panic seldom helped, and fought the urge to be subsumed into the pack mentality that overwhelmed all of those around him. He pushed himself back against the fence to let the anticipated stampede progress without him. The noise and naked fear on the faces of the other refugees tugged at the calmness given him by the familiarity of urgency. He saw a toddler trampled to unconsciousness by adults and he caught his breath. The extensive awnings to his right, which had seconds ago protected patient if malnourished queues of starving refugees, abruptly flashed into bright orange flames then blackened and withered.

"Lasers!" a voice yelled.

Berat crouched lower and squeezed his waif-like body further back into the wiry mesh of the fence. The heat increased and he knew the machines would roast him alive if he did not flee. People's hair caught fire and their clothes burned. The air filled with screams and shrieks and the crackling of human skin. His engineer's sense of logical order took over, noting the pattern of the waves of death from the attacking Caliphate Lapwings as they swept past in the most efficient geometrical orderliness.

Amid the terrifying chaos that paralysed many of the refugees, at a certain point he judged the time to have arrived and he knew he had to run. He forced his legs to overrule his mind's reluctance. He sprinted towards the nearest entry point and noted the local guards—retired Austrians—looking at the sky in fear.

As he ran, he collided with other refugees, reeled under the impact, righted himself, and then others ran into him and almost knocked him down. He skirted around burning bodies and debris. He ran through the gates of the camp. He glanced up for an instant at the evil black shapes that had turned for another pass before he scurried on, south towards the Danube. More yells of concern and fear told him the Lapwings attacked again.

The straight road took Berat downhill. Other figures staggered and limped and tried to find shelter. Behind him, deadening ruptures and the thumps of falling masonry came to his ears, the ground beneath his feet trembling as though it were also scared of the merciless enemy in the air.

He stopped when he came to an ornate, wrought iron barrier that prevented him from falling off the stone bank and headlong into the Danube. He grasped the top horizontal bar. The river below churned onwards, right to left, dirty brown water carrying flotsam of splintered wood and cadavers, both human and animal.

A heavy explosion erupted behind him. He turned to see the roof of a smart townhouse collapse inwards, ejecting a cloud of sparks and smoke. Panic chilled Berat's skin but his engineer's calm logic did not fully desert him. A wave of distant black dots descended in curved geometric elegance. He had no choice but to leap into the river if he were to survive. However, if he did so his journal would be ruined. A voice in his head observed that it hardly mattered whether water or flame were the cause of his journal's destruction.

The approaching black machines loomed larger. With no time to spare, Berat shrugged his rucksack from his shoulders. As soon as it fell to the ground, he grasped the metal bar and hurled himself over the barrier and into the murky waters below. The cold water shocked his fatigued body. The weight of his filthy sweatshirt and trousers seemed to increase ten-fold and terror gripped him at the realisation his flimsy clothes could drown him. With his eyes shut tight against the water, he felt certain his ears played tricks on him as a sound of thunder came from above. He realised a Lapwing must have passed overhead and boiled the surface above him. As if in confirmation, heat surged through the water around him.

But however bad the surface would be, he had to breathe. He yanked and his sweatshirt came apart at the seams. Amid increasing panic and with his chest tightening further, he pulled the parts of the sweatshirt from his arms and torso, his body twisting in the current. Suddenly, his left foot hit a rock or stone. He drifted to his left and his feet found the bed of the river. With his remaining strength, he pushed in that direction. Cooler water surrounded to him. His right foot stepped on the slippery stones and then he pulled himself through the water with his arms—the action was too full of desperation to be called swimming. His head broke the surface in an agony of effort and he gasped in a breath. At once, his feet slipped off the stones and the current took him under again. He flailed and lurched under the water, breaking the surface when he thought he would have to gulp in the foul liquid.

He dragged himself into a stony inlet between two ageing brick jetties where the water was only a metre deep. He heaved in breath after breath trying to recollect how much of the water he had swallowed. He hawked and spat, alarmed at the bacteria that might have entered his body. An overwhelming urge to get away from the river and then this town gripped him. He splashed through the shallows and climbed the rungs of a short ladder up to street level, taking care that his hands and feet did not slip on the lichen-covered metal.

The breeze drove palls of black smoke across the burning buildings. Berat's soaked trousers hindered movement but he decided not to remove them or the sodden boots on his feet. Ten minutes later, he sat on the ground weeping. He held his battered rucksack with his journal inside, miraculously unscathed among the wreckage.

Chapter 11

Private Agnes Queues of the British Royal Armoured Corps stowed her Pickup and sat in her seat among the row that lined the fuselage of the Boeing 828. She pulled the straps from behind her over her shoulders and clipped herself in.

On her left, her friend Phredd said with a toothy grin: "Remain still until assistance arrives."

Agnes smiled back, but inside her stomach fell. It had become a standing joke between the two young women: if a soldier were mortally wounded, their Squitch would not tell them this fact, but would simply advise them to 'remain still until assistance arrives', even if it knew death would occur before any assistance could be provided. Everyone in uniform knew the reason was to save the injured soldier from unnecessary panic if the Squitch told them they were about to die.

The doors of the autonomous air transport clunked shut. Agnes heard a hiss as the cabin pressurised. There came a slight vibration when the engines powered up and the aircraft lifted off the ground. Looking outside, she glimpsed brown and barren fields fall away in the fading daylight. The aircraft banked and accelerated.

The sergeant's gruff male voice spoke in her ear, sounding as nervous as she felt: "Right then, boys and girls. Now it's time to roll up our sleeves and get stuck in…"

He wittered on, describing their objective using a range of clichés that grated on Agnes's nerves. She snapped her eyes closed and wished she could do the same with her ears. She counted backwards through all of the recent Fridays that had led her to be in this uniform, in this autonomous air transport, on the way to the south of France to reinforce troops there who were falling back more quickly than the genius super AI had anticipated.

Ten weeks had passed since she'd decided to sign up, to 'do her bit'. Her dad said he was proud of her, but she knew he also worried about losing her. Some of her friends, like Phredd, supported her because they joined up also; some just wished her luck, and a few mocked her for volunteering to be cannon fodder. She recalled the sneer on Jason's handsome face. She used to like Jason. He'd been one of the less immature young men on her course at university, but when he explained that self-preservation should be the priority of any sane person, she bit down her instinctive reaction at his selfishness and walked away from him.

The sergeant stopped talking. The AAT shuddered a fraction when it reached its cruising altitude and accelerated further. Agnes caught glances from others in her troop and wondered what might be going through their minds. Her thoughts returned to recent memories of her decision to take advantage of the government's scheme to allow university students to put their courses on hold if they joined the Armed Forces, with a guarantee of continuance after the war. The popular cynicism among her troop, over half of whom had also been in further education, was that there would be no universities left to return to, even if any of them survived.

She sensed someone watching her. She glanced left to see Phredd's warm eyes regard her. Agnes smiled back with genuine affection, but despite Phredd's advances, Agnes had tried to drop subtle hints that Phredd was not her type, in every sense. But it had been tricky when Phredd kept on complimenting her on her eyes, her complexion, her hair and her make-up.

"You okay?" Phredd asked.

Agnes nodded. "You?"

Phredd gave a half-smile but her lower lip trembled.

"It's going to be all right," Agnes said.

"Oh yeah? When?"

Agnes looked at Phredd and said with care: "One step at a time. And let's keep an eye out for each other, agreed?"

Phredd nodded.

Agnes stared ahead to the other side of the fuselage, noting eight minutes on the countdown to in-theatre arrival. Her thoughts drifted again to home, to all of those people she—

"Okay boys and girls, listen up," the sergeant said, breaking into Agnes's thoughts.

Agnes glanced at Phredd and saw that her friend also worried about what they would find when they disembarked.

The sergeant went on: "We've got an increasing probability that we'll have to disembark under fire—"

Agnes joined her peers in groaning aloud at the news.

"Now just take it easy, everyone," the sergeant whined, as though the object of his admonishment were himself. "We've drilled for this. We've been trained for this. Other NATO troops are in trouble and need our help."

There came a pause. Agnes deduced that another soldier must have asked a question, and the sergeant gave his answer to the whole troop. He said: "We're going in under a screen of high-altitude SkyWatchers and lower-level PeaceMakers. In addition, we've got BSLs across the line as well as tanks in support. Enemy fire will be kept at the furthest possible distance. You only need to clear the AAT when instructed and move to cover, just like in training."

Tears welled in the corner of Agnes's eyes. Rumours came back to her of higher ranks and officers lying to lower ranks when they were about to land in a hot environment, but she'd never believed them. Super artificial intelligence had long-since resolved the problems of incompetent commanders who sent their troops into battle to die senseless deaths because they regarded war as some kind of sport. Today, each NATO soldier enjoyed the best protection the super AI could manage, and that was pretty good.

Agnes's spirits lifted. The arrival countdown dropped to under two minutes. She ran through her personal checklist before the sergeant called for all troops to do the same. In her ears, Agnes felt the changing air pressure as the AAT descended. She rolled her head to loosen her vertebrae and then pushed her shoulder blades back and forth.

Phredd's hand squeezed Agnes's thigh.

Agnes glimpsed the fear in Phredd's watery eyes.

Phredd mouthed 'I love you'.

Agnes didn't know how to respond, so she smiled. Then, she mouthed back: 'Thank you.'

Phredd smiled.

Agnes wondered how gently she could let Phredd down when this was over.

The sergeant's shrill voice invaded the women's intimacy. "Attention, all troops. Thirty seconds to touchdown. Follow disembarkation instructions from your Squitches."

Agnes didn't want to give Phredd the wrong impression, but the immense significance of what they were about to do weighed heavily on her also, so she put her hand on Phredd's hand and squeezed.

The AAT landed with a bump and Agnes's Squitch came to life. It placed digital directions over her vision and instructed: "Disembark." She released the straps holding her and grabbed her Pickup from behind her seat. She followed Phredd as the line of troops exited the AAT from the rear ramp.

"Follow the deployment pattern," the Squitch said. "Friendly forces are in retreat from the south. Hostile forces are in pursuit."

Agnes continued chasing after Phredd. They exited the AAT and jogged across a dry field of brown grass towards a ridge of trees at the base of a hill. She looked left and right to see other teams of troops following their own dispersal patterns.

"Caution," her Squitch advised, "friendly AATs approaching."

The digital indicator in her vision did not prepare her for the ear-splitting noise when the small autonomous air transports raced overhead. She exhaled and continued running, gripping her Pickup with both hands, wondering what the full tactical picture looked like. Sweat prickled her face and chilled her skin as it rubbed against the fabric of her uniform. How close to the front line had they been dropped? Were actual Caliphate warriors about to emerge through the trees? Why couldn't the PeaceMakers deal with—

"Danger," the Squitch advised. "Enemy forces are approaching more rapidly than anticipated. Return to the AAT now."

"What?" Agnes queried out loud.

"We've got Spiders on the way," the sergeant yelled in barely concealed terror. "Do what your Squitches tell you, now."

Agnes spun on her heels and began to return to the AAT. From the corner of her eye, she noted Phredd and the other troop members also running over the brown grass towards the squat, ugly transport.

Then Agnes heard the words she dreaded. Her Squitch said: "Danger: Caliphate Spider approaching from the south. Distance eight hundred metres, closing over irregular terrain. You are its target. Take defensive action immediately."

"Oh no," she muttered. Although the British Army's thorough training took over and allowed her to defend herself, part of her spirit reeled at being thrust into combat so abruptly. Without conscious thought, Agnes knelt, activated her Pickup, and fired at the target the Squitch lit up in her view, sensing rather than seeing the other members of the troop do the same. As the shells hit the Spider, she felt relief that she did not fight alone, that others had also targeted it. Soon enough its shielding dissipated and it exploded in a vast fireball that reached into the sky and set dying grass alight.

Her heart froze at what came next. Her Squitch said: "Danger: three Caliphate Spiders approaching from the south. Distance seven hundred metres, closing over irregular terrain. You are among those targeted. Return to the AAT now."

Agnes turned and ran, noting that others remained kneeling and firing. A few seconds later the Squitch ordered her to stop, turn and fire. As she did so, dismay surged inside her when she perceived they were still more than a hundred metres from the AAT. A dissenting voice at the back of her mind questioned why the super AI did not bring the transport closer.

She resumed firing while other members of the troop retreated towards her, Phredd among them. A few seconds later, the three Spiders blew up in quick succession, closer than the previous single one. A wave of hot air washed over her; she caught her breath and then lurched as the shockwave seemed to try to pull her forward. She struggled to get some moisture back into her mouth and throat.

"Return to the AAT, now," the Squitch instructed.

Agnes staggered onwards. Her spirits lifted as she got closer to the transport. Suddenly, it exploded with a deep thud that reverberated through the ground under her feet. A pall of black smoke curled in on itself and lifted skywards. Burning debris fell to the brown grass soundlessly. Urgent shouts and commands of other voices pierced her shock. She glanced around in rising panic. More indicators in her vision flashed red as the dangers multiplied. There were numerous targets at the ridgeline where the trees began, but part of Agnes's mind refused to accept what her display showed her.

Someone tugged her arm. Agnes looked and Phredd's terrified face implored her. But instead of offering some kind of explanation, Phredd whined: "I'm scared. What's happening?"

Agnes answered: "I don't know. We should take cover, but I'm not sure where."

The Squitch said: "Fire at the indicated targets approaching from the east immediately."

Phredd let go of Agnes, spun in that direction, knelt, raised her Pickup, and opened fire.

Agnes copied her. But when she fired at one of the numerous targets along the treeline, a sudden, vast and blinding white light grew in her vision to encompass and blot out all else. An indeterminate space of time passed. Agnes abruptly felt removed from events. A deep emptiness emanating from her sinuses created a certain calm. She chose not to fight it, not to try to find the reason or the source for this drastic change in circumstances. There came a tingling

91

from her limbs, also distant, as though they were occupied elsewhere and not currently available for her exclusive use. An indistinct brown mass filled her vision, but it did not trouble her. She recalled she'd been in a battle, but that seemed to have been a long time ago and quite far away now. She thought she might move her limbs, but the tingling persisted; pins and needles remaining stubbornly in the way of her doing something useful like getting up.

Agnes became aware of someone speaking in the distance. She wondered if the words might be directed at her. She found the intrusion mildly irritating. A warmth had begun to descend over her; a feeling of peace, the result of her choosing not to resist, not to fight anything any longer. She wanted to rest. She wished the tingling from her limbs would stop, because if it did, she felt certain she'd be able to sleep.

The voice grew louder as her last strength waned. She decided to ignore the words and sleep anyway. A sleep would help. She would rest. But the voice continued: "Remain still until assistance arrives. Remain still until assistance arrives…"

Chapter 12

Anger surged inside Dahra Napier at her aide's casual indifference. "Crispin, do not, ever again in my presence, be so racist. Is that understood?"

He stepped back in apparent shock, which placated her to a degree. He defended: "I am not a racist, boss. I just think the rag—, er, the Caliphate warrior we captured, and the fact that he's going to die when we scan his brain, is not something you need to lose any sleep over."

"Ah, but it is," she admonished. "And do you know why?"

His chin jutted; she waited for him to argue. He remained silent.

"Because if we treat them as they treat us, we are no better than them."

"If you say so, boss."

"Don't patronise me, Crispin. I do not care if we have only days or weeks or months left before all this is destroyed, but I absolutely will not concede something that is a cornerstone of our cultural and moral superiority."

She hoped Crispin would get the message, but he shrugged and replied: "I suppose that might make some people feel better."

Dahra stared, aghast. She said: "Have you become so jaded in your role? Did your recent medical event cause some deeper damage? Perhaps you would like to consider passing on your responsibilities to one of your subordinates?" She turned away from him and strode across the spacious lounge to the coffee machine on the oak desk. She poured a cup of the black filter coffee and listened to Crispin's reply.

"No, boss," he answered with a tone of mollification. "I did not mean to suggest that."

Dahra gripped the coffee cup, tensing every muscle in her hand. She let a little more of the burning anger seep out, as though she were squeezing the last drops of water from a sponge. She said: "I'm hardly a stranger to cynicism, Crispin. Heaven knows we've had to weave some webs over the years. But life and death? Now that is something which constitutes more than simple political point-scoring, a little bit more than coming off best at PMQs, yes?"

Crispin did not reply.

She turned to face him and paced back across the room. "I won't do it, you see? I won't let the enemy best us in the one way—the one last, single way I can resist—over which I can retain a scintilla of control. I absolutely will not let these beasts drag me, and by extension England, down to their disgusting, foul level of utter contempt for the intrinsic value of human life."

The paling of Crispin's face convinced her that he understood.

She went on, feeling the poisonous injustice of this awful reality seep into every pore of her skin: "No human being has the right to take the life of any other human being in any circumstances. Without that fundamental tenet, we have no right to call ourselves civilised. Now, of course, that has all gone to the dogs, quite comprehensively. But that Caliphate warrior was entitled to due process, and to be tried, convicted and sentenced according to our laws."

"I think the military situa—"

"The military situation is irrelevant," she broke in, anger surging again. "All forecasts confirm the certainty of our ultimate defeat, the only question is when. But that is in any case besides the point. The scan of this young man's brain that the French institute will perform will kill him as certainly as if we had executed him. And I find that morally repugnant. And the more they hurt us, the more I will not debase myself by sinking to their level."

She took a gulp of the bitter coffee and stared into Crispin's eyes, wondering what he really thought. Had his brush with death at the beginning of March affected him very much? She doubted it. She recalled distant memories of their scheming and how often his darker skills had facilitated her small policy victories in the House. She said: "Anyway, I hope I have made my point. What is happening today?"

"Do you feel up to doing some interviews?"

She tutted and said: "Reassuring the country after yesterday's battering? What could I possibly say that might help?"

Crispin nodded in understanding. "You have some free time between the civilian and military sitreps."

Dahra sighed and thought of her husband and their children. And then she thought of all the millions of other families. She said: "Perhaps I could visit some of the victims?"

Crispin nodded in approval. "Nice idea for a little good publicity, boss. I'll let the press office know—"

"No, you will not," she broke in, giving him her most withering look. "I just want to see how we are coping, as a city, as a people, as a country."

"Okay," he replied with a sheepish look that disappeared when his right eyelid began flickering. He shook his head and said: "Things are really wrecked, boss. There are transport breaks everywhere. We've got construction replicators clearing rubble and trying to repair—"

She placed her hand gently on his shoulder and said: "I can see; I do have my own lens... Perhaps we can just go for a walk?"

"A walk? Oh, right. I'll get security to send some people—"

"No, you will not," she repeated. "I don't think my personal safety will be at any risk on this day. Come along, I want to go now."

She led her aide from the room. They walked in silence along the beige corridor and descended in a lift deep under Downing Street. They entered the warren of routes beneath this part of Whitehall. The walls became a militaristic grey. Dahra dealt with the multitude of on-going issues in her lens as she strode purposely in the direction of the river. From the corner of her eye she observed heads turn and glance briefly as other people recognised her. No matter. They followed long corridors and crossed many junctions.

From beside her, Crispin also dealt with the mountain of problems. "Yes, the PM will attend today's COBRA... No, MacSawley, not now. Just be patient and piss off... Hello? Thank you, yes, the PM would like to go for a stroll and will be at the east gate in a couple of minutes... No, we do not require security. PM's insistence, don't argue."

Dahra said: "If they want to, they can; it's not that important."

Crispin went on: "Yes, go with the AI's recommendation then... I'll redirect you to the PM's office, a person there will help you... Of course she'll be at the NATO sitrep this afternoon..."

At length, they arrived at a guarded doorway. The young, cleanshaven soldier nodded in nervous recognition and Dahra sought to put him at ease with: "Good morning. Do you know what the weather is like outside?"

The young man's wide green eyes glanced at Crispin and back again. He stammered: "Er, a little warm, ma'am."

"That's not unusual for June," Dahra replied.

The soldier's disquiet seemed to worsen.

"Is something wrong?" she asked.

"No, ma'am. It's just, well, TT, er, General Tidbury might not be best pleased with you leaving without—"

Dahra raised her hand and twitched her eye. She had to wait a few seconds until a thumbnail of Terry resolved in the lower left of her vision. She said: "Terry, my aide and I are going for a stroll outside. We do not require an escort. However, a rather handsome young man guarding the exit here seems concerned for our safety. Would you reassure him?"

Terry smiled and replied: "Leave it with me."

Dahra waited for a moment.

The young soldier's wide face had blushed to a delightful shade of puce. He spluttered: "Yes, General Tidbury. Of course, General Tidbury," before twisting an angled lever and pulling the door open.

Dahra and Crispin stepped outside. The unnatural, oppressive heat made the air feel heavy. The metal door clunked closed behind them, ringing an introduction to the worst of the enemy's destructive efficiency. All at once, she observed the reality; that which screens and reports had sanitised to a degree now presented itself to her in raw, uncompromising detail.

"Christ," Crispin whispered, "I can't even imagine how many bodies must be buried in all that debris."

She didn't answer, biting back the urge to weep at the vast mountains of rubble and palls of dirty black smoke that

97

lined the opposite side of the Thames. She walked onto the grass and past the Iraq and Afghanistan Memorial towards the river. A bough on an aged oak had sheared from the trunk, and the interior splintered wood gaped a bright tan.

"Perhaps that's far enough, boss?" Crispin said. "The river will not look good."

Dahra did not reply. She strode on, crossing the road. On her right there rested a heap of burning autonomous vehicles. She arrived at the bank where the floating debris reinforced the sense of resignation that had been building since she emerged outside.

On the opposite side of the filthy river, giant metal, multi-tailed scorpions crawled among the ruins. These were the construction replicators. At this distance they looked small and overwhelmed in this unfamiliar environment of such vast destruction. Their rotating appendages, which in normal circumstances could throw up walls and roofs and construct entire buildings in mere hours, beavered through the wreckage sorting and filtering and pausing only where they excavated human remains.

Dahra sensed Crispin standing behind her. She asked: "How has the super-artificial intelligence prioritised reconstruction?"

"After saving trapped and injured victims, it puts clearing the debris and re-establishing communication links and transport routes at the top of the list," came Crispin's cautious reply.

"Where are the flyers?" she asked.

"Airspace remains closed on the military's orders."

"For how long?"

There came a pause as she assumed her aide checked. He said: "If the attack really is over, then it won't be long, maybe half an hour."

"I think the bereaved need to have their loved ones back as soon as possible."

"Would you like to talk to the emergencies minister?"

"No, thank you." She had left with the notion of speaking with ordinary Londoners, of trying to connect with the people to share their grief, which in some small way might assuage her desire to atone. But now she saw chaos of a magnitude that defied belief.

"I think it's time to go back inside now," she said. Dahra turned around and walked back to the main Ministry of Defence building, which she noted had escaped the attack unscathed. The images of blasted and blackened walls and all the detritus spread over roads and which hung at strange angles from partially collapsed floors stayed with her.

She reached the metal door and stopped. She turned back to her aide and asked: "That Caliphate warrior; do you think he is already dead?"

Crispin nodded. "Probably. I've been told the scan itself is quite quick…"

His words trailed off and he kept staring at her, so she said: "What is it?"

"Boss," he answered, "the military are going to want to do these scans on all enemy combatants we capture alive. Like with this one, they'll argue that we need the intel—"

"Yes, yes," Dahra broke in. "That makes perfect sense."

"I thought you should know this in advance."

Dahra sighed. Every day she knew the end drew nearer, nearer for all of them. With the outcome of this awful war in little doubt, what did it really matter? "And I shan't stand in their way," she said before turning back to the metal door. It opened. She stepped through it and returned to the darkness.

Chapter 13

The bullish face of Polish General Pakla scowled out from the screen in the back of Sir Terry Tidbury's Toyota Rive-All as the vehicle sped out of London. Terry sometimes wished he could escape all the technology, especially when he needed to think, and now the Tense Spring had ended so abruptly and events had accelerated, he did need space to think. He'd hoped the brief journey from London to his home on the south coast would give him a chance to consider the enemy's most recent moves.

"Thank you for speaking with me," Pakla began in diffidence.

"No problem, general," Terry replied. "What can I do for you?"

"I asked the institute for any data—absolutely anything at all—as soon as they get it—"

"Asked?" Terry verified with a raised eyebrow.

"Well, insisted, I suppose I might have," Pakla conceded. "But they replied it will take up to two weeks before they can help us. This is crazy. We do not have that time, not at all."

"Yes, I know, general," Terry replied in his most even voice. "I spoke to the director of the institute after this morning's briefing and he is quite aware of the urgency of the situation. He promised something useful in a couple of days."

Pakla's eyes flicked from side to side and Terry wondered what epithets the Polish general was choking back.

Terry said: "I'm not sure we should pin too much on what's inside that warrior's brain, general."

"I was having similar thoughts, if I am honest. I have much—too much—frustration with this undefeatable enemy."

Terry nodded in sympathy and replied: "I don't have a lot of time for the 'predictions' the computers keep giving us regarding what life inside the Caliphate is really like."

"Pah," Pakla concurred, "no one knows what really goes on there. How can they force us to retreat so easily if they are so poor and backward like the computers tell us?"

"We'll find out soon enough if there's anything of use in that brain."

Pakla paused and his chin jutted. In his accented English, he confided: "I still carry a hope there will be, general. My troops do their best. They are the best. But they face not one but two enemy armies. The enemy, he… What is the English word? He harry us. Constantly we are falling back. The troops have to watch as we leave civilians to the mercy of the enemy. And if the rumours are true, we know the enemy, he have no mercy.

"From time to time, I have local commanders. They have good ideas to frustrate the enemy advance. But these are always temporary. Troops are… demoralised. Even in case they delay the enemy, they know it does not matter, really. They are not stupid. They know how this war will end. And this great attack, yesterday, many of them lost people, important people."

"And your job, general, is to make sure they maintain their fighting effectiveness," Terry said, "despite what your troops think they 'know'. Morale is one of our most important challenges. If that collapses, the end will come sooner than the computers' direst predictions. One of our many jobs is to ensure that does not happen. Is that clear?"

"Of course, you are right," Pakla replied in a tone of defensiveness. "I would not dare speak for the NATO soldiers of other European nations, but the Polish soldier will never resign. Too many times in history we were expected to lose, and we did not."

Terry allowed himself a rare smile. He said: "And that is precisely why you and your troops have the most difficult front, general."

As Terry expected, Pakla took the compliment. The Pole said: "I realise this. And I am grateful. But with respect, General Tidbury, time runs out. We need an advantage, however small. Or our forces will be defeated very quickly."

"I understand, general. Let's hope we get an advantage soon."

Pakla acknowledged Terry's answer with a curt nod and the screen went blank. Terry leaned his head back in the seat and exhaled. He could hardly begrudge his subordinate generals at the sharp end an opportunity to vent their frustrations.

The vehicle sped along the motorway, green and brown countryside flashing past as the trees and plants and crops wilted under the merciless summer sun. Disorientation clouded his mind. The high sun told him the time of day, but he felt as though it might have been five o'clock in the morning or eight o'clock in the evening.

"Information," the vehicle announced.

"What is it?"

"Squonk is requesting your approval on the latest withdrawals. Would you like to review? If yes, please specify—"

"Yes, on the screen, now," Terry said with impatience.

The screen in front of him lit up with familiar sections of front he knew to be suffering severe pressure from the enemy.

"Squonk? How well are the delaying tactics working?"

The map of the Franco-Spanish border enlarged as Squonk appraised the British general: "The enemy's super AI operates on a near-zero-delineation matrix which randomises its anticipation of NATO forces' defensive tactics, as I and the other NATO forces' super AIs forecast. This means it now reacts post-factum rather than attempting to anticipate NATO's defensive manoeuvres and counteract them in advance."

Terry wondered if Squonk's tone had not included an unintended edge of satisfaction.

The super AI went on: "Nevertheless, the enemy's overwhelming numerical superiority in arms as well as men limits the effectiveness of NATO's range of preventative measures." Indicative blobs and arrows resolved on the map. "Here, here and here, the enemy has been delayed by more than thirty minutes compared to the previously assessed—"

Terry broke in: "Give me the numbers, Squonk. First, how many NATO troop lives have you been able to extend compared to when the invasion resumed yesterday morning; second, how many non-combatant lives have you been able to save in the same period?"

The tone of Squonk's voice did not waver as it replied: "First, two thousand, seven hundred and seventeen, although between fifty-three and eighty-two percent of these troops' lives can be expected to be lost in the next seven to twenty-one days. Second, over twenty thousand, however nineteen th—"

"That's enough," Terry barked, not needing another reminder of how many thousands of innocent civilians his forces were failing.   "Approval is granted to all current withdrawals."

"Confirmed."

"Current emergency notification settings remain unchanged."

"Confirmed."

The screen in front of him went blank and Terry let out another sigh. A voice in the recesses of his head dryly noted that he'd gone over thirty-six hours without proper rest. Europe's destruction and complete subjugation under another empire—brutal, ruthless and wholly without mercy— constituted an immutable certainty, and his only responsibility was to manage as best he could the final destruction of cultures that had endured for centuries.

A sudden depth opened in his throat, an endless void through which he could not breathe nor swallow nor continue to exist. Water welled in his eyes and he immediately hated himself for such weakness. History had chosen him to oversee the unforeseeable, to manage the deaths of innumerable soldiers and civilians as though he were a mere functionary in a poultry farm overseeing the wholesale slaughter of chickens for their carcasses to be cut up and packaged for—

"Sir Terry?" the Toyota Rive-All inquired, breaking into his thoughts.

"What?"

"Your blood-sugar level is dropping to a potentially dangerously low level. You are entering the initial stages of hypoglycaemia."

"How long?" Terry asked, mistakenly believing he had asked a different question, while the chicken carcasses were pulled and boned and packed.

"Please repeat the question."

"I said how long, you stupid bloody machine."

"The question is imprecise. Please clarify."

Suddenly, Terry gasped and caught his breath. The vast, breathless void in his throat vanished. He coughed and returned fully to himself. He asked the Rive-All: "How long until we reach journey's end?"

"You will arrive at your home in slightly less than eight minutes."

Terry paused, the double meaning of his words reverberating around his skull. Journey's end would come soon enough. He asked: "Is my wife at home?"

"Affirmative."

"Send a request to our home's super AI to ask her to prepare her poached eggs."

"Done."

"Good," Terry answered as exhaustion swept through his limbs.

Chapter 14

22.00 Saturday 3 June 2062

Sergeant Rory Moore paced among the trees in the darkness, breathing in relief now that the sun had finally gone after such a punishing day. European air seemed somehow lighter to him than English air. Starlight hued the leaves and branches shades of grey and blue. Cooler, light breezes floated among the trunks as he stumbled further from his unit.

He blinked hard to force the day's images from his mind: an elderly man, white hair soaked in sweat, a look of terror in his eyes as he disappeared under tons of collapsing rubble; fifty or more Hungarian youths, who had attempted to form some ridiculous, ill-equipped irregular platoon, burning alive when a Lapwing broke through and caught them in an alleyway; an autonomous air transport filled with retreating troops and casualties crashing into a medieval church and bringing the elegant spire down on their heads.

He spun around to make sure he was alone. The forest remained silent. He said: "Give me an encrypted link to

Captain Philippa Clarke, 21 Engineer Regiment, Royal Engineers, currently seconded to 2nd Fren—"

His Squitch broke in: "Encrypted comms are not available at this time."

"So use my personal encryption."

"That is not permitted."

Rory held his frustration in check and said: "I can't even use that despite my rank?"

"Affirmative."

"Make the damn connection anyway."

There came a crackle of white noise and he heard Pip's voice: "Hello, mate," she said.

"Can you talk?"

"Sure, but give me a minute."

"Okay."

He heard a door closing and footsteps hurrying. "How is Operation Certain Death going on your section of the front?" she asked.

Rory chuckled and said: "Combat hasn't changed you then."

"Maybe. Has it changed you?"

"I... I don't know," he stammered, discombobulated more by the sound of her voice than her question. "I've seen a lot of bad shit recently."

"Me too," she said. "This afternoon we had a Spider break though the line. There must have been more than three hundred refugees crowded around a water rep—"

His Squitch said: "Muted. It is forbidden to reveal operational details."

Rory sighed.

"Can you hear me now?" Pip asked.

"Yeah."

"Nothing like a private conversation, eh?" she said.

"And this is nothing like a private—"

"Conversation," Pip finished with him.

Rory felt a small but deep aperture roll open inside him. He had to control the vast emptiness it exposed. He said: "I miss those days."

"Do you remember when that ultra-Graphene ribbon buckled and you tried to stop me from—"

"Yeah, yeah, I remember," Rory interrupted. "Look, Pip, that's what I want to talk to you about."

"Wow, I can't remember the last time you called me 'Pip'."

"That's not important. What is, is that we both know where this shit is going to end."

She scoffed and replied: "We won't be here to see it when it does."

"We don't know that. We can't be certain."

"Don't be simple, mate. We're going to go the same way as Pratty and Crimble and—"

"We've got far better chances than all of those poor bloody refugees," he countered.

"True," she conceded after a second's reflection.

He walked on, moving further into the dark forest. He nearly fell down when an invisible depression swallowed his foot. He staggered, regained his balance, and said: "If we get through the next few weeks—"

"Don't you mean days?" she broke in. "I'm wondering why they're not advancing twenty-four seven."

"Just ask your Squitch."

"Right."

"Their warriors are only human, just like—"

"They don't need their fucking warriors," Pip spat. "They can win with their machines alone."

"You're not reading the reports?" Rory asked in surprise. "Mate, those bastards aren't in a rush. They want to thieve every single bit of wealth they can."

His Squitch broke in: "It is forbidden to reveal operational details."

"For fuck's sake," Rory murmured.

"Didn't catch the last bit," Pip said.

"Not important."

"Okay."

Rory heaved in a breath and said: "I just want to be sure that if, somehow, we're both still in one piece when those bastards have overrun Europe, we'll see each other again, before the end. We'll find a way. I... I don't want to think I'll never see you anymore." There, he'd said it.

Pip's voice softened and she replied: "That is so sweet."

Rory wondered if she patronised him. She sounded genuine, but he felt certain he'd missed something. He mumbled: "I suppose it's not going to happen, I know. But if—"

"You're right about that, mate," she said. "In the extremely unlikely event we both end up at the white cliffs of Dover defending against the raghead's invasion of Blighty, then yeah, I'll hitch a lift on the nearest flying pig and we'll have a beer together, deal?"

Rory choked back a flash of emotion, reconsidered, and let it out. He said: "I'm not joking, Pip. Before this war ends, I'll come and get you. And when I do, I'll hold you and never let you go. So do not fucking die, got that?"

There came a moment's silence, then she whispered: "Yes, okay."

Chapter 15

07.42 Sunday 4 June 2062

The muscles around Maria Philips's injuries tingled with the 'geno-jitters'. As the nanobots in the GenoFluid pack strapped to her chest sped through her veins and arteries, many of them clustered around nerves in the areas that needed to be repaired. Some bots acted as painkillers while their compatriots rebuilt damaged tissue close by. But this caused a gentle sensation of tingling which made small muscles around the injury tremble and shudder. The super AI considered this discomfort to be immaterial to repairing the damaged tissue.

Maria turned her head with care and looked at her friend Nabou in the bed next to her. Nabou's eyes shone with relief despite the GenoFluid pack clamped around her neck. "You all right?" Maria whispered.

Light reflected off Nabou's ebony skin when she smiled and nodded.

Maria turned and glanced at the blisters of paint on the ceiling. Large, dirty white flakes peeled outwards and hung down, resisting gravity. In the bottom-left of her vision, a small set of bars on a digital chart increased a fraction. The geno-jitters faded. A sudden wave of pain rippled across her chest and she gritted her teeth against it. In concern, she blinked and raised the graph. The painkiller bots were disengaging; the repairs to her body would soon be completed.

Doors at the far end of the ward clunked open and then cracked shut as two people entered. Maria did not lift her head to look: the display provided the answer to who they were.

The doctor's terse male voice barked: "Come on, you people there. I've got more casualties than beds and you lot are good to go." He approached Nabou, placed his hands around the GenoFluid pack on her throat, and prised it from her with, Maria thought, greater care than his demeanour suggested. He handed the pack to an assistant and muttered something to Nabou. Nabou nodded in comprehension. He left her and approached Maria.

Nabou rubbed her neck, sat up and muttered: "Great to be up to speed."

The bars in the graph in Maria's vision abruptly turned green. The words: 'Repairs complete' scrolled along the bottom of her view followed by a summary of the work the GenoFluid bots had done, including number of cells repaired, destroyed, discarded, repurposed, split, merged and estimates of how these repairs had returned her life expectancy to its pre-injury level. Her lens displayed the names of the doctor and his dowdy, bored-looking assistant.

He smiled as he tapped the control panel on the GenoFluid pack and lifted it from her chest. He said: "I expect you're feeling a little discomfort."

"A little, yes, but I suppo—"

"Yes, it will pass quickly."

"Okay then. Thanks," Maria said.

"Good," he answered with a tight, empty smile that, Maria reflected, might be evidence of overwork as much as indifference.

She stared after him as he moved on to the next bed, in which a teen only a few years younger than her lay on his side, the GenoFluid pack about to be removed from his hip. She rubbed her collarbone and her fingers drifted into her armpit. The residual pain there indicated that slight bruising remained. She swung her legs out from under the sheet and sat up. She glanced at Nabou and asked: "How long do you think we've got?"

Nabou copied her and gasped in shock when her bare feet touched the floor. She said: "Oh, floor's cold. Minutes. If we're lucky, I reckon."

"So let's get dressed and see if we'll get time for a quick game."

"Gin rummy?"

The friends collected their kit from under the beds, dressed in cubicles immediately outside the ward, and moments later sat in couches in the expansive reception area, each holding a corn-based plastic cup of NATO-standard tea.

"Hurting much?" Nabou asked.

"A little. But the bots said it's only residual bruising. You?"

Nabou's white teeth shone against the onyx of her perfect skin. "Not a thing."

"Good."

"You saved my life, Maz."

Maria shook her head in dismissal, a familiar feeling of awkwardness making her blush as she always did when she became the centre of attention. She shrugged and evaded: "You would've done the same for me. Come on, we're mates. We look out for each other."

Nabou's expression softened. She said: "In some cultures, that's a debt that can't ever be repaid."

"And in others, it isn't," Maria said brightly, wanting to change the subject.

Nabou said: "It's okay, Maz. Let's each of us take what it means to us, all right?"

"Yes, fine… How about we see if we can reach our families?"

"Right," Nabou perked up, "good idea."

"Rats," Maria said. "Are you getting that?"

Nabou's shoulders sagged. "Yes," she murmured.

Headquarters ran a reassignment communication that had priority. With the British Army's legendary heavy-handedness, the comms in Maria's lens were truncated by the notification that she had been reassigned to a squadron in the east.

Nabou said: "At least they are keeping us together, Maz."

"There are two enemy armies on the Eastern Front, you know."

Nabou reached out and placed her hand on Maria's forearm. The inherent beauty in her friend's ebony skin struck Maria again when set so starkly against her own dull, mottled, pink flesh. Maria met Nabou's stare as she said: "We will be all right because we will take care of each other. Yes?"

Maria felt nonplussed at the intensity of Nabou's declaration. She replied with a smile and said: "As if there could be any doubt?"

"So, we have got eight minutes before our transport arrives. Let us try to reach our families."

Maria blinked her acceptance of her redeployment and then requested priority contact with her brother, Martin Phillips.

A thin cursor winked in the lower-left of her vision. She held her breath.

There came a short buzz and her brother's voice announced: "Can't talk now, Maz."

She blurted out: "They've redeployed me to the e—" but she stopped when she realised he was no longer there. She wondered why he'd accepted the request if he'd been unable to talk. She decided he must have thought he could. Maria muttered under her breath: "I just wanted to talk to you for a moment. Because I'm scared witless. For all of us, dear brother."

She glanced up to see Nabou's smiling face nodding, the singsong tones of her native language falling from her mouth like an aural waterfall.

Chapter 16

Martin Phillips accepted his sister's comms request without thinking, realised he shouldn't have because of the circumstances, barked: "Can't talk now, Maz," and tried not to think if he would ever talk to her again.

Ominous black dots raced and pitched and dived in the sky above him. His fellow retreating NATO comrades ran to the left and the right of him towards the deserted town of Auch in the south of France. Features of the local terrain overlaid with attackers and defenders filled his vision. His chest ached as he gasped in breath after breath, forcing his legs to keep pounding forwards. All of the troops ran in retreat, away from the front, away from danger.

A genuine attack from a merciless enemy revealed the appalling limits of the British Army's Basic Fitness Test. Since the command to retreat had been given mere moments ago, he'd lost count of the number of soldiers who he'd passed as they struggled huffing like beached whales, staggering forwards on legs obliged to carry too much excess weight, as the enemy approached at lethal speeds. Like him, those who'd taken their fitness with more than a pinch of salt obeyed their Squitches' directions, hurried on, and stood the highest chance of surviving the engagement.

"You will shortly be attacked. Prepare to defend yourself," his Squitch announced without fanfare.

"Jesus," Martin hissed through regular breaths now he'd settled into his running stride. Light sweat on his forehead made the ridge of the helmet itch his skin. He checked with a palm that a magazine sat in his Pickup.

He drew closer to a copse of wizened birches and young oaks in front of him. He wondered if it might conceal either AATs or land transports, anything that would carry him behind the lines. He silently thanked his Squitch again for keeping him the necessary few seconds in front of the enemy. He'd been lucky. Then again, he'd worked hard for his luck. He pushed memories of burned NATO troops to the back of his mind, lest the recollection of them might inadvertently increase his own chances of joining them.

"Stop and lie flat on the ground now," his Squitch ordered.

A grunt escaped him as he broke his stride and fell down on the hot, dry sandy dirt. Dust particles itched his nose and throat and he nearly gagged. A flash of white light burst overhead, and the dusty earth shuddered as though in an earthquake. He gasped as the change in air pressure forced—

"Roll one metre to your left now "

Martin did so without conscious thought, just as training had taught him. The ground shook again. He forced his eyes open but saw only azure sky mottled with contrails and dirty-grey palls of smoke.

"Remain prostrate."

"If you insist," he crackled through the dust in his throat, trying to expel a fraction of the stress. He clenched his buttocks against an abrupt pressure from his sphincter, and he regretted his decision earlier in the morning to have extra eggs with his fried breakfast. The terrifying thought came to him that his bowels would likely void themselves if he were killed. Shit, literally.

"Danger: Caliphate Spider approaching from the southeast. Distance five hundred metres, closing over flat terrain. You are its target. Take defensive action immediately."

Martin rolled onto his front, turned to the right direction, and brought his Pickup to bear, bodily urges forgotten. His lens displayed a digital scene of chaos. He aimed at the approaching dot, helpfully highlighted for him. He pulled the trigger not understanding how his small, limited efforts might in any way affect the battle around him. He fired shells that flashed over the dusty scrub and disappeared into the hazy distance.

For hundreds of metres on either side, NATO soldiers struggled to retreat, lumbering towards him. Breezes blew waves of dust to his right. The individual Spider closing in on him took shape. Martin appreciated the fear-inducing nature of its movement. He fired until his magazine emptied. Lying on his front, he struggled to reach for another, not taking his eyes off the troops staggering away from danger. Abruptly, they vanished in a gout of sandy dirt that erupted skywards. Martin felt the crumpling thud in the ground around him.

"Stand up and continue retreating," his Squitch instructed.

"What happened?" he asked, forcing himself to raise his body to a crouch against an innate desire for self-preservation. Instinct urged him to keep as low as possible, a yearning he suspected governed every soldier under fire on a battlefield. He turned his back to the attacking forces and ran, trading speed for keeping his head down so that his spine ached with each alternate heavy boot pushing through the sandy dirt.

"The attacking Spider was destroyed."

"Don't evade the bloody question.   How many casualties?"

"Your question is imprecise. Continue retreating. In three hundred metres, you will descend into dead ground. Proceed as quickly as possible. The enemy's advance continues within anticipated parameters."

Martin swore aloud and forced his body upright and into a fast jog. Images of Maria, their wastrel brother Mark— forever addicted to his stupid gaming—and their worried parents in their terraced house in East Grinstead flashed in his mind's eye. Recalling familiar scenes helped him combat the fear that made his breaths shallow and his stomach ache.

The sandy terrain descended in front of him.   His confidence crept up as he pictured the horizon behind him climbing higher, hiding his puny body from all the hardware that wanted to blow him to kingdom come. He glanced at other figures to his left and right. His lens denoted their names and ranks and units, but he did not recognise any of them.

"Lie down flat now," his Squitch ordered.

He fell down into the fine-grained dirt yet again and panic rose in his throat. He held his breath and willed his body deeper into the ground.

"Prepare to continue retreating."

"What? Explain."

"The enemy's axes of attack are separating—"

"Consolidating gains?"

"Negative. The enemy is responding to deployments of NATO reinforcements—"

"We still have reinforcements?"

"Continue retreating now. There is a dry riverbed one hundred metres in front of you. Enter it and head north to the abandoned village of Embats to regroup."

"How far is the village?"

"Eight hundred metres along the riverbed."

"Right," Martin said. He reached the bank of sandy limestone and slid down the rocky, dusty side into the wadi. Stones and chunks of larger rock scraped and clattered along with him. He paused, feeling almost safe for the first time since the enemy's attack had begun. The sounds of battle drifted over the ridge above him while his lens placed the distant threats hundreds of metres away.

"Proceed north along the riverbed," his Squitch instructed.

"I need a piss," he said to delay having to move.

"The probability of injury or death is increasing while you remain immobile."

He urinated at the side of the wadi. He gave up trying to recall what had happened to those nearest to him when the attack began, and strode along the barren riverbed, wondering how many decades it had been since this part of southern France had seen enough rain to make the river run. Contrails filled the hot blue sky above. He put a new magazine in his Pickup. Other troops entered the wadi, dishevelled and looking confused. It struck Martin that normal discourse felt so alien. No one spoke to him and he did not attempt to engage them. He found it easy to imagine the violence each of them had witnessed and somehow this seemed to give everyone an automatic right to privacy from those whom they did not know.

He trudged around a bend and a dilapidated farmhouse came into view. Frustration grew when he glimpsed faces that looked stony and bitter and full of resentment. Martin realised then that morale must have been beaten to death by the enemy's onslaught. How could any of them hope to survive?

A voice cried out: "You. In here. Turn right, in the back."

He glanced up at the entrance to the farmhouse. A petite figure stood by the doorway pointing at the approaching survivors. She struck him as one of those females who had something to prove. At once, he shook his head in self-admonishment that he should judge this situation by the standards of peacetime. God knows someone needed to lead this defeated rabble.

"You. In here, quickly. Turn right, in the back."

He didn't expect that she should be so young, so lithe and attractive, yet have such battle-weary eyes. Martin saw from the woman's insignia that she was a captain in the Royal Engineers. He choked down a flirtatious rejoinder and obeyed the same command when she barked it at him. Other faces were downcast.

The stomping feet and murmurs and huffs of frustration made flakes of sandy lime fall from the damaged ceiling. Laths of wood splayed out from what had been partition walls and the fine particles of crushed sand and lime added to the discomfort in his nose and mouth.

The lithe captain appeared in the rotting doorway and she announced: "We've still got a few stragglers coming towards us. I've told Squonk to tell them to get their act together because we need to move out ASAP, and we—"

"Oh, yeah? Move out to where?" a gruff, patronising male voice shouted out. "We're about to get either blasted or fired, sweetie-pie."

The small woman spoke audibly without shouting: "If you want to live longer than the next five minutes, shut the fuck up. All of you."

The room fell silent.

Finally, an indicator flashed in Martin's eye giving her name: Capt. Phillipa Clarke, Royal Engineers. She eyed everyone and Martin felt a wave of self-assuredness emanate from her, in stark contrast with their desperate situation. He twitched an eye muscle and the text of her file ran up in the corner of his vision. He blew air through his teeth on reading of her exploits in a terse, military summary. Stillness around him indicated his fellow troops had done the same.

Captain Clarke announced: "First, you are all going to deactivate your Squitches, Pickups and all other kit. Second, you are all going to put your BHC sleeves on. Then, if the enemy doesn't see us, we are going to hop to safety... like good little bunny rabbits."

The caustic smile did not obscure the depth of emotion in her eyes, at least to Martin. A surge of protectiveness for her welled inside him, similar to the feeling he had for his little sister, Maz, but also different. He recognised the difference and stamped on it; not now, not in this danger, and not with a superior officer. Those feelings had no business making themselves felt in wartime. He heaved in another breath and joined the others in deactivating his equipment.

Captain Clarke pushed through the assembled troops, heading towards the rear of the farmhouse. She advised: "Step on it, you lot. Without your BHC sleeves, you are finished. Got that?"

Chapter 17

Sweat prickled the back of Sir Terry Tidbury's bald head as his adjutant, Simms, looked at him with a blank face but eyes that betrayed the severity of the positions the NATO armies were in.

The door to the COBRA meeting room clunked shut with the police commissioner's exit, and Terry and Simms were alone. Terry said: "What on earth do they think we in the military can do about such things?"

"Societal cohesion worries them, Sir Terry. The prime minister and her director of communications seemed to suggest that the relentless news of retreat was responsible for—"

"The retreat is responsible for nothing," Terry broke in, frustration accelerating his breathing. He went on, slapping the back of each chair as he paced around the expansive but worn conference room table: "Squonk, how many NATO troops have been killed in action in the last hour?"

"Two hundred and twenty-one."

"And how many have been killed since the resumption of the invasion?"

"Eleven thousand, nine hundred and—correction; twelve thousand and seven."

"And why have we taken so many casualties—top reason only?"

"Overwhelming enemy strength."

"You see?" Terry said, slapping the back of another chair. "None of these civilians has an answer to that simple fact: overwhelming enemy strength."

Simms raised a thin eyebrow and asked: "Who does?"

"Not our exalted computers, without a doubt," Terry said. "Look at them. They can't even manage the retreat without losing thousands of our own troops. And then these politicians ask me for some 'good' news because more and more civilians are killing themselves."

"I would venture to suggest they are grasping at straws, Sir Terry."

Terry heard the tone of diplomacy in Simms's voice. He looked at his adjutant's impassive face and said: "Futility breeds strange reactions."

Simms nodded.

"Come along, let's return to the War Rooms."

The two men left the COBRA meeting room and strode along mostly deserted corridors. Simms's presence helped Terry think and concentrate on the innumerable problems the continental retreat presented him with. He glanced up at his adjutant's angular head and said: "Societal cohesion is their job, not ours. And retreat is all we're going to be doing until the end of this Dante's Inferno, for Christ's sake."

"If I may suggest something, Sir Terry. I think the politicians are so… nervous because what the civilian populations of all the European countries specifically lack is any sliver of hope. Leaders fear a breakdown where evacuations descend into chaos, the injured cannot be treated, and people's morals collapse absolutely."

"The absence of any sliver of hope is one benefit of the damned computers, Simms." Terry answered with irony. He stopped as the doors to a lift opened. Stepping in, he allowed Simms to select their destination. Once the doors closed, Terry resumed: "Too many people seem to get some kind of perverse satisfaction poring over the permutations of the forecasts of our demise. And almost all of them are public. Is it any wonder civilians are killing themselves rather than waiting for the inevitable?"

"The media disseminate more and more outlandish descriptions of what will await us when enemy forces finally dominate us," Simms said.

"And we can't help that. I thought the PM's jackal was supposed to keep them in line now he's had a cloned heart put in?"

"The domestic media are but the half of it, Sir Terry. All kinds of cults and obscure… freaks? are popping up and trying somehow to own our doom-laden future."

"Indeed."

"And it is still days before we can expect anything from the brain-scanning institute where we sent that captured warrior."

"And there's no guarantee that what we extract from his head will give us even a clue, much less any hope."

"But it will surely bring some clarity, will it not?"

Terry smiled at Simms's stiff enunciation; the man's unshakable demeanour had always impressed him, but there were times he wished Simms might relax a little. He replied: "A brief glimpse of the enemy before he crushes us? I suppose it might count for something, although now I can't think what."

Both men paused at the entrance to the War Rooms. Knowing that Simms would be up to date because he had one of those detestable lenses, Terry asked: "What's waiting in there?"

Simms's eyebrows came together as he replied: "Slightly more than a little, Sir Terry."

The door slid open. Terry entered and barked: "As you were," to avoid any unnecessary waste of time on military courtesies. He approached the central display and demanded: "Squonk, update operation Defensive Arc."

The space over the flat surface came to life with a multitude of colours. The British Army's super AI spoke while a three-dimensional topographical map of localised areas of Europe zoomed, pirouetted, withdrew, rotated, and zoomed again. "Army Group East is being driven back more than seven minutes ahead of previous forecasts—"

"So update the damn forecasts," Terry muttered, not wanting the computer to remind him of its mistakes.

"Updates are currently running at three trillion per second. As per your orders, they are probability-filtered to take account of the limitations of human physiology."

"If you were an animal, I'd put you down. Continue."

"Elements of the Polish First Armoured in sector 161 are suffering greatest attrition as enemy forces gained the advantage in poor visibility."

"And you couldn't compensate for it?" Terry asked, contempt for the computer fading as he analysed the digital representation of the terrain to the east of Munich. "Go in there, further on Sectors 160 through 164.

Detailed indicators resolved in the air over the digital land, coloured differently for military casualties, civilian victims, and estimated numbers of enemy warriors.

"The enemy could be planning to break through there before beginning to encircle formations north and south. What are you doing to prevent that?" Terry asked.

The three-dimensional map withdrew and flashes of light denoting other units lit up as Squonk replied: "The indicated reinforcements will arrive on-site with three minutes' tolerance."

Terry noted the details of what units had been assigned to which sections. There came a light thump on the console and he muttered, "Thank you, Simms." He lifted the mug of tea to his mouth and blew the steam away before ordering: "Squonk, withdraw and show the extent of current enemy jamming."

The topography shrank and horizontal lines of light encircled the display at differing distances, ranging up towards the ceiling. Digits appeared stating the comparative altitudes from a hundred metres to thirty thousand metres. Inverted cones of white noise materialised along the entire Eastern Front, smothering the terrain that NATO had already lost. Terry's gaze followed the cones up to their points of origin near the ceiling and imagined the enemy's satellites up there, in space, out of reach, unassailable, playing the pivotal role in the chaos on the ground below.

"We need an answer to their jamming," he mused under his breath.

Suddenly, red flashes pulsed at points along the front between Prague and Munich. Terry held his breath. Operators at the comms stations behind him began muttering confirmations. On the other side of the room, the female operator at the NATO comms station nodded and spoke softly: "Thank you, SACEUR, that's affirmative. TT is on the premises." She held her arm aloft, turned her head and said: "General, SACEUR requests immediate secure comms."

Terry glanced at Simms, turned away from the display and went into his office. He threw the door closed and ordered: "On the desk-screen, Squonk." He sat in the chair and gulped down the hot tea, steeling himself for the inevitable.

The face of General Jones resolved on the screen in Terry's desk. "General," Jones began, "we have a situation here."

Terry felt a sense of fathomless unfairness. At times like this, the vastness of his military experience, training and ability deserted him, and he hated himself for feeling weak. He answered: "I see, general. But what choice do we have? The computers ensure that events move too quickly for—"

"Damn the artificial intelligence, general," Jones broke in. "We still call it. This is no different from exercises."

In a flash, the suggestion came to Terry that his commanding officer might be struggling to cope with the certainty of oncoming defeat. Terry forced this abrupt realisation to the back of his mind.

Jones kept talking: "So what do we do, general? We have fifteen seconds to decide between thirty-five troops being killed in Sector 161, which will leave over two thousand civilians exposed, or twelve troops dead in Sector 164 which will leave eleven thousand civilians at our enemy's mercy. So call it, general."

Terry said: "Sir, you require me to make the call on the enemy's unanticipated attack?"

"Damn right. Six, five, four, three—"

"Squonk: give priority to Sector 161 now."

"Confirmed," Squonk answered at once.

Terry met Jones's glare and said: "That was, as I believe you Americans used to say, a no-brainer."

Jones's face moved back from the screen but his expression didn't change. He said: "You just condemned all those civilians to God-knows-what under their new masters."

Terry shrugged and said: "But I had to defend our remaining assets, sir. Every last soldier matters in trying to stem the tide." He wanted to contradict himself that in truth it did not matter in the slightest either way, because in a few weeks at the most, all involved would likely be dead. He could not understand why General Jones saw things any differently.

SACEUR exhaled and said: "Perhaps there may be one soldier who makes some kind of difference, although I doubt it myself."

"But you prefer not to leave such decisions to the computers, is that right?" Terry asked, playing a hunch.

The American's eye twitched. He said: "If we're going to lead, general, we need to know how it feels to make decisions that cost lives."

"I couldn't agree more, sir."

"Good. The artificial intelligence has too much control over who lives and who dies. That's all for now." Jones's face disappeared.

Alone again, Terry said: "Squonk? Tell me how many ti—"

But Squonk broke in: "Note, recalibration after the most recent battlefield action now shows that total defeat of NATO will most probably happen thirty-seven minutes sooner than previously forecast."

Terry ignored the interruption and asked: "How many times since hostilities resumed three days ago has SACEUR intervened in decisions reached by super artificial intelligence?"

"None."

"At all? Not battle, tactical or strategic?" Terry queried before taking a long sip of tea.

"Affirmative."

131

A rueful smile formed on Terry's face. The shocking resumption of the enemy's invasion was bound to lead to all kinds of unexpected ramifications. He spoke aloud: "But I would never ask a subordinate to make a decision I could not make myself. Shame on you, SACEUR." He put the mug of tea down on the table and looked through the window at the rest of his staff sitting at or standing over their stations. His mind drifted back to the COBRA meeting and the civilians' concerns that the suicide rate was increasing too rapidly. "It doesn't matter," he said to his subordinates even though they could not see or hear him. "I wonder how many of you will live long enough to envy the dead?"

Chapter 18

Berat Kartal huddled in the bushes on the edge of a park on the outskirts of a German town that seemed deserted. The light faded but the heat did not. Rays of thinning orange sunlight hued the shrubbery a deeper green. Motes of dust and flying insects flashed and passed through the beams. He tilted his paper journal forwards to better illuminate the page and again resisted the urge to prod around his hip. His body was now so emaciated he could and did spend inordinate amounts of time poking and pushing the skin that covered his bones. Despite himself, he pushed the skin behind the iliac crest of his hip bone and the void there swallowed his thumb. He would never had guessed starvation could reveal such obscure spaces in his body.

He shook his head in an effort to focus. He reread the previous entry to recall what he'd planned to write when he heard a rustling from the other side of the gravel path in front of him. The noise stopped. Whatever it was, Berat knew it would be starving. Every living thing was starving, except obese humans, because they were mostly dead. What had made the noise: marten, dog, fox? He waited but the rustling did not recommence. The light continued to fade.

He huddled over the open journal and wrote with his pencil: *I can hardly believe tomorrow marks four months since this odyssey began. The measure of time feels somehow meaningless. It could be four hours or four hundred years since I fled my old life in the dark of that terrifying night in my lost homeland. The face of every soul I have encountered haunts my sleep, for I can never stop wondering what has become of them. Surely some of them have survived; they cannot all have been killed, can they?*

I saw many more refugees today, away on the other sides of fields and streets in towns that are mostly in ruins. Today I also spotted some military forces, including some ground vehicles and aircraft. They were heading south/southeast, so I was reassured that by heading north, the enemy had not in fact overtaken me, as I had feared. I came across yet more people struggling to make way, and they booed and jeered when our military passed by. Why should they do that? Do they think those men and women in uniform look forward to a battle they are sure to lose?

I have passed through one town and two villages today. The paper I stuffed into my boots helps me walk with less pain, but the heat of each day is truly formidable. I found some shade and slept in the middle part when the sun was hottest, and now will push on for as long as I can because the moon is rising and the night seems to be clear. Earlier, I came across a peach orchard wherein the automated watering system must have been functioning until quite recently. The peaches are not ripe and lack any real flavour, but I ate as many as I could stomach (three), and carried as many as possible away with me. I thought of this as 'lucky', as having good fortune, but is it? My stomach hurts now and I have already had one painful movement. It is so strange that anything at all should emerge from that orifice. Am I so far gone I can no longer eat anything at all?

The daylight is ending now, and once again I feel my spirit fading with it. But I shall move on, for now the enemy is always at my heels once again. But, in truth, I still know not why I keep going, for my destiny must be the same as every other poor wretch whom I have come across on this fantastic journey.

Berat slipped the pencil into its sleeve in the spine of the journal and closed it. Night had almost fallen and he used the last of the light to navigate his way out of the park. The bright, full moon rose further and coloured the paths and trees and debris and bodies in sickly shades of yellow and white. As he trudged on, Berat reached into his rucksack and took out one of the hard, green peaches. He walked and gnawed on the flavourless fruit, and told himself again not to think too much, lest his fate became too inescapable.

Chapter 19

Captain Pip Clarke leaned back on the plain wooden chair and sipped from the bottle of alcohol-free beer, wishing it were the real thing. Her head lolled to relieve the exhaustion of the last few days' retreat. Her eyelids lowered and the demons returned. It seemed to her almost every time she closed her eyes these days, some awful aspect of her experiences resurfaced, goading her to relive a terrifying moment. This evening, the Spanish special ops guys resurfaced, and her memory replayed unbidden their contact with the Spiders on that stony beach in February. They stood again in their defensive square, blasting away at the Spiders as the machines closed in from land and sky, with the best weapons NATO had, but they still didn't last more than a few mo—

"Hi. Am I interrupting?"

Her eyes jolted open to see a stranger's unassuming face in front of her. He had a high forehead and an off-centre dimple in his chin. "Yes, as a matter of fact you are," she answered in irritation. She closed her eyes again and tried to recall where she'd seen him before.

"Okay, right," he said. "So I won't keep you. I just wanted to say thanks for saving my life."

"Yeah. You're welcome."

"You've saved a lot of lives the last few days, Captain Clarke."

She sighed and looked at the man. "You have no idea how sick I am of people telling me that."

"Right. Well, you're not the kind of soldier I would want to piss off, so I'll be sure not to mention it anymore," he said with an affable smile.

Pip knew that in normal circumstances, she'd react, but the weight of the recent past had begun to crush her spirit, bit by bloody bit. "Look," she began, "I'm sick of people complimenting me for doing my job. It's really pointless."

"Some say it's good to be around you, that you're some kind of lucky charm."

Pip choked back an offensive response. She said: "Leave me alone," with as much venom as she could muster.

He raised an eyebrow and said: "Okay, but this is the trailer. Others are bound to be coming and going. If you wanted to be alone, you could've gone for a walk outside. We're well behind the lines here. It's quite safe."

Pip smothered the terror that rose in her mind at the idea of going outside at night, alone. She glanced around the trailer before recalling that the only reason why three-quarters of the seats were empty was because so many troops had become casualties, and those who hadn't needed to sleep if they had no other duties.

"And let's be honest," the man said, "this is an older model. It's a dump. And the water replicator's almost done in."

She felt her expression soften.

138

"My name's Martin."

"Call me Pip," she replied.

"It was on Sunday," he said, scratching his left shoulder with his right arm. "In the old farmhouse at Embats. We were falling back, massively in the shit."

"I remember."

"You got us out of there."

"I was doing my job."

"So were all of us, I think, but we were—"

"We were outgunned and outmanoeuvred," she finished for him. "Like always." She took another swig from the bottle. "What're you doing here?" she asked.

"You don't have your lens in?"

"Would I ask if I did?"

"I'm a forward observer."

She scoffed and asked: "You must have been lucky to get out at all."

Martin shook his head and said: "Not lucky, just not overweight."

"Yeah, it's a major problem."

"I read your bio. That was some evac at the start of the war."

She sighed and said: "Yeah, so people keep telling me."

Pip noticed how Martin seemed to pick up on the trace of irritation that returned to her voice. He heaved a breath and said with a sheepish look: "I said what I wanted to, and like I said, I don't want to mess with a soldier like you. Thanks for chatting." He got up and left the trailer.

The door clicked shut and Pip took another pull from her bottle, suddenly glad it contained no alcohol. Martin-the-forward-observer seemed nice, and perhaps, in another life... Sadness welled inside her once more. She wanted to be part of a team again, not in charge of anyone.

She thought of her old squad, memories that felt as though they had been formed years ago instead of months. Pratty, with his funny moustache, had been blown to pieces on the night the invasion began. Crimble, left in the Spanish mountains with a gangrenous arm and no medical facilities. She hoped he might still be alive somewhere, somehow. The only member of the old gang she knew still lived was Rory Moore, now a sergeant on the Eastern Front. Talking to him on Saturday had been wonderful, but the passion in his insistence that she must not let herself get killed seemed to go beyond their platonic friendship.

She missed all of them, but most of all she missed the anonymity. Now she was someone, one of the few to have fought the Caliphate up close and lived. The shell of who she had to be in front of everyone else lifted a little further away from who she really was. And the void between the shell and her true self expanded with every hour of this bloody war.

She scoffed at her own gravity; they were all going to be chewed to a pulp in Operation Certain Death anyway. Perhaps Martin-the-actually-quite-handsome-forward-observer would be worth getting to know a little better, before it was too late?

Chapter 20

Medical orderlies Maria Phillips and Nabou Faye sat opposite each other in the busy canteen and wolfed down the hot *ogbono* soup. The chilli overheated Maria's mouth but she welcomed the distraction. The friends ate in silence. Maria's limbs ached from the relentless work, constantly assisting casualties by moving the injured and organising the repatriation of bodies and parts of bodies.

Nabou's face of black porcelain grimaced and she said: "I think there's too much chilli in this."

"It's all right," Maria said, keeping her voice low. "Besides, you specified it."

"Yeah, I know," Nabou replied. Her face became a frown and she added: "I feel like a robot, Maz."

Maria noted the now-familiar mood swing in Nabou, where her relentless energy and enthusiasm vanished abruptly, replaced with sullenness. "Me too," Maria sympathised.

"They should only use robots to fight this stupid war."

Maria said nothing, her experience with her brothers, Martin and Mark, guiding her when to speak and when to listen.

"I know they mostly are," Nabou went on, "but seriously, why do real people have to be involved at all? They could just let the machines smash each other to bits, tally up at the end and that would be that."

"But it wouldn't, would it?" Maria said.

"Sometimes I struggle to care about any of this, Maz, you know?"

Maria nodded.

"Because that's the next point, isn't it? If we are certain to lose, why fight at all? The AI knows. The AI tells all the politicians that we're going to lose. So why bother? Are we supposed to hold them up long enough all the civilians can kill themselves?"

"I don't know, Nabou, but we both joined up for the same reason, to help. Right?"

Nabou's face hardened in a way Maria hadn't seen before.

"Right?" Maria repeated.

A sheen of clear liquid formed on the whites of Nabou's eyes that reflected the ceiling lights. She said in a strained voice: "But it is always the same. Their machines smash our machines and drive us back. All. The. Time. It is not as if NATO soldiers even do that much fighting."

Maria laid her spoon down in the soup and covered Nabou's hand with her own. Red light suddenly flooded her vision. A siren sounded in the canteen. The crash of twenty pairs of legs pushing chairs back from the flimsy trestle tables drowned out a multitude of curse words.

Maria hurried with everyone else and in a few seconds had exited the canteen into the hot Austrian sun. Familiar crumps of explosions came to her ears, oddly reassuring for their distance. Outside, no one spoke. Her Squitch told her: "Retreat to the rear area and await evac."

She scrolled through the wealth of data superimposed over her vision and the reassurance vanished. She demanded: "Probability of Spiders breaching defensive perimeter?"

The super-AI responded: "Increasing incrementally. The battlespace is too fluid to give accurate estimates."

"This is crazy, Maz," Nabou said. "This is the strongest part of the line. We should not—"

"Let's go to the station," Maria said, knowing the lieutenant-colonel would likely tell the super AI to prioritise casualty evacuation. But Nabou's concerns infected Maria like a stubborn virus: they'd been told to expect a day of stability where they'd have a chance to send some of the injured either behind the lines or back into combat.

Her Squitch broke into her thoughts: "Avoid the clearing station. Go towards the grid reference indicated now in your vision. Autonomous aircraft FR417–010 will arrive in three m—"

"What?" she shrieked in confusion as a digital path illuminated to steer her away from her patients and over to an empty part of the field. "Did you get that, Nabou?"

"Yes, and I think it is bullshit."

"I will not leave the casualties."

The Squitch's tone did not waver: "Then you are likely to be killed along with them."

Nabou said: "Oh, new, higher-level bullshit."

Maria smiled at the more familiar tone of her friend's voice. Nabou drew level with her and returned her smile.

Nabou said: "How much does it know that we do not?"

The Squitch spoke over Nabou's question: "You must retreat as indicated."

143

A comms' signal flashed in Maria's vision and a panicked voice shouted: "Everyone follow what your Squitches tell you—now. The retreat just accelerated. Unit Foxtrot One-Seven, get yourselves over—"

The commentary stopped as Maria was not its intended audience. "What do we do?" she asked Nabou.

"After what happened last week, I do not want to spend another few days with a GenoFluid pack strapped to any part of me."

Maria grunted her agreement.

"But… we do have ninety seconds before that transport lands."

"If we could save even one—" Maria stopped when Nabou suddenly turned away and broke into a sprint. Maria ran after her friend. At once, a sensation inside her urged caution: black dots littered the intense blue sky above, while pasty smudges of black smoke hung in the air at widely varying altitudes. Maria felt small and vulnerable.

"Come on, Maz," Nabou yelled over her shoulder.

Maria put her head down and lengthened her stride.

Her Squitch said: "You must follow your orders and proceed to the evac point." Maria thought she heard a hint of prissiness.

Nabou slowed to jog as they approached the clearing station, an arrangement of flimsy units the size of shipping containers. She said: "I wish we were allowed to switch that thing off."

"Me too," Maria agreed. She stared at the array of single-storey white huts, each of which held half a dozen wounded brought in from previous engagements.

"Come on," Nabou urged. "We have not got long." She ran to the nearest doors. These slid apart at her approach and she went inside.

"Shit," Maria cursed, hurrying after her. Red digits in the bottom-right of her vision counted down to the arrival of the evacuation transport. The doors parted and the blast of cooler air from inside contrasted with the heat of an average summer's day in northern Europe.

"You, stop!" yelled a male voice.

Maria entered the hut and froze.

"Maz, tell him, will you?" Nabou asked in frustration, standing in front of a tall, overweight doctor.

Maria looked from one to the other and said: "Why are you here? We've got to evac now." She noted the doctor's name when it appeared in her vision next to his bald, oval head.

"No," the doctor replied. "I will look after them," he insisted, glancing at the occupied beds around the hut.

The double meaning of his words came to Maria. Her forehead creased in frustration. She said: "They're going to die anyway."

Nabou's shrugged and she said: "We must go, Maz. We will have to run to get the transport."

"Come with us, Doctor Glenza. Please?"

The man shook his head. Maria could not understand why he should behave like this. She only knew him by sight, but his military record was admirable. Had he broken down? Was there another reason for his reluctance to get out while they still could?

"We must leave now, Maz," Nabou insisted.

"Yes, go" Doctor Glenza agreed, repeating: "I will look after them."

Maria stared at him as Nabou strode past her and through the doors. "How?" she demanded.

His expression collapsed and he pleaded: "Please, just go. They'll be here soon."

Maria backed away from Glenza, not sure what to make of him. Suddenly, a figure on one of the stretchers rose up and emitted a howling: "No!" before pulling itself to its feet. Maria stepped back in shock. Dried blood the colour of rosewood stained the upper half of the soldier's uniform and a GenoFluid pack covered his head. Sightless, he thrashed around, hitting the stretcher and then nearly stumbling when his arm swished through empty space.

Maria grabbed the man before he fell. "Control yourself," she urged. "The bots will knock you out and you'll certainly die here."

His blind head cocked to one side. "Why?"

"Can you run?"

"What?"

Maria strengthened her grip on his forearm and placed her other arm around his shoulders beneath the pack. "Let's go," she said, propelling him towards the doors.

"Wait," Glenza called. "I can look after him."

The doors opened and Maria felt like she'd stepped back into an oven. Huddled over, the wounded soldier kept moving forward. She said: "We need to leave now. We've got a transport."

The soldier didn't reply.

Ahead, the hot, dry field stretched out in front of them. In the heat haze an indistinct aircraft shimmered as it came down to earth.

"I can see you, Maz," Nabou spoke through the comms in Maria's ear.

"We're going as fast as we can," she shouted through gasps for air. The wounded soldier had begun to flag.

"Just go as fast as you can. I think the transport will wait for others," Nabou said.

Maria instructed. "Squitch, tell the bots in the pack to give this casualty more pace."

"Confirmed."

Doctor Glenza's round face came back to her mind and she shuddered again at his demeanour and what his plans might be. He must know the position would be overrun in moments—what did he expect to achieve? It unnerved her to realise that triage no longer meant the best use of limited resources on the battlefield, but actually abandoning all casualties when the enemy surged. Could qualified and experienced military doctors go to pieces so easily?

The wounded soldier's legs galloped a little more quickly. Maria murmured some encouragement as they ran to the transport, although her left arm ached from the effort of supporting him. She slowed him when they reached the squat, ugly aircraft capable of holding thirty or more troops. "Okay, we're at the transport now. I need you to lift your leg half a metre up. Can you do that?"

The blind soldier grunted and raised his left leg. It hit the doorway flange and he fell forward. Nabou grabbed one of his arms and pulled him in. Maria followed.

"I'll buckle him up," Nabou said, sitting the man in a fold-down seat against the fuselage.

"Thanks" Maria answered, collapsing in a seat on the opposite side of the aircraft. Urgent shouts came from the entrance as it slid closed. Maria looked at the impersonal, grey metal and wondered what it must feel like to be left on the other side of it. Her eye caught Nabou's glance of concern and Maria knew that her friend entertained the same thought.

The medical transport's engines hummed and Maria's stomach fell when it lifted off the ground. She glanced at the wounded soldier she'd rescued from the casualty clearing station. With a twitch of her eye, she called up his details: Sergeant Rory Moore of 103 Squadron, 21 Engineer Regiment, Royal Engineers. Her respect grew when she read his summary and that he'd been in the war since the very beginning. Now, his injured head lolled forward but the straps held him in place, stopping him from falling on the floor as the transport accelerated away from the battlespace. The GenoFluid pack that completely obscured his face was advanced in repairing a wound he'd received during an earlier retreat.

Beyond the digital representations in her view, she caught Nabou's lingering stare. "Okay?" Maria asked.

Despite the background noise, Nabou's voice sounded clear in Maria's ear: "Yes, Maz. Sorry about that back there."

"It's nothing. We had very little time."

"I didn't know what to do."

"I said it doesn't matter."

"That doctor, what was wrong with him?"

Pain flashed at the side of Maria's right eye, under the bone. She shook her head and replied: "I have no bloody idea."

"This keeps getting wor—"

Nabou's voice broke off when the Squitch interrupted: "Caution: you may be required to disembark under fire."

"Worse," Nabou finished.

"Trip's been all right so far," Maria said, looking again at the wounded soldier.

Nabou said: "You did well to get him out, Maz."

Before Maria could answer, the Squitch broke in again: "Stand by to disembark. When the door opens, turn right and run two hundred metres into dead ground and await further instructions."

"Jesus," Maria breathed, her headache worsening.

Nabou said: "This is wrong. Why are we coming down so soon?"

"My Squitch isn't giving me anything," Maria said.

"Mine neither. It is horrible to be kept in the dark like this."

The display in Maria's eye noted the transport's rapid descent. She glanced around the fuselage at a dozen or so others like her and Nabou, and wondered briefly about their stories, what each of them had seen and experienced. She doubted any of them had endured the extent of action that Sergeant Moore must have. She observed his head as it came back up and turned left and right, like a blind animal using its other senses to gather information. But he'd have his sight back in a few hours, if they survived the evac.

The transport's descent made the air ripple unpleasantly in Maria's ears. The craft thudded into the ground, a door on either side of the fuselage slid up, and suddenly everyone was calling and moving.

"Exit the transport now," her Squitch instructed needlessly.

The people around her moved with urgency but in good order. She grasped Sergeant Moore's right forearm and he stood. Nabou supported him from the other side.

"Sergeant Moore, we need to leave the transport now."

"I still can't see shit," Moore replied.

"We will help you," Maria said. "Move forward now. In two steps you need to—"

Sergeant Moore fell through the doorway and collapsed into the sandy dirt. Maria followed Nabou and jumped onto the ground.

He groaned and said: "Great bedside manner."

"Sorry," Maria said, which Nabou echoed.

Maria had to hold back a smile when Nabou smirked.

"I've been in deeper shit," the sergeant said as the medical orderlies pulled him to his feet.

"We need to get to dead ground. It's not far."

"Just point me in the right direction. My lens is still buggered."

Maria again put her arm around his shoulders and propelled him along. Behind them, the transport's engines gave a thin shriek as the aircraft took off.

Hurrying ahead, Nabou craned her head and said: "I do not like it, Maz. We have not been taken back very far at all."

"Relax," Sergeant Moore said. "Leapfrogging."

"What?" Maria asked.

The man slowed to a trot, heaving breaths from under the GenoFluid pack on his head. "Are we there?"

"Almost," Maria said.

He said: "The super AI saves more of us—well, loses fewer of us—if it leapfrogs. Tactical withdrawal, get it?"

Maria shook her head in resignation, even though he was blind and did not see it.

Nabou said: "That will work provided that the enemy's super AI does not account for it."

Maria said: "We're orderlies, we don't get much tactical data."

The injured man went on: "Doesn't matter. We're all finished anyway. We're all going the same way as Israel and Turkey and everywhere else."

They slowed to a fast walk and Maria caught the look on Nabou's face. "That is what I have been saying," her friend said with an uncharacteristic hint of churlishness.

Maria didn't know how to reply. Deep inside she knew it as well, but knowing and accepting were two very different things. "We're not finished yet," she said in defiance.

The Squitch spoke in her ear: "Proceed northeast."

"Come on, let's go," Sergeant Moore said, evidently having been told the same thing.

Maria held him as the three of them changed direction. The sun baked the dusty earth with greater intensity in the dead ground, and an overwhelming futility possessed Maria. With the land rising on either side of her, she looked at the backs of the other stragglers in front and had the feeling that if it weren't for the super AI, organisation in the NATO armies would have already broken down.

"Sergeant," Nabou began, "how far have you retreated?"

"You mean since I got this?" Moore clarified, tilting his head.

"Yes, sir," Nabou replied.

"Call me Rory. I dunno. The shrapnel mashed up my eyes along with my lens... But that clearing station was supposed to be my location till the pack had finished. At least according to Glenza. Mind you, he struck me as a funny bastard."

Maria swapped a glance of raised eyebrows with Nabou.

Sergeant Moore continued: "The last few days we've only been leapfrogging backwards. Terrible. You've only just got in theatre, then?"

"Yes," Maria answered. "We were reassigned from England."

Rory grunted and said: "You're going to be back there pretty soon, if you live long en—"

Rory lost consciousness.

"Shit," Nabou said, the sudden deadweight making her stop and struggle to remain upright.

Maria rushed back and helped Nabou lower the sergeant to the ground. "Great," she said with irony, "the bots have put him to sleep."

"How are we supposed to get him out now?"

"We need a transport," Maria said, wondering if one were close enough.

Chapter 21

11.42 Saturday 10 June 2062

American reporter Milton Mitchell began the last twenty minutes of his life in much the same manner as he'd spent the majority of his adulthood: railing against the overwhelming unfairness with which fate had treated him, mostly in the form of, first, his alcoholic parents, and second, his vicious, barren wife.

He stared at his reflection in the mirror without seeing the vast bitterness in his eyes, only feeling the depth of his resentment. He finished lathering the foam around the lower half of his face, washed his hands, and picked up the razor blade. The floor suddenly dipped and Milton lurched, cursing: "Goddammit." He steadied himself, glanced through the porthole on his left, and muttered: "And that idiot captain said the crossing would be smooth."

With care he drew the blade up his throat to his chin. After a few strokes, a communication icon flashed in his vision, from his piece of shit of an editor. He twitched an eye muscle to reject it and finished his shave. When he had dabbed his face dry and thrown a sweatshirt over his head, he returned the call.

"What did I tell you about taking my calls, Milton?" Lilith whined.

"Yeah, yeah. Please spare me and stop sounding like my ex, 'kay?"

"I wanna put you out reporting live ASAP, which means now."

"What the f—" Milton choked. He kicked the thin metal door of the closet and the size of the resulting dent surprised him. "We agreed I'd go live at midday. What's changed?" he asked.

"Jesus, why can't you keep up?"

"I was shav—"

"The wires are screaming that the Caliphate's ACAs are out over the Atlantic. Looks like they might be going up for Ireland or maybe Iceland."

"That's not news anymore, Lilith. Smashing up Europe is what they been doing for a while now."

"Don't get wise with me. Get your ass on the deck of that boat."

Milton sighed, muted the connection, uttered a profanity, and unmuted.

"I want you to give it the 'how freakin' great America is to be sending all this aid to Europe when they most need it' shtick."

"I know the script," Milton answered as he put his leather jacket on.

"Is your donut charged?"

"Think so," he said, checking he had the device in his jacket pocket.

"So, c'mon. Go, go, go. Get up there and you'll be going live to over twenty million Americans!"

The connection ended and Milton sighed again. There had been a time—it seemed so long ago now—when reporting live to millions of viewers and listeners had given him purpose. But that was before Abigail, ten years ago; before his near-fatal drug addiction caused by her refusal to have kids. Of course, the refusal was a cover because she couldn't have kids. But when they started dating he'd told her he wanted kids. And she didn't tell him she was barren. The bitch.

He pushed the door open and nearly tripped on the flange as he stepped over it. Merchant shipping smells invaded his nose: salt infused with oil, old paint, rusting metal. He used both arms to pull himself up the steep and narrow metal stairways. He wanted to get across to the right side of the boat—one of the crew had explained 'port' and 'starboard' to him, but he couldn't recall which was which.

Abigail: spoilt daughter of the media outlet's owner. She'd been so petite, so demur, so *feminine*. This had only lasted till they began cohabiting, then she turned into the vixen from hell. But he'd been trapped: she could always call daddy and Milton would be out of a job, struggling to find work at one of the few outlets that weren't super-AI run from commissioning to editorial to transmission. Abigail was a freak with the body of an angel and the heart of a vicious, callous man, craving control and domination. God, he hated her. Soon, he told himself again, soon he'd find somewhere to escape to and he'd get away, no matter how much she threatened him that he'd be finished if he ever did leave her.

"Yeah, that was her all over," Milton muttered aloud. "Always controlling, always the bitch-boss, like the sole reason I was put on this fucking Earth was to serve her—"

The comms icon in his lens flashed. He blinked incorrectly and instead of rejecting the contact, he accepted it. "Milton? Milton, are you in position now?"

155

"I'm on the top deck," he answered, angry with himself for the mistake. "I still need a few minutes."

"What? Your convoy is about to be attacked."

"Get outta here," Milton replied in dismissiveness. "We only left Norfolk yesterday. Shit." He broke into a trot to cross the vast cargo deck, feeling small and lost among the stacked metal containers that rose around him in sheer columns a hundred feet high. Confusion swept through him: how could the convoy be under direct attack? They were still thousands of miles from mainland Europe.

He broke into a run when he finally made out the right side of the boat in the distance. The *Endless Horizon* was the largest merchant vessel afloat, and crossing its upper cargo deck took far longer than he'd expected. He staggered and nearly fell when the deck moved on the swell again. Low cloud bore down from the sky and he cursed when the first drops of rain hit his face.

A general alert addressed to everyone on board arrived in his lens, notifying the crew that an attack was imminent and instructing everyone to take cover and find the nearest fire extinguishers, and remind themselves of the drills they'd practised before leaving the mainland United States.

"Milton?" Lilith trilled, sounding like Abigail.

"I need to get to the right side of the boat so folks will be able to see—"

"See what?"

He slowed to walk, breath heaving from exertion and frustration. "The closest US Navy ship, Lilith." Then he added: "This is all bullshit, anyway. No way can those ACAs make it out this far. It has to be a scam, some kind of glitch."

"You wanna see?"

He recognised his editor's tone. "Really? Have you got it?" he asked, curiosity overriding all other feelings.

"Incoming now."

A different icon flashed in his lens. He raised it, a restricted military comms channel which showed Caliphate ACAs approaching the convoy. He swore again.

Lilith said: "Hang in there, hun. Syndication's gonna make you a star, Milton!"

Another warning arrived from the ship's super AI notifying him that if he did not take cover at once, he would lose his press accreditation and be confined to his quarters for the rest of the voyage.

"Shit, you're right. Okay, okay. Is this gonna be chit-chat or am I going solo to donut?"

"Solo, as long as you can keep it interesting. I'll tell you when to sign off."

"Give me ninety seconds," he pleaded, not relishing the idea of losing his accreditation and being stuck in those miserable quarters for the next five days. He hurried down similar narrow, steep metal stairways as quickly as possible without slipping. He descended three levels and decided it was enough. He had to do the piece. He'd just have to try and talk his way out of trouble afterwards.

"Lilith? Okay, I'm good in fifteen."

"You're on in fourteen, thirteen, twelve…"

Milton withdrew the small metal donut from his jacket pocket and twisted the top and bottom halves in opposite directions. It hummed and flew off to hover a few feet away and slightly above him. He glanced over his shoulder, taking care to align his body how he wanted to appear on all the millions of lenses and screens around the world. With a blink, he connected to the donut and perceived, in the corner of his eye, a thumbnail of the view from it: his head and body, with the right side of the *Endless Horizon* behind him, her massive bulk disappearing into apparent infinity.

Lilith spoke in his ear: "Three, two, one."

Abruptly, all his concerns vanished. Lilith had been right: with the convoy under attack this report could go down in history. His professionalism kicked in as it always had: "Hello, everyone! This is TRI-CBS's Milton Mitchell coming to you live from the Atlantic Ocean. I'm on the *Endless Horizon*, part of Convoy SE–07. Protected by the might of the US Navy, the American merchant marine is making another heroic effort to rush materials to support NATO's endeavours to defend Europe. Now, you may be wondering why, if we look around here, you cannot see any other ships."

Milton looked on as the donut took his vocal cue and panned out from the side of the ship to show the ocean, unusually choppy with gusts of wind blowing crests off the waves which drifted on the breeze like beer foam blown from the top of a glass.

When the donut panned to face the distant, white-flecked horizon, he continued: "Well, the reason for that is despite SE-07 being a convoy of over eighty merchant and navy ships, they are in fact spread so far apart as to be over the horizon. Now, I know for a fact that the nearest warship to the *Endless Horizon* is just over there, right where that plume of smoke is rising…"

Milton's words trailed off. The image from the donut, again acting on what Milton had said, zoomed in on the curling, twisting funnel of black smoke as it drifted with the same absence of direction as an alcoholic trying to make his way home.

Lilith spoke in his ear: "Keep talking, Milton. Dead air's no good."

"Well, uh, that sure looks like, um…" he fumbled trying to recall the name of the US Navy ship that had been closest to the *Endless Horizon*. But then something else caught his eye.

"There appear to be some black things coming toward us now."

The image from the donut adjusted to focus on one of four approaching Blackswans. Its compressed ellipsoid body and protruding fins sped only a few feet above the waves. As it drew closer, individual parts of it broke away.

Milton continued: "It appears to be breaking up. I think what might'a happened is that these machines have flown too far from wherever they were launched."

The view from the donut showed the Spiders break out from their housing in the frame of the Blackswan, their own power units activating. They fanned out and accelerated ahead of the Blackswan.

Milton maintained his commentary: "Well, the machines are certainly breaking apart now, likely due to the fact that they have, maybe, uh, run out of fuel? Wow, look at that," he exclaimed when the lead wave of Spiders suddenly pitched up vertically and climbed into the sky.

"I wonder what that means?" Milton said, questioning why the *Endless Horizon* didn't have its own defences, and relied solely on the Navy.

The donut followed the Spiders' paths. They rose to several times the height of the massive merchantman and then dived down towards the water.

Milton watched at least twenty of them splash at high speed into the waves. He reported: "Well, uh, I really, really wanna believe that they have crashed or malfunctioned, but if it's true—" he broke off when a deep shudder ran through the deck. He gripped the wet, cold metal rail and peered over the side, at the Atlantic a hundred feet below, and thought he glimpsed faint orange flashes.

"Impossible," he muttered, his audience forgotten. Another alert flashed into his lens: the ship's artificial intelligence advising him to abandon ship. He caught his breath. The *Endless Horizon* listed hard to starboard. Milton grabbed an upright metal post. He glanced down to see the vastness of the ocean rushing up to meet him, embrace him, and swallow him.

In the few seconds left to him, Milton Mitchell turned back towards the donut still hovering close by and shrieked: "Abigail—I fucking hate you!" Then, over four hundred thousand metric tons of cargo ship keeled over, swamping him in her embrace, and together they sank.

Chapter 22

Terry Tidbury put the most recent casualty figures to one side in his mind. He sensed his wife, Maureen, waiting on the other side of the kitchen, likely keeping their food hot.

He deactivated the screen and said: "Thank you."

She retrieved the baked salmon and potatoes from the oven. As she put the plates on the table, she noted: "After what happened today, I wonder if the Americans might pull out of the war."

Terry looked at her in surprise. "Impossible," he said. "They'd have to abandon NATO. Walk away from a hundred and twenty years of mutual support. Unthinkable." He lifted a bottle of white wine from the elegant steel cooler on the table and unscrewed the cap. He filled two glasses and said: "I don't think today changes so much."

With a mature elegance Terry adored, Maureen lowered herself onto the chair and picked up her glass. "I rather think it does, dear," she said in a tone Terry recognised for its significance.

He lifted his own glass and said: "Cheers."

Maureen reciprocated. They drank.

"Why?" Terry asked, wondering what he could have missed in the day's events.

His wife picked up her knife and fork and said: "If those blasted flying bombs can reach that far, perhaps they can reach all the way to America?"

Terry said nothing and savoured the slice of warm salmon flesh melting on his tongue.

"It's not as if the USA doesn't have its share of isolationists," Maureen noted.

"It always has," Terry countenanced. "But this time it's too important."

Maureen didn't eat, saying: "I really wouldn't be so sure, Terry. They can see the war in Europe is lost. Look at it from their perspective, hmm?"

"I have," Terry insisted, "and I cannot see them abandoning NATO now. SACEUR is one of their best generals."

Maureen ate. Terry sipped his wine, unnerved by his wife's appraisal. The silence lengthened.

Maureen said: "I was in touch with Alf earlier today."

Terry smiled at the mention of their oldest son. "He sent me a comm, too."

"Good. It was a nasty break, I was worried."

Terry shook his head and said: "That kind of accident happens on selection training. He'll be fine in a couple of days. Did Toby get in touch?"

"Yes, he thought he might be allowed some leave soon."

"Hmm, I hope it's not because he's my son."

"He insisted it was normal rotation."

"Well, I drummed it into those boys not to expect any special treat—"

"Yes, Terry," Maureen broke in.

Terry noted the faintest trace of irritation in her voice. "And I hope they don't get any bad special treatment because I'm their father."

Maureen smiled. "The boys will be all right... for as long as any of us will be."

Silence descended again. Terry enjoyed the food. He took a quartered piece of lemon from a small plate, squeezed some juice on the remaining salmon, and asked his wife: "Do you believe it could be possible? About the Americans quitting? Just turning their back on Europe and NATO and leaving us to it?"

He watched his wife pause and consider her response, and for the ten thousandth time he blessed the gods or fate or whatever guided life on Earth that he had found her.

She answered in a measured tone: "Their president seems... unsure? I don't think she expected to have to deal with such an emergency—"

"None of us did."

"And I think she would like it if she could find an easy way out. It would be popular with a lot of the American people, Terry. Don't forget, until a few months ago very few people in either America or Europe had anything to do with the military. I remember one of your speeches last year when you spoke about NATO becoming a 'home' army because there weren't any more threats—"

"Yes, I remember," Terry said.

Maureen's face tilted in that familiar look of explaining that which she deemed to be blindingly obvious. "And think about the problems they had before the war, with all those unstable people joining their military forces and causing all kinds of problems. I think the thing is, dear, that so much has happened since February, people have forgotten a lot of what used to be considered normal before then."

Terry sat back in his chair and admitted: "You could be right."

"And despite everything, in America those people haven't gone away. Yes, like a lot of us they have been shocked and perhaps even stunned into silence, but with that awful attack today—"

The screen in the wall flashed the notification of an incoming message. Terry ignored it.

"Thank you," Maureen said before going on: "so close to their own country, it could really affect things there. I'm certain there will be pressure to stop throwing good forces after bad, Terry."

He stared at his wife, considering. Finally, he turned away from her. "On screen," Terry instructed.

A familiar face appeared. "Earl? Hey there, buddy. How you doing? You and Jones got that damn Caliphate beat yet?"

Terry smiled and replied: "Call me back in the morning, Suds."

The face of Lieutenant-General Studs Stevens of the USAF smiled back. The smile faded and an uncomfortable sense of foreboding chilled the skin on the back of Terry's bald head.

"It's great to see you again, Maureen, keeping the leash on your British bulldog," Suds said with his easy American charm.

"Will you be coming to Britain soon?" Maureen asked.

"I'm not really sure right now."

"That's a pity. I'm planning to do a Beef Wellington on Friday."

Suds laughed and said: "For sure I'll be there—great!"

Terry laughed as well, the kind of forced chuckle to show appreciation rather than because anything especially amusing had been said.

The American looked back at the general and his voice deepened: "You know, Earl, this is just a social call."

"Of course," Terry replied, his nerves tingling because Suds had used their private code for an important message. His memory flooded with recollections of their first meeting all those years ago. Now, the ways that Suds described the details would provide Terry with information no one monitoring the conversation could ever guess.

"You recall that joint NATO exercise we met on, when was it, March '43, right?"

"Right, how could I ever forget that wet March?" Terry replied with a thoughtful nod. The exercise had in fact taken place in February 2044, and this meant Suds believed their connection to be insecure, albeit monitored by friendlies.

"You remember what happened on hill 214 on the first day?"

"The tactical advance?" Terry queried.

"Nope, the withdrawal."

"Ah, that. Yes, General Brady suggested that I send fire teams to outflank you, but—"

"No, he didn't suggest. He pulled rank and ordered you to. But when they got there, I'd already deployed the latest AI Sentinels."

Terry smiled. "That's right, Suds, I'd forgotten. Those Sentinels were terrible machines. The ammo always jammed."

"Nope, it was the gyros, right? Damn things kept falling over 'cos they kept mixing up their horizons."

Terry had all the information he needed. He communicated this to Suds with: "You're right: it was the gyros. Ah, those were the days. It doesn't seem that long ago, does it?"

Suds' eyes narrowed: "You bet. It's funny how the memory can play tricks."

"It's like nothing is exactly how you remember it."

165

"That's right," Suds confirmed.

There came a pause as the two men stared at each other.

Terry said: "It's good to reminisce, Suds. Thanks for taking my mind off our current issues for a while."

"Sure. All the best to your family, Earl. I hope we can meet up soon."

"The same to you. Thanks for calling."

Suds nodded and the screen went blank. Terry blew air through his teeth.

Maureen sipped her wine and then asked: "Just a brandy, or a brandy and cigar?"

Terry looked at his wife with vast admiration and said: "You were right, dear. Suds has just told me there is a real possibility that the US will pull out of the war. Thank you."

Chapter 23

Polish Major Kate Fus spat the strong mouthwash out of her mouth. She watched the globules of pale green liquid as they rolled into black cracks in the dry earth. Questions swirled in her mind: how could any of the troops under her command survive the next week, how could NATO slow the enemy's unstoppable advance, and what might be happening in her homeland?

The sky above her brightened and the shadows on the cracked ground faded like her prospects of surviving this war. She walked around to the other side of her command vehicle and re-entered it. "Bolek," she said, addressing the Polish Army's super AI, "windows please, usual configuration." The shrubs, bushes and withered trees in her dead-ground position appeared around her. "Give me an overview of the plan for today."

The screen offered a digital layout of her location, a mere five kilometres from the German border. Forty-eight hours earlier, the entire Eastern Front had all but collapsed under the enemy's renewed onslaught. A line of over two hundred kilometres had been pushed back as though NATO forces were little more than a tiresome irritation. Now, she commanded a bulge in the line that she expected the enemy would want to squash. "Where are the reinforcements I asked for?"

"None are currently available."

"For the sake of the Lord," she muttered. "What about the retreat plan in this section? There are only two bridges in Černá v Pošumaví and too many hills to go around the town. What happens when the enemy blows those bridges?"

"Alternatives will be considered as the retreat develops," Bolek replied with an evasion to which Kate had become accustomed.

"Current probability of imminent attack?"

"Between thirty and thirty-five percent, as displayed on the screen in front of you, major."

"Why so low?"

"Based on the enemy's movements to date, the probability reflects the multitude of issues which enemy forces have to consider against the munitions they have brought to bear."

"But this part of the line represents an abnormality. So far, I have not witnessed anything like this in the enemy's tactics."

"Such situations have occurred before, although not on any part of the line for which you have been responsible."

Kate sighed and asked: "Location of General Pakla?"

"En route to SHAPE."

"Show me on the screen."

The map in front of her changed to show the location of the general's transport. *Her* general. He would arrive in a few moments so perhaps she might have a chance to speak to him later in the—

An incoming comms signal flashed from Captain Fiala, again. Out of all of the troops under her command, she could always rely on Captain Fiala to have a question.

She tapped a green oblong on the display. "Yes, captain?"

"Good morning, major. I only wanted to let you know that the inducer responsible for laser coherence-length variation on one of my BSLs is showing a malfunction. It may render my part of the line comparatively weaker. Given everything else for which you are responsible, I wanted to be sure you knew."

"Thank you, captain," Kate replied. "Bolek?"

The Polish super AI replied: "It is a minor hardware malfunction."

"Are any repair crews sufficiently close by?" Kate asked.

"Negative."

"There you have it, captain," Kate said. "Thank you for letting me know."

The connection ended. Kate knew it wasn't worth asking Bolek to organise or prioritise repairs because it would make no difference to the outcome when the attack came. "Indeed, what would or could?" she mused aloud.

"Please clarify the question," Bolek said.

Kate let her head loll back and looked at the bright morning sky above her. She said: "How can we not lose this war?"

She did not expect any insight from the super AI, perhaps a dry summary of requiring superior munitions and forces, but instead Bolek replied: "Enemy jamming is showing minor frequency fluctuations. This is consistent with—"

"Shit," Kate cursed, sitting up and slapping a panel on the display. "Attention, all troops. Stand to. It looks like we might not be getting Sunday off, after all."

169

The image in the screen in front of her shrank to display the entire length of her section of the front. She said: "Bolek, bring those PeaceMakers down right now."

"They are in transit."

"Where's the enemy? Could it be a mistake?"

The veil of white noise that obscured details of enemy-held territory withdrew to show approaching ACAs that were quickly identified as combined wings of Blackswans and Lapwings.

"Negative," Bolek answered. "Multiple contacts approaching. Forward units have begun withdrawing."

Kate swore as the number of attackers increased on the screen like drops of digital rain. After previous retreats, as much NATO hardware as possible was left to operate autonomously—all tanks and battlefield support lasers were unmanned. Thus the only crumb of comfort Kate had was that fewer than three hundred troops needed to retreat across her section of the front. There were only a handful of NATO soldiers within a few kilometres of her position.

"Bolek, why are there so many of them?" she asked, disliking the plaintive tone in her voice.

The super AI replied: "The enemy appears to have assigned more materiel to this attack than is required."

"How much more?"

"A substantial volume."

Before Kate could answer, her mobile command vehicle jolted into life. She reached for the straps, pulled them over her shoulders, and clipped herself in, muttering: "This is going to be good fun." Kate gasped when the vehicle climbed out of the dead ground and in the sky she perceived the physical enemy presence that had been represented digitally on her screen. "Bolek, get everyone back as quickly as possible, please."

"Confirmed. In progress."

The vehicle shook as it joined a road strewn with debris. A hard left turn strained the tendons in Kate's neck and then she could see the town: a white church spire giving some elegance to the patchwork quilt of grey, brown and red house roofs. Somewhere in there the river snaked, crossed by only two bridges that had to be the enemy's primary targets. She glanced at the hills which surrounded the lake into which the river emptied to the southwest, knowing that it would be impossible to escape that way.

"Bolek," she said, "why did we not pull back during the night?"

"To allow the recovery and evacuation of wounded."

"Okay."

"Warning: defensive forces will be overrun in less than two minutes."

"What? Where are the PeaceMakers?"

"Destroyed."

"Already?" Kate focused on her tactical display. To see the Caliphate dominate the battlespace was no novelty, but she swallowed in fear to see such absolute saturation. As the digital dot representing her vehicle entered the town, she noticed three other NATO vehicles approaching ahead of her on other roads.

"And the tanks and BSLs?"

"Seven units—correction, six units remain, flanking ridge 889. They will be destroyed in approximately ninety-two seconds."

"I'm getting fed up telling you not to use 'approximately' with precise numbers, Bolek," Kate admonished as she scrutinised the display. The three other NATO vehicles converged, two from the east and one from the north, while she approached from the southeast. All four of them would come together at the southern bridge. They had to cross it before the enemy destroyed it. She recognised their call signs and knew the men and women in the vehicles: the two commissioned officers were captains responsible for the residues of their troops, while a handful of non-coms had been assigned in-theatre to monitor performance issues at first hand.

Her vehicle shook continually and she glanced through the windows to see the familiar debris of war. With an ominous feeling, she noticed the other vehicles slowing as her own accelerated. She said: "Bolek, what is going on? We are going to get hit soon, so why are you slowing the others down?"

"As the senior officer, you have priority."

Kate's chest tightened. "No, no, no," she said, shaking her head as the other vehicles came to a stop. This would cost valuable seconds. "But we will all die," she cried.

Bolek's tone didn't alter: "Negative. Enemy forces are projected to destroy two of the other three vehicles."

"Get the others across that bridge while it is still there," she hissed.

The super AI countered, "You are the most valuable in-theatre asset to Polish and NATO forces. Your successful evacuation from the battlespace must take priority over junior ran—"

"No!" Kate yelled. "Override, do you hear me? I repeat: override and evacuate the junior ranks, *now*. You will not sacrifice the lives of others to save me again. Is that clear?"

"Confirmed," came Bolek's impassive reply. Then: "Major, you have a comms request from General Pakla."

"Reject," Kate answered, catching her breath at the unalterable path on which she had embarked.

She watched the other NATO vehicles accelerate, converge, and speed over the bridge. A second later, a Spider hurtled in and hit the middle span of stonework. Her vehicle slowed as it approached the bridge. Small pieces of stone arced through the air while the majority of shattered chunks fell into the water. When the view cleared, she counted the three vehicles escaping through the streets on the far bank. With an odd sense of satisfaction, Kate looked down at the blinking comms icon in the display and whispered: "Not today, my general. I am sorry. Goodbye, dear."

Bolek announced, "This vehicle has been targeted and will be attacked in fifteen seconds."

"Alternatives?"

"Exit and attempt to surrender."

Kate smiled at Bolek's asininity and glanced at the river between low buildings. "What is coming to get me?"

"Enemy Lapwings are clearing this sector."

So she would burn rather than be blasted to pieces. "Stop," she ordered.

The vehicle stopped. At once, she unclipped her restraints. "Open the door; activate my Squitch."

The door pivoted open as Bolek said: "Ten seconds. Nine. Eight..."

She leaned behind her and grabbed her Pickup from its secure mounting in the floor. She slapped a panel next to it that opened to reveal magazines of ammunition. She scooped up as many as she could in a single handful. Pushing off from one foot, she landed clear of the mobile command vehicle and nearly fell when she stubbed her foot on a piece of broken masonry.

New senses assailed her: the heat, dust and a stench of burnt wood. She leapt towards a single-storey building on the far side of the road. Her ears split under the deafening crack of a thousand slate roof tiles exploding. In a few steps, she reached the whitewashed wall and threw herself around the corner, falling to the ground. Kate pulled herself up into a ball and read from the display in her lens that her mobile command vehicle had been destroyed.

Her Squitch advised: "You are in enemy-controlled territory. You should seek cover and wait for friendly forces to retake the battlespace."

Another smile creased her face at the idiocy of the comment, as though this were a training exercise. In the sky over the town, the fighting went on. PeaceMakers vanished in clouds of smoke. She hoped the three remaining NATO vehicles would be able to escape the area and perhaps fight again. Facing the deserted Czech town, her spirit sank at the sight of Spiders crawling and scrabbling among the buildings to disappear for Lord-knows-what reason in explosions that sent judders through the ground and into her boots. Window frames and roof joists burst into flames as Lapwings pirouetted and soared and dived and dealt invisible laser pulses to anything the enemy deemed worthy of the slightest attention.

Her Squitch notified her of General Pakla—*her* general—trying to contact her. She pulled herself into a sitting position with her back against the whitewashed wall. Her throat tightened in fear and longing and defiance. She fought the urge to hear his voice a final time, to say sorry, to say goodbye. But she knew from his schedule that he was with his wife now. He must have somehow escaped from her for a few minutes...

She opened a flap over a small pocket on her right thigh. She pulled out a thin, circular device the size of a large coin. Kate placed her right thumb in the central depression to confirm her identity, and holding the centre firmly, with her left thumb and forefinger she twisted the outer rim one-hundred-and-eighty degrees, deactivating the Squitch. All of the data in her lens vanished. She put the device back in its pocket and closed the flap.

She grasped her Pickup and lifted it out of the dust. On her left, she collected the nearest magazine and inserted it into the rifle. She gathered the others and stuffed them in her tunic. She didn't expect to have the time to use them, but kept them close to her body in expectation they might hasten her end. She checked that the Pickup remained deactivated. She climbed to her feet.

Kate moved to the corner and with care peered at the road and her mobile command vehicle. Flames crackled from the windows and black smoke rose skywards. She found the abrupt removal of her Squitch more disorientating than she'd expected. But she also believed the rumours that swirled around all of the NATO armies about what it took to survive behind enemy lines. She stared at the sky and sensed a lessening of activity. The buildings of Černá v Pošumaví burned and hissed and groaned. Roofs fell in and walls collapsed. If any civilians remained, they must surely be dead.

Kate closed her eyes and composed herself for a moment she hadn't expected to have. She activated her Pickup and trusted her aim was still good. She stepped out and advanced along the side of the burning building, holding her weapon defiantly in front of her. Emotions clashed as the end approached. A certain calmness at having embarked on an irrevocable course steadied her limbs. A childish thrill at doing something so extremely dangerous made her spine tingle. And under it all there flowed a strange fatalism. She'd never expected to survive the retreat; she'd only hoped perhaps to last a little longer. At least those junior ranks had not been obliged to die so she could live.

Out on the street there came the sound of whining, a coarse grating of metal on concrete that must have been made by some kind of vehicle. Major Kate Fus squinted and when a sudden gust of wind swept the billowing smoke aside, it revealed a large, tracked vehicle—certainly not anything recognisably NATO—trundling towards her. It looked to be driverless, with a bulbous front giving way to a rear of high, straight lines. She brought her Pickup to bear and opened fire.

Chapter 24

21.26 Sunday 11 June 2062

Professor Duncan Seekings inhaled the warm evening air as he scanned the farmland visible from the west side of the Porton Down military research establishment in southern England. The deep orange sun sank into the misty horizon and a chill breeze wafted over him, making him shiver. After a curious conversation with his friend, Graham English, over a quick frame of snooker earlier in the day, he had been preoccupied with the next generation of NATO weapons and how they could be designed, tested, and mass produced before the inevitable happened and those rotten Middle-Eastern-types overran all of Europe.

As a result, he was running a little late for an important and secret meeting to discuss the latest research. Duncan concluded that perhaps his friend's constant admonishments—that he did not sufficiently attend to the less interesting aspects of the race to find answers to the New Persian Caliphate's war on Europe—might have some merit.

Gravel crunched under his feet as his gangly legs took him back to his office. He muttered to himself: "Graham's not half as clever as he thinks he is. Still reckons the snags don't matter. And the snags always matter. I wonder if the French fellow can see that the snags matter? Perhaps having him and his people at Aldermaston will help them focus?"

He arrived at the door of the office and ducked as he entered. "Lights, standard," he barked. He stopped. glanced around at the well-organised space and admired the misshapen piles of books and papers. He noted food crumbs and other detritus on the carpet and recalled that he'd barred all of the facility's cleaners from his office because they constantly annoyed him by moving some of his books to a shelf on the wall.

"Has the meeting begun yet?"

The Ministry of Defence's super AI answered: "All participants have arrived."

Duncan tutted and frowned. "Damn and blast it. I could do with a cup of tea first. Oh well." He picked up his VR glasses and put them on as he fell back into the worn couch in the middle of the room.

"—completely secret. Although I am sure all of you already understand this, it does nevertheless deserve repeating."

Duncan looked at the front of the conference. Bjarne Hasselman, secretary general of the North Atlantic Council, NATO's governing body, had just finished speaking. The man seemed bothered, which did not surprise Duncan. On his left sat the lanky, young French scientific genius Louis Reyer, and on Hasselman's right sat a pretty lady. Both appeared small next to Hasselman's bulk. As Duncan watched, the name 'Jill Hayes' and 'Specialisation: quantum statistics' digitally materialised in his vision.

"Hmm," he mused, muting his own voice so no one else at the meeting would hear him. "So the stars of the show are there. Jolly good."

Hasselman spoke, his European accent truncating his English pronunciation: "Given that time is of the essence, I will hand over to Monsieur Reyer and Ms Hayes at once. As most of you know, Monsieur Reyer is leading the team at Aldermaston in England dedicated to designing the next generation of NATO ACAs."

"As if we're ever going to last long enough to do that, but still," Duncan muttered, conscious of his own frustrated efforts to increase the firepower of future weapons.

"And, if any of you are concerned that this objective might not have sense," Hasselman added, "we are making plans also to continue the defence of Europe in remote locations once the majority of the fighting will have died down."

Duncan did not find Hasselman's imperfect use of English especially reassuring. He shook his head in disbelief but stopped himself from voicing his bemusement at such a ridiculous suggestion.

The Frenchman next to Hasselman gave a gentle cough and began speaking in more heavily accented English than the secretary general: "Hello. This meeting is to give everyone here an update on our progress, and hopefully to answer any questions as to how we must proceed."

Duncan glanced to his left and then his right to see fifty or more other participants. As his eye alighted on individuals at random, their names and specialisations appeared in the air. He nodded in thoughtful appreciation at the range of permanent representatives, generals from all branches of member states' armed forces, and specialists from fields as diverse as mathematical physics, applied statistics, and condensed matter physics. No more than a handful, including Duncan, knew what was to be announced. He recalled his own efforts to help Reyer's team the previous week, but more important work on improving weapons' performance had obliged him to abandon his investigation into the extended Pauli exclusion principle.

Reyer went on: "We have identified a potential advantage in our fight." A large screen behind the Frenchman came to life with an enlarged representation of a Caliphate Spider. Its parts were all labelled: appendages, joints, explosive compartments, super-AI core, the cryo-magnets that generated the shielding, and the propulsion unit. The image zoomed in on the last of these as Reyer spoke: "If we look closely at the power source, we can see the muon fusion chamber, a little over three centimetres in diameter, able to generate sufficient thrust to give the Spider—and indeed all other machines that the Caliphate has—their quite fantastic speed and dexterity. This is larger than any muon-based fusion device we thought possible. It is positioned inside a high-pressure containment field which is in fact the most important reason for its successful functioning. However, there is a very big flaw in its design."

Duncan sat forward on his couch in his office, thoughts of tea abruptly forgotten. "Here we go," he muttered.

"It should be able to function with at least twenty-five percent greater efficiency than it does." Reyer glanced at Hayes.

Hayes clasped thin fingers together on the table in front of her. As the image of the power unit enlarged further, she said: "The pressurisation inside the containment field allows a number of issues to be overcome at the quantum level. I shan't bore you all with an in-depth explanation of Fermi-Dirac statistics, but the groundwork looks like this:"

Several equations and comparative graphs resolved on either side of the image. Hayes continued, her words clipped: "Obviously, those of you assisting us will want to familiarise yourselves with these developments. However, the issue which we believe concerns all of us is the apparent under-utilisation in this model."

"Hmm, looks clear enough to me," Duncan said aloud. "Wonder if the other, military bods will get it?"

The image of the muon-based fusion device enlarged further, looking like a vast, elaborately carved candlestick holder. Some of the equations and graphs disappeared while those that remained moved to new positions closer to the parts of the power unit to which they related.

Hayes went on: "According to our best calculations, this unit should be able to output this much more energy:"

Comparative statistics materialised and were highlighted on the screen demonstrating the woman's point.

Reyer said with, Duncan thought, a trace more smugness than the situation warranted: "Ladies and gentlemen, we appear to have discovered a flaw in our enemy. The next generation of NATO machines can utilise this shortcoming and be better than theirs."

"Excuse me," said a voice. Duncan glanced and a general from the German Army had an incredulous expression on his florid face. "But how is this even possible? Our enemy is using the same level of super-artificial intelligence we are, *ja?*"

Reyer raised a hand but the general continued: "How could such intelligence make such a mistake? *Ja*, I am a soldier and maybe I am not understanding the science and equations and all this… piffle. But in military matters, I know my enemy will not make any mistake he does not have to, especially with such very good advices."

Reyer gave a Gallic shrug and replied: "And I am a physicist, not a detective. I only research and establish facts, general. I do not know why this muon-based fusion device is designed the way it has been, I only know that it should—and can—be more powerful."

The German spat: "Impossible," and looked thoroughly unimpressed.

Hasselman put out a placating hand and said: "General, given that we still know very little about the enemy, I believe it would be wrong to draw conclusions that are not based on hard evidence. I am sure there is an answer as to why this should be the case, but I fear it will have to wait for now." He stared at the other participants before adding: "Perhaps it is sufficient that we can acknowledge some good news for once?"

"Professor Reyer," said another voice, and Duncan noted the speaker was General Sir Terry Tidbury. "Does this 'lack' of utilisation also apply to weaponry? If we were able to produce more powerful devices, what impact would that have on missile payload and pulsar energy and frequency?"

Reyer answered: "Professor Seekings in England is leading these efforts. Would you like to answer that question, professor?"

Duncan sighed and said: "We have many variables to deal with at this initial stage, most of which—"

Reyer broke in: "Professor? Can you hear me?"

"Damn and blast it," Duncan said when he recalled that he'd muted his mic. He activated it and said: "Yes, thank you. Well, we have several variables to, er, consider, Sir Terry. Forecasts suggest a modest increase, er, in weight capacity, meaning that we would, for example, er, be able to add possibly two or four missiles to an equivalently sized ACA. Regarding the pulsar bursts, it would be a question of frequency. Er, research is continuing."

"Thank you, professor," Hasselman said.

"Have you come up with any actual designs yet?" asked another member of conference.

Hayes answered: "Not yet, no. We first need to have the propulsion system agreed and approved. It is the most important issue and will affect the other design parameters."

A strident female voice asked: "Will they be completely new designs or would upgrading current machines save effort?"

Hayes replied: "We are working with the super AI but so far it looks like we will have completely new designs."

Duncan sensed a positivity among the audience, even though attendance was virtual. He muted his mic and spoke aloud: "Well, it's certainly a novelty to be talking about future developments that may favour us instead of the enemy."

Hasselman spoke: "Very well. If no one has any other questions, I think we should let Professor Reyer and his team get to their—"

"Sure, I got a question," someone broke in.

Duncan glanced and saw the interruption came from Dan Griffin, an American space warfare expert who he recalled had attended previous meetings.

Griffin's voice carried heavy sarcasm: "Assuming you guys can work out the power-unit design, and then you can work out the ACA design, exactly how long is it gonna take to manufacture, test, and bring these new weapons to full production?"

The three people at the podium looked at each other. Finally, Reyer said: "Obviously, we will do our work as quickly as we can, but there are many—"

"How long?" the American insisted.

"Bloody bore, no manners," Duncan muttered.

Reyer gave another shrug and said: "Four to six months."

There came audible gasps from most of the attendees. Duncan sighed and watched as half a dozen people shimmered and vanished, leaving the conference with a shake of their heads.

"Why so long?" Griffin pushed.

Jill Hayes, her face a mask of suppressed anger, said: "Because, as you probably know, not everything in military ACAs can be replicated. The power unit—whatever its final spec—will need heavy elements like europium, among other components. These will all need to be sourced and transported—"

Another voice called out: "But NATO and Europe are going to be finished in days."

Again, Hasselman put his hands out to placate the attendees. "Please, ladies and gentlemen, as I mentioned at the beginning, plans are under way to continue the fight should nothing in the military forecasts change in the nearest future. Now, if you do not mind, I think it wisest to allow Professor Reyer to return to his most urgent work. We also have the military sitrep that will commence shortly; I am sure the general retreat is a greater cause for concern. In addition, that will be followed by a report on the refugee crisis. Now, I would like to turn to—"

Hasselman stopped when Duncan removed his glasses and thus left the conference. He leapt from the couch and paced around the office area: "Damn American," he cursed. "Everyone knows there are things we can't replicate so of course it's going to take time. Bad show, really." He strode to the kitchenette and put the kettle on.

A communication icon flashed in his lens. "Audible, Squonk," he instructed.

The voice of his friend Graham English filled the area. "You've already left? How did it go, old chap?"

Duncan took a mug from the sink and threw a teabag in it as he replied: "Interesting. There is certainly an advantage, if only we can get the time. Why weren't you there?"

"Because breaking the enemy's jamming is considered a priority, remember? And in addition to that headache, I've got a team working on some novelties."

"Oh, can I have a look?"

"Perhaps."

"Will you have some time to come down here for a bit of snooker?"

"I don't think so. It's getting more difficult to leave London."

"Hmm," Duncan sympathised, "such a bore. How about I come up?"

"Could you leave your work for so long?"

"Until Reyer and his team release the power unit's parameters, my options are limited."

"Jolly good," Graham replied. "Tell you what, I have seen designs for something so leftfield I don't quite believe it myself."

"So send me the plans, then."

"Not so fast," Graham chided. "This is tiptop secret, old boy. You'll have to come up to London to see for yourself."

"Damn and blast you, sir," Duncan cursed, his curiosity piqued. "Only no practising snooker behind my back, all right?"

"Right you are," Graham replied.

Chapter 25

English Prime Minister Dahra Napier stared agape at the screen on the wall in her office in Ten Downing Street. "My God, this is staggering," she breathed. The memorandum she read summarised in brittle, simple sentences, the initial results revealed by the *Institut Neuropsi* from the brain scan of the Caliphate warrior captured on 2 June.

"Ugly brute, isn't he?" Defence Secretary Liam Burton said, nodding at the man's picture before taking a gulp of coffee.

The head of MI5, David Perkins, said: "Clearly his destiny was as cannon fodder. It's surprising how much trouble poor facial symmetry can cause for some people." He accepted a porcelain cup and saucer from Monica the aide with a sniff and no thanks.

Dahra noted this and said: "This could be extremely important now our most useful contact in Beijing has been lost."

Perkins replied with indifference: "I don't think 'lost' is the correct word. During the last contact, they gave a coded

187

notification that their cover had been compromised and any intel they provided could not be regarded as reliable. But, as of today, they are not 'lost'."

From behind her, Dahra heard a scoff escape from Crispin. She glanced back at the screen and continued to read about the young man called Farhad Oveisi, twenty-four years old, sold into the military by his parents at age ten. When the scan was performed, he had an IQ of 68.278. She read in silence until she reached the end.

"Very tantalising," Burton said.

"All personnel with sufficient security access have been notified of this memo," Crispin added.

"Squonk," Burton said, "where and what is Tazirbu?"

The Ministry of Defence's super AI replied: "Tazirbu is an oasis town in the Sahara Desert with a population of about five thousand."

"But according to elements of this man's memory, it's one of three main centres of enemy ACA production. His recollections imply a thriving armaments production centre," Burton said.

"Current data on Tazirbu is twenty-seven years old," Squonk replied.

"My God," Dahra breathed. "But how? They were supposed to be backward, medieval, with constant internal wars, uprisings and coups. It was supposed to be a sealed dictatorship that cut itself off so no one outside could see how bad things were on the inside. Look at this, look at what they've taken out of this man's head. Surely the only question is how it's taken this long for the Third Caliph to attack…" Dahra's voice trailed off in shock.

"According to this memo," Liam said, waving his one empty hand at the screen, "this individual was 'given' into the Third Caliph's 'care' because his district benefited from numerous social improvement projects. Consider his recollection of that network of water replicators, sufficient to ensure enough water for sanitation and farming in his village indefinitely. And that memory is fourteen years old. That's hardly what we'd expect to see in a malfunctioning society."

Dahra smothered her shock and gathered herself. She would not allow herself to be perceived as weak in front of the male colleagues in her cabinet. She looked at Liam and said: "It's only a small part of the Caliphate's total area. The capital is Tehran and the district he comes from is close to there."

Liam said: "But that ACA production facility is in the middle of the Sahara, thousands of miles to the west. Imagine it, PM: what if our worst nightmares are in fact true?"

Dahra nodded and said with unintended irony: "They pretty much already are, Liam."

The defence secretary said: "Supposing the Third Caliph has unlimited resources, construction replicators, food replicators, and super artificial intelligence to run it all for him? Simple brutes like this can do the invading and kill anything his ACAs miss, but, militarily speaking, he does not need an officer corps because the bloody computers will execute everything for him. And if he has munitions plants all managed by super AI, the possibilities are endless."

"Up to and including the complete destruction of Europe," Dahra noted before turning away from the screen and sipping her green tea. She preferred to have Terry explain the military issues to her, for he seemed the ideal patient uncle, while Liam was more passionate about the services of which he used to be a member. Liam, she reflected, would make a good bodyguard. She looked at Crispin and asked: "Is Terry available?"

Her aide's eye twitched and he said: "Sorry, boss, he isn't. Shall I leave a ping?"

"Yes."

Liam addressed Perkins: "When does this French institute say it will give us more detailed information?"

Perkins replied: "It will need some weeks to provide complete data but has promised to let us know as soon as it picks up on anything that might affect the course of the conflict."

"Good," Burton said in satisfaction.

The door to Dahra's office opened and the foreign secretary, Charles Blackwood, entered. Dahra smiled at the thought that nothing would ever affect Charles's sartorial elegance. He stuck his hand in the jacket pocket of his suit and could've passed as a model on the catwalk as he flashed the room a smile and said: "Sorry I'm late."

Dahra shook her head and asked: "Late for what?"

Blackwood's eyebrows rose and he glanced from Crispin Webb to Liam, then to Perkins and back to Dahra. "The call with Madelyn Coll, the current president of the United States of America?" he offered with faint trace of irony.

Dahra recalled something about a call with her opposite number in the White House, but the shock of the memo had left her nonplussed.

Crispin Webb said: "Yes, boss. It was scheduled for midday, but the French institute's memo came as a bit of a surprise, and I didn't want to interrupt you."

"And?" Dahra said.

"I would have, had the Yan—er, had the Americans, been ready on time, but Coll still isn't available."

Dahra turned back to the screen and said: "This is significant. Finally we have some idea about that awful place."

"With respect, PM," Perkins began in his familiar disdainful tone, "we've always had 'ideas' about the New Persian Caliphate. Our computers have repeatedly extrapolated what could've happened within the regime after it closed everything but its major ports—"

"I know, Mr Perkins," Dahra broke in testily. "But anything like this was certainly at the extreme end of the probability scale."

"At least we have some confirmation, at long last," said Charles Blackwood, accepting a coffee cup from Monica with a flirtatious smile.

"And we can be one hundred percent certain it's not planted evidence," said Perkins, his narrow nose seeming to sniff the air. "Pity a little more faith was not put in my department's reports over the last few years instead of those computers. The reality this simpleton's memories prove is actually far more extreme than anything our intel from China surmised."

Dahra wanted to reprimand Perkins, but she had to concede that she too would have been furious in his position.

Perkins shrugged and added: "Hardly matters now anyway, I suppose."

"I think it does," Liam Burton argued, his chest expanding. "Battle's not over yet, mate."

Dahra sensed the anger under Liam's words but Perkins seemed oblivious.

The head of MI5 replied: "Might as well be. We'll all be dead soon enough, and if this place isn't flattened in the battle, it'll be swarming with... what do you army-types call them? Ragheads?"

Dahra glanced at Charles Blackwood to see an amused smirk on his face.

Liam answered darkly: "It's a shame the attorney general can't hear you. I wonder if there isn't a law against defeatist talk like that."

Perkins scoffed aloud and said: "Yes, when NATO losing thirty thousand troops in the ten days since hostilities recommenced and the imminent collapse of societal cohesion itself isn't enough to keep us occupied, why not—"

191

"Gentlemen," Dahra broke in, "if you don't mind. I have to go cap in hand to the US president yet again, so I'd be grateful if you could control yourselves."

"Besides," Perkins went on, "I thought the army's big job now was to get the precious Royal Family safely to Canada or wherever—"

"Mr Perkins," Dahra insisted, "control yourself or get out now."

Perkins tilted his head and murmured: "My apologies."

Dahra doubted his sincerity but she looked at the others, including the now-seething Liam, and said: "That goes for all of you. Keep your testosterone under control. Thank you. Charles, jump in if you think I'm missing something."

Blackwood nodded.

She added: "And it is a possibility that I will miss something. Liam, once again, what are our priorities? What do we need most of all?"

Liam tore his eyes off Perkins and replied: "Everything, PM, it's as simple as that."

"Really?"

"Oh, yes. Yesterday, I spoke to Sir Terry, I spoke to the people at Aldermaston, Porton Down, and considered the super AI's forecasts. My gut says more troops would be preferable because that helps with morale. But on the logistics side, we're lacking all the equipment we can't replicate."

Dahra nodded and said: "Well, that makes it straightforward." She turned and addressed Crispin: "Can't they at least tell us how long she's going to be?"

Crispin held up an index finger and said: "Here we go."

The memo vanished from the screen to be replaced with the oval head of Madelyn Coll sitting behind the Resolute desk, flanked by four white, middle-aged men.

"Good morning, Madelyn," Dahra began, trying to imbue her voice with some enthusiasm. "Thank you for agreeing to talk with us so early in the day."

"Hi, Dahra, how's it going over there?"

"We are keeping well for now," Dahra replied, choosing to overlook the banality in the president's question. "Have you seen the memo?"

Coll frowned, "I don't think so. What memo?"

"About Oveisi, the captured Caliphate warrior, from the French institute? They scanned his brain, extracted his memories. We had the first summary delivered a couple of hours ago."

One of the men, whom Dahra recognised as Coll's letch of a Secretary of State, Warren Baker, leaned forward and whispered in her ear.

When he withdrew, Coll said in a whining voice: "Ah, no, not yet. But I hear it's a big help for you guys."

A wave of exhaustion swept over Dahra. She did not know how to connect with the president. "Well, yes, hopefully," she fumbled. "We shall have to wait and see."

Coll glanced down at something on her desk. "Yeah, right. Anyways, I need to level with you."

"What?" Dahra said, now wholly confused.

"You wanna talk about more help, right?"

"Er, yes. I thought we could discuss in particular—"

"Nope," Coll said with a shake of her head. "Not gonna happen."

Dahra's chest tightened and she hoped she'd misheard. She heaved in a calming breath and said: "Why? Is there a problem?"

Coll's eyebrows rose. She asked: "Did you see what happened over the weekend, Dahra?"

"Yes, of course, and we share the pain of your lo—"

"And the people of the United States of America thank you for your sympathy," Coll broke in with a sardonic sneer.

Dahra wondered what on Earth must be happening. She appreciated it was only seven in the morning over there, but—

"But the problem we have, in addition to the loss of our ships and their valuable cargoes, is that they were attacked on our goddamn doorstep."

Realisation dawned on Dahra. At once, she knew she had to gain control of the conversation. She said: "With all due respect madam president, over five hundred kilometres from the Eastern Seaboard is hardly on your doorstep. As far as we know, those machines were almost certainly at the limit of their range."

"What did she say? What did she say?" Coll repeated, looking at the men around her.

Dahra swallowed and her heart rate picked up. She sensed worse was to come.

Coll leaned forward and continued, her voice intensifying: "I have got the press and most of Congress demanding I reassure them that those machines cannot reach the continental United States."

"Well, don't you think that's obvious?"

"What?"

Dahra held her arms open, trying to placate the woman on the screen. "Because if they could, they would have by now, don't you think?"

Coll stood and walked around the Resolute desk. She wore an unflattering, light-blue two-piece suit and Napier thought of offering Blackwood's sartorial assistance.

Coll said with anger: "And what if they're building better machines? What if they couldn't hit us a few months ago but can now?"

"My experts here advise me—"

194

"I don't give a shit what your experts say—"

"Please, Maddie," Dahra implored. "Don't stop helping us."

The president's face softened a fraction. She said: "The political pressure is growing on me to quit throwing good American lives away like this."

Dahra understood at once that 'political pressure' meant insistence from Coll's campaign backers. "I know. I understand, I really do," Dahra implored. "But please remember how I helped you in February, when you wanted to attack the Caliphate with nuclear weapons for destroying Israel. That certainly would have led to Armageddon and the US would've been obliterated while the Caliphate would've survived."

"Of course I remember," Coll retorted, appearing only a little mollified. "But that was then, and we sure stuck by our NATO obligations since."

There came a pause. Dahra decided to change the emphasis with: "NATO needs more troops and more equipment."

Coll returned to sit behind the desk. A slim male who Napier recognised as a member of the National Security Council came forward, whispered something in Coll's ear, and then withdrew. Coll said: "How do I give a press conference where the parents of dead American troops ask me why their son or daughter died? What do I tell them when they and the whole world can see Europe collapsing like a house of cards?"

Dahra stared at Coll, lost for words.

"Prime minister, if I may?" Charles Blackwood said, taking a few steps closer to Napier.

Dahra made brief eye contact with him and gave him a nod of assent.

Blackwood held his hands together in front of him in a relaxed posture as he said: "Madam president, with respect, it is not dissimilar to American laws on the possession of firearms. Now, fifty thousand Americans die each year from gun violence, but the majority agree that is a necessary cost of freedom, yes?"

Coll sat back in her chair but said nothing.

Blackwood didn't allow time for contradiction: "Every year, you *know*—your government, the American people, the statisticians—that so many thousands of your citizens are going to die due to preventable gun violence."

"Yeah, but it's not preventable if we—"

"Want to be free," Blackwood finished for her, with the gentlest interruption Dahra had ever heard. The foreign secretary went on: "And this is precisely the same issue we are dealing with here. Yes, I grant you that, in all probability, the whole of Europe will fall to the New Persian Caliphate in the next few weeks and the fight will ultimately be lost, but that is not the reason for you to stop now. Madam president, Europe is free *now*, and it needs to be free for as long as possible, for as long as we can make that *now* last. Even though we may all die, that is no reason to stop protecting our freedom."

"Europe isn't America," Coll answered. "But I guess you have a point."

Blackwood said nothing.

Coll said: "We have, what is it, three convoys already scheduled, so I will leave those in place. Let's return to this subject on our next call in a couple of days."

The screen went blank and Dahra felt the breath escape from her chest. She looked at Blackwood. "Thank you, Charles," she said.

The foreign secretary shrugged. "I don't expect it to make much difference. She's beholden to her campaign donors, and if they're putting pressure on her that continued support for NATO will lead to Blackswans and Lapwings laying waste to the Eastern Seaboard, then no wonder she's getting touchy."

"You still did a good job there," Liam Burton said. "Especially given that grating accent."

Blackwood let out a chuckle and replied: "I'm glad that wasn't only me. My God, she can whine."

"Liam," Dahra said, "liaise with our contacts in the US military; and you might want to talk to Sir Terry."

"Sure. It struck me that the prep for the next three convoys is already so far advanced, she probably would have conceded them in any case."

Dahra ignored the slightly crestfallen look on Blackwood's face, saying: "It might come to it that we will be obliged to accept American irregulars into our own militaries, although I hope not."

With a glance at Charles, Liam said: "We'll do everything we can to keep the Americans in until the end, PM."

Chapter 26

Inside Sergeant Rory Moore's mind, selected memories of the previous two weeks' engagements concertinaed down into a bottomless well. He opened his eyes to see an off-white ceiling above him. A bright strip light encroached on the edge of his vision and stung his eyes. He felt tired but also vulnerable at being in bed and not knowing why he was in bed. He recalled two female medical orderlies who got him away from a strange doctor at a casualty clearing station, a transport, and the relentless summer heat. Had he taken a headshot?

A man's face suddenly appeared; thin eyebrows drawn close together in curiosity. He said: "Ah, good morning, sergeant. Don't worry. You've been sedated for some time so you'll feel a bit wonky for a while."

Rory opened his mouth to reply and felt a gentle pressure on his right forearm. The doctor said: "Don't speak now. Give yourself a few moments to acclimate. You're in a hospital back in Blighty, and your commanding officer is waiting to talk to you."

Rory let out a groan.

The doctor smiled and said: "It's all right, I'm in charge here and he can wait. Just breathe normally for a while."

The doctor disappeared. Minutes passed. The deep ache that suffused his back and leg muscles made him wonder how long he'd been prostrate, but he no longer had his lens in his eye, which meant he had to remain in ignorance. The realisation of the missing lens led to recollections of the contact which, he suspected, should have killed him. A worrying but familiar question resolved in his mind: how long could his luck hold out? How many contacts that had seen comrades killed could he hope to survive before missile, Spider or shell finally inflicted irreparable injuries? He closed his eyes and concentrated to recall the contact. He and Sergeant Heaton had been pulling back either side of a small Austrian town. Their troops were retreating behind a screen of tanks and battlefield support lasers. Rory had just ordered his people to chuck out their Footie anti-personnel smart-mines when—

The swish of the curtain around his bed broke into his thoughts. A stocky figure turned to face him, smiled, and said: "Welcome back to England, Sergeant Moore."

"Thank you, Colonel Doyle," Rory replied, damning the atrophy in his muscles.

"Not in too much discomfort?" The colonel asked, clasping his hands behind his back.

"Not really, sir. Just wishing I had my lens to help me get up to speed."

"There's plenty of time for that, young man. What do you remember about your last contact?"

"Very little, sir. Please, do sit down if you like."

Doyle nodded, turned the thin-framed chair next to the bed around, and sat facing Rory. He said: "You took quite a serious wound to your head. One of your troops managed to get a GenoFluid pack on it in time, but your evac was problematic. Complications developed and the bots in the pack put you into an induced coma."

"But it's been days," Rory said.

"Yes, your head needed a lot of repairs. Still, thank goodness for modern tech, eh?"

Rory felt a shiver as the colonel made him realise how close it had been, again. He didn't want to think about it too much in case it affected his luck. He asked: "How soon can I return to active duty, sir?"

The colonel stroked his moustache with his forefinger and thumb in apparent consideration. He asked: "I completely understand your enthusiasm, sergeant, but are you sure you want to?"

"Of course," Rory replied with a shrug, and then winced at the pain.

"Very well, but I want to be certain you know there's a training posting that is yours if you want it. Anyone looking at your service record since February would certainly conclude that you had contributed a great deal to the war effort."

"Colonel, thank you. But the training I gave during the Tense Spring really was enough. Besides, the coordinators have got all of my lectures on record—"

"You've been through even more in the last two weeks."

Rory sighed, a wave of exhaustion sweeping over him. He said: "It's always the same, sir. We retreat, that's all. We lose ground. We lose people. We just lose."

Rory's eyelids became impossibly heavy and forced themselves down. He wished again he had a lens to tell him what the hell was going on. As consciousness left him, he asked himself if he really had just been talking to the colonel.

Chapter 27

The three old friends sat around the worn circular table and contemplated the future that remained to them. The oldest, Ondra, lifted the bottle of *Slivovice*, unscrewed the cap, and poured the last drops of the plum liqueur into each of three glasses, his withered hand trembling a little.

Martin observed the twinkle in Ondra's eye as he poured, the same as it had been for the thirty years they had known each other. "Is it truly the last bottle?" Martin asked with amused regret.

"I am certain," Ondra replied with a nod.

Jan, the youngest by a few months, scratched his white beard and rubbed his index finger in the deep wrinkles at the corner of his eye. "It is," he confirmed. "I even checked in Ondra's secret stash which he thought we did not know about."

Ondra lifted his glass and said: "Of course I knew you knew about it. That's why I only kept just enough there to convince you."

Martin, plumper than the other men, lifted his glass and his hand also trembled. "At least," he said with pride, "I am not covered in white hair like you two relics."

"Luck of your genes, Martin," Jan said, also raising his glass.

"For us, comrades," Ondra said.

"For us," Martin and Jan echoed.

The three friends clicked their glasses and drank. Ondra made his satisfaction plain with a quiet but rumbling belch that went on for two long seconds.

"No wonder Tereza left you, you pig," Jan said with a shake of his head.

Ondra smiled despite everything, because it made sense to smile at the end. He eyed his two friends: "Look at where we have finished, eh? My Tereza, may the cold-hearted witch rot in hell, stole my life and threatened our kids before they finally grew up and escaped her grasping claws. You, Jan, Kiki leaving you like that for that skinny little shit—"

Jan held his hand up to stop Ondra, but the *Slivovice* loosened tongues and feelings in ways that might have caused an argument on a normal Saturday night. But this was not a normal Saturday night. Jan finished for Ondra: "Yes, but he was a rich trader. What chance did I have, eh? You knew at the time, friend. We were always away from our wives for one reason or another—can we really blame them? In some ways I am not so sad. Kiki is for sure very safe in some mountain retreat in New Zealand now I expect."

"If that were me," Martin said, arms resting on his protruding belly, "I am not sure I would be so happy."

Jan waved his hand in dismissal and said: "We all choose our feelings, friend. What we cannot choose are our fates."

There came a pause. Ondra patted the remains of the white hair on the side of his head and said with warmth: "And you have had the worst of all of us, Jan."

Jan scoffed and responded: "Ha, until now, maybe. First Lada and those damnable super-cancers. After she died, I wondered if they would find the cure, and I know I will not live to see that."

Ondra asked: "You never heard from Radek?"

Jan waved a hand again: "No, of course not. I will never know what got into that boy once he lost his mother."

"I remember him," Martin mused. "He was such a handsome lad."

"Yes," Jan replied. "But he got his wanderlust from Lada."

Another pause settled over the men, each looking at his empty glass and the empty bottle.

Martin stroked the black stubble on his ample chins and asked Ondra: "Are you absolutely sure you do not have another bottle stashed away somewhere?"

Ondra grinned. "I am sure I do not."

Jan said: "We do not have to do this now, not tonight. We can wait a while yet."

"Yes, but for how long?" Ondra argued with a shrug. "The reserve power in the generators will run out in less than ten minutes, and then we will have no food and no water. And we have used up all of the *Slivovice*."

"But we could still wait," Jan said. "See one last dawn, feel the sun on our faces a final time. We haven't been above ground in months now."

Martin turned to Jan and said: "We agreed, Jan. If you really want to stay, you can do so but on your own, with no light, no aircon, no food and no water."

Jan's expression lightened as he said: "If you put it like that, I suppose there is not much else to do. And we should all go out together."

"It is what we agreed," Ondra added.

Jan pushed the rickety chair back and stood with a groan. "At least I can stop with the medications, finally."

Ondra also got up and stretched to his full two-metre height. "And not only you," he said. "The discs in my spine have been killing me for longer than I can recall."

"That's because you constantly refused to go to the doctor," Jan said. "He could have given you a simple injection of bots that would have fixed your backpain and then gone out in your pee."

"No," Ondra replied, "I always said no bots in my body, and I have kept it that way."

"Here we go again," Martin said, pushing his overweight body up from the chair, "one last rollout for the great conspiracy theory of our times: that medical bots are the government's secret way to control us. Is that right?"

Ondra raised his hands in mock offence. "Yes, and what of it, eh? Those bots can go anywhere in your body and do anything, and I would rather suffer in pain than let any of them inside my body. Come on, let's get on with it. The reserve power will go in a few minutes. Time to carry out our last mission."

The three friends left the small, windowless kitchen and walked along an off-white corridor. Ondra noticed Martin limping. "Are you all right?"

Martin said: "Yes, just the meniscus tear playing up again. Do you think we can at least surprise them?"

Ondra glanced at him and replied: "More than forty-eight hours have passed since they overran this area, which we can be certain of because that was when the main power went out. By now, they are probably halfway to Prague and I suspect Krakow is already on fire."

They arrived at a door. Ondra opened it with a wave of his hand. Once inside, artificial lights came on, illuminating a series of cabinets on the left, and the length of the shooting range on the right. The air carried the unmistakable aroma of spent cordite from a million rounds fired over the decades.

"We are running out of time."

The old men moved with as much agility as their advanced years would allow. They opened the cabinets and selected their preferred holsters. More grunts and groans reverberated off the bare walls as they put the holsters on.

"Here is my one true love," Ondra said, picking up the only rifle in the cabinets.

Martin let out a chuckle and said: "At last you can activate it out in the open."

"When we were in the army, I always preferred the earlier PKU–28. That was a true beauty, as light as a feather and no recoil," Jan said.

"Yes, but it was not smart, was it? It belonged to a bygone era," Martin answered, holstering a Glock 33 with several clips that slotted into pouches around his ample waist.

Ondra slid magazines into his own holster as he said: "The PKU–38 was the first really smart assault rifle, and it will always be the best."

Jan tutted and replied: "I still do not think a rifle is the right weapon for this fight." He holstered a new Sig Sauer 889 and ammunition.

Ondra walked to the door. "Have you tried one of those PKU–48s the army uses now? No refinement in it; it is only functional."

"Yes, yes," Martin chivvied. "Let us go."

Ondra slid open a small panel on the wall. A thin tray emerged, coming down from vertical to horizontal and stopping with a click. On it sat a dozen earbuds. "Want one?" he asked the others.

Without speaking, the other two took an earbud and each inserted it in his ear. They left the room. Ondra activated the older version Pickup.

A new, metallic voice in his ear said: "Calibrating. Stand by."

"Did you get that?" he asked his comrades.

Martin and Jan confirmed with nods and grunts.

The three men walked with a new purpose in their stride that belied their advanced years. They reached the foot of a stairwell.

Martin, already out of breath, said: "Can we take the lift up?"

Ondra chuckled and said: "Why not?"

At that moment, the reserve power cut out, plunging the men into darkness.

"*Pro kurva,*" Martin cursed.

Jan laughed, a deep bellow, and said: "Okay, goggles on."

Each of them strapped old-fashioned night-vision goggles over their thinning hair and began the ascent up four flights of stairs. Twelve minutes later, they reached the ground-level exit of the Ostrava-Stará Bělá shooting range. Ondra and Jan waited while Martin recovered his breath.

Ondra wagged a finger and reminded them: "On the other side of this door is the same neighbourhood we have lived in for the last thirty years, more or less. It is the same activity centre. On the right, there is the sports field the school has been using for years, with the hills leading to the Polish border beyond that. Those hills will still be there. On our left, there will be the tennis courts, the café, and the car park. Nothing has changed. Got that?"

Martin, his breaths slowing, said nothing. Jan said: "Ondra, let us get this over with. We shall be fortunate to get even one of them, you understand?"

Ondra replied: "But they do not even know we are here. Think," he urged his lifelong friends, "their machines will have moved on. Their best warriors will be at the front. We have around us now all the dullards and brutes and rapists. We can avenge the wrongs in our last stand."

Martin checked the magazine in his Glock and said: "And you can take a day off sounding like a third-rate pimp trying to sell his clap-ridden wife for a snort of crack. You pompous ass."

Jan laughed again while Ondra gave a look of mock offence. Seconds passed while the three friends stared at each other a final time. Jan said: "I never thought it would end like this. I had imagined one of us being left behind when the other two had gone, lamenting us and trying to find a trustworthy replacement to run our little gun club."

"Me too," Martin said, before turning to Ondra and ordering: "Come on, big guy. It's time for action."

"Who are you calling 'big', fatty?" Holding his outdated Pickup vertically in front of him, Ondra eased the door open and stepped outside and into the darkness. His night-vision goggles did not reveal any threat.

"This is an anti-climax," Jan said as he strode out in front of them.

"Computer?" Ondra said. "Computer? What is going on?"

The computer of modest, outdated ability inside Ondra's PKU–38 replied: "There is too much electronic interference to provide any useful data."

In the warm night air, the three friends turned and looked at each other, smiling and shaking their heads in bemusement. A sudden, deep impact in the tarmac of the tennis courts made them turn in that direction. Another impact came, and then another.

The computer's voice in the friends' ears opined: "Unidentified munitions have arrived close to your location. They might be hostile. You should consider taking defensive action."

All three brought their limited weapons to bear as the appendages on the three Spiders snapped out. At once, the Caliphate machines moved towards the men. Ondra, flanked by Martin and Jan, opened fire. The men backed away. The force of the Spiders' motion pressed and then flattened the chain-link fencing that enclosed the tennis courts. They strode towards the old men.

Chapter 28

08.57 Monday 19 June 2062

Terry took the offered mug of tea and said: "Thank you, Simms. See that I am not disturbed during this meeting."

His adjutant nodded in confirmation and left Terry's personal office in the War Rooms.

Alone again, Terry said: "Squonk?"

"Yes, Sir Terry?" the British Army's super AI answered.

"Regarding the Oveisi case, estimate the potential to affect the outcome of the war. And just give me a summary, I'm not interested in the numbers."

"Minimal. Total defeat for NATO forces is a near-certainty before the extracted data can be analysed to sufficient depth to affect future tactics or strategy."

"Supposing that somehow either we could continue resisting after defeat or even postpone defeat, how much intel could the Oveisi case provide?"

"In theory, after sufficient analysis the data could prove material."

"Therefore, so could the data extracted from the brains of other injured Caliphate warriors, correct?"

Squonk answered: "Affirmative. Cross-referencing enemy strengths from the extracted memories of multiple subjects would also make a material difference in the hypothetical scenario under discussion. However, there is currently a dearth of available subjects."

Terry exhaled slowly, considering his next order. "Very well. Squonk, where practicable reassign current deployments to maximise the possibilities of NATO forces capturing enemy warriors. Flag this order top secret, only for the eyes of corps commanders and higher ranks."

Squonk queried: "Sir Terry, this will involve redeploying those NATO troops with the most combat experience into positions where they are most likely to engage enemy warriors. Do you wish to override normal leave rotations?"

Terry shook his head in bemusement and said: "Yes, I do."

"Confirmed," Squonk answered. "Sir Terry, the meeting will begin in fifteen seconds."

"Very well." Terry blew the steam as it wafted from his tea and waited. He preferred the military sitreps because the issues were those with which he felt most comfortable. The broader UN-based meetings involved too many politicians and other civilians who seemed to require an inordinate amount of explanation, often in areas—such as civilian casualties—that were not his key concern.

The screen in front of him winked into life. The African-American face of Supreme Allied Commander Europe, General Joseph E. Jones, resolved in its familiar saturnine grimace. He said nothing as thumbnails materialised along the bottom of the screen. These included generals, lieutenant-generals and other senior ranks from each national force that still held territory to defend, the commanders of the remaining military bases and ports in Northern Europe, and representatives of specific munitions suppliers.

"Welcome, everyone," Jones began with a world-weariness in his voice that Terry found disconcerting. "I assume you've all been keeping up to date with the weekend's events, so I'll make this real short. The most important point is that while increased deployment of the FT–23/D anti-personnel smart-mine has slowed the enemy's advance, collated data shows it has not done so by as much as we were hoping for."

Jones's face withdrew and a map of Europe appeared. Numerous indicators flashed with digits denoting how many FT–23/D anti-personnel smart-mines the retreating NATO soldiers were leaving behind.

"Due to enemy jamming, we can't know with any certainty how much damage these mines are doing, we just leave it to the super AI to extrapolate from how quickly the enemy continues to advance. One bright spot occurred around Arat in Romania. Intel suggests that the enemy didn't fully realise what he was up against, and the delay there lasted long enough to let several thousand civilians back while bringing up some useful hardware. This has also raised questions over the effectiveness of the enemy's internal comms. To us, it would be highly unlikely that any experience gained at heavy cost on one part of the front would not be relayed to all units. But this seems to be what happened at Arat, where our computers insist those warriors got caught out by the smart-mines." Jones sighed and added: "We could do with a few more Arats."

Terry sipped his hot tea, reassured immeasurably by the malty flavour tinged with a satisfying sweetness.

Jones continued: "Since then, however, we've seen a drop in the delay-against-projection figure, which you can see here and here. The American Abrahams N4–1A tanks are performing almost twenty percent better than we anticipated, especially when deployed with BSLs, but the British Challengers are, maybe, not doin' quite as well as we expected."

Terry cringed at the observation. He had seen reports that detailed the numerous shortcomings in the British Army's autonomous tanks, but little could be done short of a wholesale adoption of American software, which was not compatible with how the different missile systems operated.

"Elsewhere," Jones continued, "convoys SE–09 and SE–10 reached Europe without incident and have brought, among many other things, more than four hundred of the Abrahams and six hundred BSLs. Logistics is getting them out to screen Berlin and Paris if the enemy doesn't interfere in those deployments."

Jones paused and sipped from a glass of water. He continued: "Another issue that affects the timetable is that the enemy is—yet again—not following established military doctrine by neglecting to attack several munitions manufacturing plants. We know he has the ACAs available to completely flatten our ability to manufacture the arms we cannot replicate. But so far, he prefers the more unorthodox approach of terrorising the civilian populations. I remain convinced that he has to hit and disable these centres before long. Like with the resumption of the invasion itself, the longer the enemy neglects to do something he should do, the more likely it becomes that he will do it.

"Now, as our various fronts contract, this has the positive effect of shortening resupply lines. This has also led to an increase in the wounded recovery rate, which is good news for morale on the battlefield because casualties are getting better treatment. On the downside, this relentless retreat is causing bigger problems when it comes to civilians. A lot of folks in the enemy's way are having trouble moving. Although the vast majority are supportive and even willing to help our troops, we are getting increased instances of alcohol- and drug-fuelled misbehaviour. Apart from that, as I expect you've seen in your own countries, suicide rates are also climbing. Here are the figures as they stood an hour ago."

Jones took another sip of water; Terry drank his tea. The map of Europe receded and lists of numbers splayed downwards: killed in action, missing presumed dead, missing presumed captured, wounded; volumes of territory lost; civilians estimated killed, civilians estimated captured.

SACEUR went on: "We're following the pre-agreed plans where battalions and even corps are merging as the fronts contract. Again, this does give us some advantage in synergies, especially combined with increasing numbers of troops, although all of the new recruits are obviously green. Nevertheless, the headline figure hasn't changed a whole lot: all of mainland Europe will fall within the next three weeks at the maximum. To be blunt, I will be very surprised if it doesn't happen sooner. Any questions?"

"Yes, sir," said a colonel from Army Group Centre. "Is there any news on improving replication? Before this shit-festival kicked o—er, before the war started, one of the top priorities for NATO for the next five years was the objective to expand replication to include more explosive components, to make it easier to replicate more powerful explosives. Has that gone anywhere?"

Jones shook his head and replied: "No, the key impactors for increasing explosive yield still have to be mined and transported. I know that if their shielding wasn't so tough, we'd be able to use munitions we could replicate. That would help slow them up, but warfare has moved on a ways."

The colonel nodded in consideration and said: "Thank you, sir."

"Anyone else?"

A major from the French logistics corps said: "General, what about the political angle? I do not wish to repeat mere rumours, but seeing how bad our situation is, I think no one needs the extra worry that the United States Forces might withdraw from the battlefield. The English press is reporting this with some... volume? For you Americans to abandon NATO now, this would be very bad for all of us."

Jones shook his head and muttered: "Son, I'm a soldier, not a politician. All I can tell you is that if Madelyn Coll orders me to quit Europe, she will have my resignation before she finishes the goddamn sentence. Now, are we done?"

Silence greeted the general's final question. He thanked the participants and ended the meeting. Terry tapped the screen to bring up the current deployments on the British mainland. Southern England already thronged with refugees from Europe, training ranges and stores of materiel. He wondered what it would be like with hundreds of thousands more refugees, thousands of soldiers and millions of tons of equipment and munitions that must be added when the enemy obliged them to exit the mainland.

Chapter 29

Crispin Webb stabbed a button on the coffee machine and glanced back at Dahra Napier. They had a rare few minutes alone together in her office in Ten Downing Street, and the pitch of her voice had begun to rise.

She shook her head and said: "But it's been three weeks since the attack, and still the press will not let this go. I don't understand it. What do they think is going to happen? There is going to be no public inquiry 'after' this war. There are going to be no lessons to be learned because those few who survive are going to be living under a completely different regime."

Crispin took the double espresso from the machine and sipped the hot, bitter liquid. The last few days had, incredibly, seen a new opportunity present itself: a way-out Crispin had not expected. However, one of the conditions was keeping his boss in position and functioning well, which became trickier by the day. He closed several streams in his lens to better concentrate and said: "People still need something to hang their frustrations on, boss. They've been overwhelmed with the deaths and injuries, the destruction, the stories of heroism, the lucky escapes—"

"You mean they still need someone to blame?"

"I don't think it's that simple, boss. There's the genuine outrage that the mayor, Jack Stone, instructed the super AI to preserve historical monuments over hospitals—"

"But he's gone," she broke in.

Crispin paused and then answered: "But he's not been tried and he's not going to be convicted."

"That's hardly the government's fault. The courts are swamped with serious crimes, thousands of them. And they'll never be heard now."

"The problem is MacSawley at *The Mail*. If he'd let it go, it wouldn't take long to drop off most people's radar."

"And why doesn't he?" Napier asked pointedly.

Crispin swore under his breath while he looked at the floor. Knowing this rookie-mistake reaction constituted an admission of guilt that he should've handled *The Mail*, he decided to be honest, against his better judgement. He shrugged and replied: "I promised him something and didn't deliver."

Napier nodded in comprehension and asked: "And you didn't tell me because?"

"Because it happens a lot, boss. I've been leaning on all of them to be more bloody patriotic. They should be supporting us, keeping morale up. Instead, MacSawley acts as though it's just another story, and the usual games go on."

Napier shook her head. "So, let's give him an interview, then. Exclusive, yes?"

"But you hate him, boss."

"My God," Napier nearly choked, "he is a vapid, sanctimonious, vicious, thick-skulled troglodyte who thinks he is the centre of the universe because of the poison he pours out of that vile media outlet."

"Then I won't let you waste your time on him. There's not much left."

"So how do we make him stop?"

"There's one way I think I can do it and guarantee you won't have to see him."

"Yes?"

"Leak the Oveisi memo. Give him that as an exclusive."

"That could leave us open to accusations of murder. We allowed the scan to go ahead knowing it would kill the warrior."

"We discussed this at the time, boss. No one cares about a Caliphate warrior dying when so many—"

"Yes, it would be massively hypocritical of MacSawley to try that tack."

"Right."

"Okay, do it," Napier said with a nod.

Crispin twitched his eye muscles and offered to Napier: "Want to see him on the big screen?"

"Good God, no. Thank you," she replied.

"Okay. Apologies in advance for my language."

The pugnacious face of the editor of *The Mail* appeared in Crispin's vision and said at once: "Well, hi there, Cris. To what do I owe this nice surprise?"

Crispin gritted his teeth to bite down the anger of his name being shortened in a fashion he loathed, and then said: "I'd like to say how nice it is to see you, *Mister* MacSawley, but if I did, I'd be lying."

"Hardy-fucking-ha. What do you want?"

"I've got an exclusive for you."

The editor's eyes widened. "Oh yeah, what?"

"But it's got strings."

"Don't fuck me around, Cris. I've got my people digging for more shit on your government—"

"Andy, we're all going to be dead in a few weeks, max. Why the fuck are you behaving like these are normal times?"

"Because that's my job, that's why. And as far as 'all of us will be dead in a few weeks' goes, you speak for yourself, chum. Or should I say 'chump' if you're too stupid to hop over the pond when the need arises?"

Crispin held his anger, although it didn't surprise him that MacSawley would have already sorted out his escape route. He opened his gambit: "You know the French institute, the one that can scan a brain and extract all of a person's memories?"

"Yeah, so?"

"They did it on a Caliphate warrior NATO captured."

"And it shows what exactly?"

"All kinds of interesting shit about life in the Caliphate. A place we've known the square root of fuck all about for twenty years."

MacSawley nodded in consideration. "Okay. What do you want for it?"

"Drop all your fucking Jack Stone shit, okay? It's enough; he's resigned, those people are dead and lots more Londoners besides. Leave it."

"Hmm, nah, I think I'll pass."

"I'm pretty sure a competitor will pick it up. Maybe your old mucker Jezzer at—"

"Okay," MacSawley broke in, "when can I have it?"

"Give me an hour. And give the by-line to one of your third-rate hacks."

"And all I've got to do is lay off the Jack Stone shit?"

"Yeah, and if you don't, I'll come over there and fuck you like a pig."

"Ha, you wish. I'm waiting." MacSawley ended the connection and Crispin exhaled.

"So," Napier said, "that is sorted out, is it?"

"Yes, boss."

"Good. And what else have I got lined up for today?"

Crispin called up the relevant data in his lens: "Daily COBRA is now. Police commissioner for England wants ten minutes alone with you because he needs authorisation to requisition construction replicators to dig mass graves. Then you have a call with NHS England to update you on triage numbers and the lack of GenoFluid packs in the event of another aerial attack. After that you have a meeting with bosses from several tech companies looking for—"

Napier put out a hand to stop him and asked: "How many people in England have died since the invasion resumed?"

"Parameters?"

Napier's head tilted to one side and she specified: "Enemy action and suicide."

Crispin located and collated the relevant figures in his lens. He answered: "Forty-seven thousand, five hundred and one."

"And yet still we waste time with trivialities like the press."

Crispin didn't answer, deciding instead to drain the coffee in his cup.

Napier turned and headed for the door. "Sometimes I think our culture learned nothing. Nothing at all," she said.

Chapter 30

18.23 Sunday 25 June

Duncan Seekings took a sip of his light and bitter and sighed. He glanced at Graham and tutted at the smug satisfaction beaming from his friend's round face.

On the snooker table in front of him, the white cue ball had come to rest behind the yellow ball, tight to the baulk cushion. This obscured the last remaining red ball, some twelve feet away at the other end of the table, which Duncan had to hit with the cue ball if he wanted to avoid committing a foul and giving Graham penalty points. The frame was finely poised and either player could win it.

Graham sipped his pint of Guinness, the white foam on top of the black liquid leaving a slight moustache on his upper lip. He said: "So how are we handling the miss rule, then?"

Duncan's eyebrows rose and he replied: "As it should be, old boy. As long as I make a reasonably decent attempt, you can't have the cue ball replaced. Agreed?"

"But we have no referee to determine what constitutes a decent attempt."

Duncan gave his friend a tight smile, lined up his cue to attempt the shot, and said: "I'm sure we'll be able to compromise." He played the shot. The white ball hit two cushions and missed the red by more than a foot.

"Foul, and a miss," Graham said with a little too much relish. "Four points to me." He got up and moved the indicator along the metal slide to increase his score appropriately.

"Shall I have another go?" Duncan said.

"If you wouldn't mind, professor."

Duncan replaced the white ball to the best of his memory and muttered: "If I hit the side cushion a little further up."

Graham said: "I hear Reyer and his team are making remarkably good progress on their power unit."

Duncan leaned down at the table to play the shot and replied: "Given the resources they have at their disposal, I should think so." He played the shot. The cue ball again hit the side cushion but this time collided with the black ball.

"Oh dear," Graham said with obvious amusement. "You've given me seven points. Foul, and a miss."

Without seeking confirmation, Duncan collected the white ball, replaced the black ball on its spot, and put the white ball back behind the yellow.

Graham added the points to his score and said: "It is not quite as straightforward as it may seem."

"Oh?" Duncan said. He played the same shot and the white ball again rolled into the black.

"Well played," Graham said with a chuckle. "I really put you in quite a pickle, didn't I?"

"Yes, bravo."

"Anyway: foul, seven points to me."

"Not a miss?" Duncan asked, pausing to sip his drink.

"Nope, because that's put me thirty-seven points in front with only thirty-five on the table. You need a snooker, professor."

Duncan slumped in his chair, finding it difficult to care about the game. He looked at Graham and asked: "Is there even any point to Reyer's work? They can design whatever power unit they want, but it'll still take months to get better weapons into mass production. And that is time we simply do not have."

"My dear professor," Graham said lining up his shot on the red, "plans are in motion to allow us the time." He played the shot and the red rattled in the jaws of the corner pocket. "Damn."

Duncan got up and said: "Damn indeed. I've got to keep the red out... Yes, I have heard some balderdash about maintaining some kind of resistance. Of all the depressing, asinine rubbish I've had to put up with lately, the suggestion of trying to keep the battle going once we've lost the war really is the worst."

"You don't think it's feasible, professor?"

Duncan glanced back at his oldest friend and asked: "And you do?"

Graham lifted his Guinness and said with a mischievous smile: "Oh, come now. Doesn't the idea of continuing the resistance in tunnels and underground caverns appeal once we are under the yoke of our glorious Third Caliph? Not even a little?"

Duncan smiled when he realised that Graham was joking. Duncan lined up his shot on the red, which he intended to miss and lay a snooker, but potted it instead.

Graham said: "Don't worry, you can still get a snooker on one of the colours, but you must pot the black to stand a chance."

Duncan sighed and replied: "Really? And if I should get run over by an autonomous transporter, you'll be sure to point it out to me, won't you?"

Graham guffawed and replied "Right-ho, professor."

Duncan lined up on the black ball, played the shot and missed. "Balls," he said. "Frame conceded."

"Come and sit down and have your drink."

Duncan leaned his cue against the wall and sat with another heavy sigh.

"Of course such plans are being made, however futile—"

"—not to mention facile—"

"—they may be. But no option is beyond consideration."

"You've got to admit, old boy, it does all look pretty bleak," Duncan said before taking a longer pull on his drink and wondering how many frames of snooker he and his friend had left.

"And you should see some of the options," Graham said.

"I imagine the computers have offered a few."

"Not only them. Every Tom, Dick and Harry has been coming up with all kinds of weird and not-so-wonderful wonderful inventions to save their beloved England. The people in the experimental research department have been considering things day and night—"

"Yes, I do know."

"And what, professor, do you think is the kernel of the problem?"

Duncan frowned and said: "The utter futility of trying to avert that which is absolutely immutable."

Graham nodded and said: "Nicely put, but hardly very positive."

"Really, how can you expect anyone to be positive?"

Graham's tone lowered: "The key problem is the limits on replication."

Duncan looked at his friend and a distant memory resurfaced, from twenty years earlier, the only time a disagreement between them had flared into clear hostility. Again, after so many years Duncan recognised the strain in Graham's voice. What had he just said? Something about replication?

"Do go on," Duncan murmured.

"To start with the enemy: the Blackswan, the Spider and the hideous Lapwing are all protected by shielding, a commonality shared by both combatants."

"Yes, that's all right."

"The accepted wisdom is that kinetic energy is needed to wear down the field produced by the cryo-magnets. This is done with the use of lasers, missiles or other explosives. However, the Caliphate's machines have shielding that is so strong we need a disproportionate volume of kinetic energy to disable it, and then leave their machines defenceless and actually destroyable. Still with me?"

"Don't push your luck, old boy."

Graham smiled and sipped his Guinness. He let out a satisfied sigh and continued: "But the first and most important problem is replication. As we know, certain elements, including a range of heavy metals and naturally occurring chemicals, still defy replication, and this affects our ability to manufacture arms. Because our PeaceMakers and battlefield support lasers and the pulsar cannons on them still need to be built, they take too much time to produce and get to the battlefield."

Duncan nodded, "You said that was the first problem."

"Correct. The next is that even if we could replicate everything we need, we are still facing an overwhelming number of enemy machines. The forecasts vary, but it looks like the enemy could have literally millions of Blackswans and Lapwings sufficient almost to target every single person in Europe."

"You're just trying to cheer me up now, aren't you?"

"Not quite. We do have an answer: we know that the enemy's power unit is a flawed design, but we need time to exploit that. So, how do we make that time?"

Duncan's eyebrows rose: "Ask the Third Caliph if he would be kind enough to pause his forces for a further nine to twelve months?"

"Very droll. No, we need a way to destroy the enemy—or at least enough of their blasted machines—that can be mass produced by replication. What that means is something that doesn't need to be actually manufactured, but which will still be reliable and easy to use, including by civilian defenders."

Duncan battled to keep his credulity in check. He said: "Would it upset you greatly if I made a joke about compacting sufficient volumes of dandelion seeds and firing them from a wooden catapult?"

"Yes, it would. So don't, thank you."

"Very well."

"Let me show you something that, for reasons best known to itself, our super AI rated as 'Not worth further investigation'."

Duncan perked up as Graham clipped open the case on the chair next to him and withdrew a rigid sheet of A4. Duncan took it without speaking and peered at the images in the ultrathin 3-D screen.

"Now, the only sure way we can defeat a Spider is to turn its own munitions against it."

"It certainly looks simple enough," Duncan said. He stared at the main image of a metal tube with a single projectile inside it.

"Exactly," Graham enthused. "It's a single-shot weapon that is discarded after use, like a Stiletto. It can be used individually or multiples of them can be arranged into defensive batteries."

"And what projectile does the tube fire?"

Graham hesitated.

Duncan said: "Well?"

"A net," Graham replied.

"A what?"

"A net."

"What kind of net? A fishing net? A hairnet?"

"Maybe tap on the screen and see," Graham suggested.

Duncan did so. He peered at the resulting image and said: "I think I need a moment. This is either the cleverest thing anyone has conceived or the stupidest, and I need time to decide which."

"It is also top secret, professor."

"Indeed." Duncan stared at the image. With a flick of his finger he enlarged it and rotated it and looked at it from every angle. He muttered: "Hmm, so how... Ah, then... Right, that's makes some kind of sense, I suppose."

"Well? What's your verdict?" Graham asked.

"This is clever. The nano-bots in the netting tuning into the shielding's frequency then the atom-level shift to use the Spider's own munitions against it. I wonder where the snags are. There must be some snags."

"There are no snags that refinement will not rectify," Graham intoned with a trace of imperiousness. "The netting negates the shielding then forces the Spider to detonate whether it wants to or not. It is a work of genius."

"And the super AI should be able to handle the aiming, firing and other timing issues."

"But the most important thing is replication: devices up to five years old will be able to produce these things in any required number."

Duncan finally looked at Graham and said: "Yes, but does it work?"

"It needs development, refinement—"

"England only has a couple of weeks left, old boy."

Graham shrugged and drained the last of his Guinness. He put the glass on the small wooden table, stood and gestured at the snooker table, and said: "One more frame?"

"Go on then," Duncan replied, also getting up. "If that's the best last hope, what were the others like?"

Graham grimaced as he stuck his pudgy hands into the table's pockets to retrieve the balls. "Too many of them relied on components that cannot be replicated, so they were not viable as a stopgap."

Duncan also retrieved balls from pockets, leaving reds at the bottom end of the table while putting the colours back on their spots. "If we can make it work—"

"It will work."

"What's it called?" Duncan asked as he set the fifteen red balls in a wooden triangle. He collected his cue.

Graham finished putting the yellow, green and brown on their spots and said: "The Falarete."

"Interesting name. Sounds a bit Greek."

"Well spotted. Actually a mix of ancient Greek and Latin. The 'fala' part means 'shining' in ancient Greek; the 'rete' bit is Latin for 'net'."

Duncan said: "A shining net indeed," while Graham collected his cue.

"Your turn to break off, professor," Graham said.

Duncan paused. He stared at his friend and said: "Assuming you can find and eliminate the snags—which I don't think for a minute will be as easy as you seem to believe

230

given your enthusiasm for the thing—how much difference do you think it could make?"

"Oh, the computers forec—"

"No, not the computers. You, old boy. What difference do *you* think it could make?"

Graham shrugged again and replied: "You said it, professor; it is our best last hope."

Duncan placed the white cue ball between the yellow and green, and leaned down to play the break-off shot. He said: "I was being ironic."

Chapter 31

Sergeant Rory Moore drank the last of his tea and dropped the paper cup on the floor. In the view in his lens, his Squitch relayed the day's planned path of retreat. Opposite him, Sergeant Heaton did the same, staring into the middle distance.

Heaton said: "I worry about the length of the valley."

"Why?" Rory asked.

"Because if the raghead wants to, he will flatten the town at the entrance and then charge us down. And we'll be stuck in a funnel."

Rory shook his head and replied: "We've got more BSLs backing us up now. Units to the northeast and southwest. And tanks at the other end of the valley. The forecast is that it's going to take the enemy at least six hours to advance to the village anyway."

"Aye, six hours for the bastard ragheads, but not for their ACAs. And the colonel will pull those BSLs back before they get fried."

"Yeah, they've been bringing more of those shite Lapwings on this section."

"Nasty buggers."

"But even then, if it got that bad, we'd just call in transports to evac us out."

"And what happened the last time we 'just' got transported out?"

Rory touched the side of his head where he could still feel the tiniest indentation in the bone of his skull. "Oh, yeah. But that was just a bit of bad-luck shrapnel."

Sergeant Heaton said: "You took a lump of metal in the head that would've been your lot in any other war in history."

"Luck of the action. Shall we get a toddle-on or what?"

The compact Yorkshireman tutted and said, "Aye, if you're going to start coming out with more of your Nancy southern words, then we should get on."

The two sergeants left the windowless utility room, exiting into a long corridor inside the abandoned sports facility.

"You know why the raghead's bringing up the Lapwings?" Heaton asked.

"Because they're all vicious, mad twats?" Rory offered.

"Apart from that."

"No, why?"

"Because those can better help them clear the Footies."

"Easier than blowing everything up with Spiders, I s'pose."

"Aye."

They arrived at the main sports hall and pushed through the double doors. The forty men and women who comprised their squads were all at various stages of preparing to move.

Heaton spoke in a loud, commanding voice that Rory liked hearing: "Right, you lot. Has everyone been briefed by their Squitch?"

Nods of heads and murmurs of confirmation greeted the question.

"So you all know what's what. Assemble at the start line in five. And don't leave anything behind."

Rory looked around at his own troops and accepted a couple of nods of acknowledgement from his corporals. In Rory's lens, his Squitch provided summary reports from each of his four corporals concerning the apportionment of arms and equipment among each four-troop team in the platoon.

"Good," Heaton said. "The Footies are all accounted for."

"Yup," Rory agreed. "Let's get the boys and girls out in the field and get these things down. I don't want to waste any time."

"Aye," Heaton said, before looking up at Rory and asking. "Do you want to go first this time?"

"Yeah," Rory smiled, "why not?" He walked back to his troops and swapped observations and banter with the four corporals under his command. Rory checked each team over, a hankering for past times asserting itself. He hadn't realised how straightforward being a corporal had been. Now, he found it tricky to let his corporals get on with their own jobs. Rory kept a keen eye on each soldier's visible attitude. He knew some of them were nervous, perhaps one or two even scared, but in front of him they made sure not to show it and kept the banter up. Good.

The troops left the sports hall and began the day's pull back, the detestable 'fighting retreat' which Rory felt was the same as running away only given a veneer of military professionalism. The town through which they stomped seemed to be deserted, but Rory knew from experience that non-combatants remained to take their chances with the new regime. From time to time, civilians would confront the soldiers with despair, frustration or even anger, but it made no difference. If a fifty-something man couldn't evacuate because his ninety-year-old mother refused to leave the house she'd lived in her whole life, it was not Rory's problem. Sometimes they passed disturbing sights, especially if the town or area had previously seen ACA action. Their Squitches recorded everything anyway, not that anyone would be left to analyse who had been dead or alive at this stage of the war.

At predesignated road junctions, most of the squads separated to cover more ground. In each squad, two troops tossed out FT–23/D 'Footie' anti-personnel smart-mines from loaded tubes strapped to the backs of their webbing. One other soldier carried the team's Stiletto single-shot missile-launchers while the fourth carried grenades and most of the ammo for the team's Pickups.

Rory twitched his eye and spoke: "Oscar zero-three, what's the delay?"

"Nothing, sarge," came the breezy reply. "Lily's found a starving moggy, or I should say the cat found Lily."

"Roger. Don't make it suffer before you put it out of its misery," Rory answered with a grin.

Walking next to him, Heaton chuckled and said: "That'll get Lily on your side."

They retreated along roads and avenues, past parks and streams, and the heat of the morning grew. The banter died away and Rory sensed the mood darken. Sweat ran and irritated skin that struggled for air under uniform, webbing and arms. The typical small German town displayed the signs of its abandonment: moss and weeds pushed up through every crevice in tarmac and paving slab; the shutters on the closed shops were covered in a fine dust; and despite Rory's earlier joke, there lay the occasional dead pet among the gardens and hedgerows. Rory tried to peer into the windows of the houses they passed and once or twice he thought he made out curious eyes staring back, but if the local authorities hadn't been able to get these civilians out in the preceding days and weeks, his troops would certainly not.

"Caution," his Squitch announced without warning. "Enemy ACAs approaching from the southeast."

"All teams, form back up," Rory ordered.

Heaton dropped back to Rory and said: "The end of the town is half a klick around that bend. Then the sides of the valley steepen and we're in the funnel."

Rory shrugged and said: "I think it's not such an issue. Look at what we've got on our side."

"Aye, but I've been thinking about Brass's general order to retrieve wounded enemy—"

"So?" Rory asked, confused.

"What if the ragheads also want to catch some of us alive, eh? We'd be right in the frame and no mistake."

Rory shook his head and answered: "No. No way, fella. They already know everything about us, don't they?"

"Aye, but on this section of the front, we're the units furthest from any hardware."

Rory conceded Heaton's point about location but dismissed his main concern. Before he could say anything, however, the corps commander addressed them over the comms system: "Two platoon, two company. Continue on your designated route. Form your platoon up and keep a sharp eye out. We've got a few friendlies that should take care of things above your heads for long enough; if not, you'll be transported out."

Rory swapped an ironic glance with Heaton.

The commander went on: "The enemy's main strategic target on this section of the front has to be the manufacturing facilities five klicks northeast, so you should be all right. Out."

Rory heard Heaton mutter: "For fuck's sake," and smiled.

His Squitch then said: "Enemy ACA contacts approaching from the southeast."

"Teams," Heaton called out, "dump any remaining Footies and let's get out of town."

On the four-lane highway that led into the valley, Rory watched the squads return. As they formed up, they swapped bits of kit. The soldiers responsible for deploying the Footie smart-mines discarded the empty containers and collected magazines for their Pickups.

"Come on," Rory urged one team.

A black-haired gangly man who was activating his Pickup asked: "Hey, sarge, why is it we have to drop the Footies? Why can't we have an ACA that flies about and drops them instead of us?"

Rory raised his eyebrows and suggested with thick irony: "Oh, I dunno, Jake. Maybe because our ACAs are just a little bit busy with some other jobs?"

"Oh, yeah, right. Thanks, sarge," came the deflated reply.

Rory chivvied the rest of his teams and noticed Heaton do the same. He ran across to the Yorkshireman and said: "Standard pacing, okay?"

"Okay," Heaton agreed.

"Don't worry," Rory said in reaction to Heaton's frown of concern. "At least we've got the Yank Abrahams tanks at the far end of the valley, not those bloody Challengers."

Heaton nodded ahead and said: "That valley is not going to be a picnic."

Rory shrugged and asked: "You want to stay here and take cover in the buildings?"

Heaton threw a friendly sneer in return.

Rory smiled and called out: "Okay, everyone, standard pacing, look sharp and listen to your Squitches."

The two columns of NATO troops fell into step, each soldier with their Pickup ready. A glimmer of pride ran through Rory at his troops and their professionalism when out in the field—

"Danger: Caliphate Lapwings approaching from the southwest. Take defensive measures immediately."

Forty male and female soldiers moved at the same time, bringing weapons to bear while dispersing to put more space between each other on the road.

"Bloody hell, it's not even nine o'clock yet," Heaton said in a misguided attempt at levity.

Sweat chilled the back of Rory's neck: he suddenly recalled how much he hated the overwhelming sense of nakedness when the enemy attacked. He scanned the bright blue morning sky above the buildings for the tell-tale black dots.

His Squitch advised: "Return into the town."

Keeping low, he began moving back the way they had just come. He turned around and glanced at the troops dispersing in all directions to put further distance between each other. Rory counted at least half a dozen troops shoulder their Stilettoes. The super artificial intelligence guided each soldier to play a role that would give all of them the greatest chance of defending the whole platoon successfully.

Double-storey town houses dotted the sides of the road, most still in good shape. In the middle of the road sat a broken autonomous private vehicle capable of holding a large family or group of people. Rory heard the bright song of a blackbird close by.

"Danger: Lapwings closing on your position, PeaceMakers on interception courses. There is a possible risk of injury from falling debris."

With a twitch of an eye muscle, Rory opened a private channel with Heaton thirty metres behind him and said: "Here we go again."

Heaton murmured his reply: "I'm beginning to think you had the right idea about taking cover in the town."

"We need to get everyone back there to be on the safe side."

Streaks of light appeared in the sky, coming towards the ground at high speed.

"Yeah, it was an action like this that got you sent back to Blighty for repairs."

"Thanks for the reminder, sergeant."

The PeaceMakers disappeared behind the line of the buildings due to the slight incline on the road.

Rory's Squitch said: "Friendly forces have engaged the enemy."

From the southwest came hissing sounds as a flight of missiles streaked into view, following the PeaceMakers.

With a twitch of his eye, Rory opened comms to both squads and ordered: "Move up to cover among the buildings and stay sharp for falling debris." Then he added, based on his own recent experience: "And be aware that 'falling' does not mean that it comes down in a nice, straight line at ninety degrees. Keep your eyes open and your heads down."

There followed a moment's pause before a series of deep crumples vibrated through the ground and into Rory's boots.

His Squitch announced: "The flight of enemy ACAs in your vicinity has been destroyed. However, you should exercise caution while continuing to withdraw."

Rory's lens lit up with Heaton's communication. The Yorkshireman said: "Just like that?"

Rory recalled the first time he'd met the enemy, in Spain, and the carnage their weapons had caused and the friends he'd lost. Four long, hard months later, it seemed NATO had finally caught up. "Looks like it," he answered.

"Okay, do you want to or shall I?"

Rory smiled in relief and said: "You can."

Heaton said: "Okay, everyone. Looks like we got the upper hand this time. Let's back it up nice and slowly and get through the valley. Remember: we've done our job: half a ton of Footies are waiting for the advancing ragheads, and they'll slow the bastards down."

As everyone formed up once again, the corps commander spoke in Rory's ear: "Two platoon, two company. Your section of the front is clear but be advised the enemy is projecting stronger jamming surges down—your loc—best to g—ey. Out."

Rory turned in sudden confusion to look at Heaton, but his Squitch announced: "Caution: enemy jamming is interfering with comms—"

Heaton exclaimed: "What the fuck is going on? Their jamming's never affected our comms like this."

Rory spun around to face the rest of the abandoned town again as his Squitch answered Heaton's question: "Caution: anti-personnel smart-mines are being detonated."

Rory asked in shock: "Detonated? Detonated by whom?"

The Squitch answered: "The highest probability is by enemy warriors."

"No shit," Rory said, aghast.

"Why are they sending their troops in like this? What's the point?" Heaton asked.

Rory held a hand up to quieten Heaton and the NATO soldiers who had already stopped moving. He forced himself to think. Enemy jamming could, might block comms with the corps commander, but at least their Squitches should still communicate with each other due to the troops' proximity. He recalled the last time he'd been this close to enemy warriors, at the tunnel entrance, and their kit had worked fine throughout the contact.

Time passed and the distant crumps of Footies exploding grew closer. Ominous palls of smoke rose above the buildings.

Rory glanced back at Heaton and waited. The explosions stopped.

Heaton whispered: "You think they were dumb enough to walk right into the Footies?"

"Dunno. You've heard the rumours, their grunt-ranks are supposed to be as thick as shit."

"But what about their officers?"

"I reckon the super AI is their number-one 'officer'."

"Yeah, but either the officers or AI should've told them to stop walking into those mines and blowing themselves up."

Rory said: "Maybe there's something in this particular town they're after?"

Heaton looked incredulous. He said with irony: "Aye, I suppose that fountain with the stone dolphins we passed half a klick back would look rather fetching in the Caliph's front garden."

"What do we do? We've got jamming coming down and a load of Footies have gone off."

"But how can the jamming affect our kit? It shouldn't be able to."

Rory shook his head and said: "Must be because we're right underneath it. With these weather conditions—"

"Then we can do what we bloody well please."

"Don't think so. Before we lost comms, I think he ordered us to continue pulling back." Rory signalled up at the sky, "And from those contrails it looks like shit is still going down further along the line."

"You think maybe we should go back into the town and check on the ragheads who set those mines off?"

Rory shrugged and said: "What for? Remember the last time we came up against these fuckers, at the tunnel entrance?"

"Aye," Heaton said. "Personal shielding."

"Exactly. They could be triggering those Footies to get us to backtrack and I don't think we should fall for the trap."

"But it's fair to assume enemy troops set the Footies off," Heaton said. "And if they're the same as those we had contact with in Hungary, then it is also fair to assume the Footies that have gone off did not kill them. I don't think we should withdraw over open ground."

Rory glanced around again at the well-kept houses surrounded by hedges and the single abandoned vehicle in middle of the road. He said: "Wouldn't hurt to rest up during the worst of the heat and see if any of the ragheads have got the balls to come on. Our time-on-objective is eighteen-hundred and we could run that distance in a couple of hours if we had to."

"Good call." Heaton turned and moved back among the troops.

Rory lifted his Pickup and made sure it was activated even though he already knew. His Squitch announced: "Danger: Caliphate warriors approaching from the southeast. Stand by to open fire."

Rory sensed the whole platoon react. Team members traded shouts of advice and encouragement; soldiers ran, leapt over hedgerows and took cover behind walls, as their Squitches were instructing them what to do. Rory's own Squitch overlaid digital indicators in his sight of the buildings in front of him. He padded to the left and drew closer to, of all things, a bicycle repair shop, probably the only commercial premises on the entire road.

Seconds dragged out to minutes. Rory concentrated equally on keeping his breathing shallow and on the tactical display in his vision. All manner of vignettes from previous engagements cycled through his memory, honing his reactions. Sweat collected in his eyebrows and a drop ran down his nose. It tickled his skin and he wanted to sneeze.

At that moment, his Squitch announced: "Multiple targets closing in on your position. Bring your weapon to bear and stand by."

Rory raised his Pickup and aimed it where he most suspected a Caliphate warrior might emerge. Suddenly, he felt a wave of hot air on his left, as though the bicycle repair shop breathed fire at him.

The next instant, he came to laying in the middle of the road in a rage of pain and shock. All around him, weapons' fire rattled in short bursts. The stench of burnt hair assailed his nose and hard, black tarmac chilled the side of his face.

"His Squitch urged: "Multiple targets directly ahead. Open fire now."

He forced himself up and looked for his Pickup. It lay a short distance away, but something in his eyesight wasn't right. He dragged himself to his weapon.

"You are moderately injured. Aim and fire now," his Squitch urged while from every direction volleys of shots rang out.

He lifted the Pickup, hauled his damaged body into the fire position and then noticed the chaos in his display. He pulled the trigger but his Pickup registered a malfunction. He counted four figures crouching by walls about a hundred metres ahead, but every few seconds there came a green flash off them. They might pause or stagger a little, but Rory doubted they were injured. The firing from close by sounded well controlled, as though the platoon were experienced campaigners instead of green troops.

However, his display told him eight soldiers were already dead with three more injured. He swore and began shuffling backwards on his front, looking for a discarded weapon.

Sergeant Heaton spoke: "How are you doing?"

"Yeah, fine," Rory answered. "You?"

"Pinned down behind the vehicle fifteen metres behind you. The ragheads don't seem to be advancing. I've sent my best two teams to outflank the bastards."

"On my way," Rory answered, noting a smear of blood on the road as he pushed himself backwards. His left leg felt like shit.

A volley of shots rang out, followed by a piercing shriek of agony.

A private suddenly leapt out from cover and sprinted forwards, firing his Pickup. The young man screeched: "Fuck you, toss—" when his head exploded like a blood-red melon inside which a bomb had gone off. The decapitated corpse twisted a little as it flopped to the ground and rolled over.

More shouting and curses came to Rory's ears in between the bursts of weapons' fire. Rory analysed casualties and deployments, shaking his head at the sheer unfairness of the enemy enjoying such advantages.

After several more minutes of crawling backwards, Rory felt himself pulled in behind the vehicle to cover and saw five others, including Heaton. Able to sit up, Rory perceived that his injuries were not severe despite the blood on his leg. His Squitch confirmed this.

A series of hisses followed by rapid explosions erupted from the enemy positions. More gunfire rattled and shook the air.

A young private spat: "That's got them," and leapt up. Rory glanced at Heaton, who nodded and also stood. Rory pulled himself up and looked. Four soldiers approached two bodies slumped against blackened walls. Rory picked up a Stiletto and activated it, waiting for the inevitable: there had been four contacts in his view and only three warriors were accounted for. He scanned the buildings and yelled: "Where's the fourth one?"

"All four are dead, sarge," one of the privates called. "Over here, one's on top of the other."

Satisfied, Rory lowered and deactivated the Stiletto. He limped up the road.

Heaton slowed down and drew level with Rory. He said: "This doesn't make sense—"

"You're fucking right there," Rory broke in.

"Why attack without support? Where are the next wave? Air support? Were these shits trying to prove something?"

"Dunno," Rory said, his limbs becoming heavier with exhaustion. "Maybe you were right? Maybe they wanted to capture us?"

A new voice spoke in Rory's ear: "Two platoon, two company. Are you receiving, over?"

At the same time, Rory's Squitch indicated that the higher-level jamming had gone.

"Er, yes, sir," Rory answered. "We had a contact—"

"Right-ho," the corps commander said. "SkyWatchers show your position and that you have a wounded enemy there, yes?"

"No, they're all de—" he stopped when Heaton indicated that one of them was still alive. Rory limped after

Heaton as the Yorkshireman hurried over to a pair of warriors locked in an embrace blackened by explosions.

"Okay," the commander said, "that makes it critical. Preserve the life of the enemy at all costs. Is that clear?"

"Yes, sir," Rory replied, confusion mounting.

"I've redirected transports to evac your platoon… what's left of it, anyway. Damnable business. Oh, and keep silent about this engagement until debrief, clear?"

"Crystal, sir," Rory said.

"Good show. Out."

Heaton said: "Okay, let's get packs on the wounded. Use your own first if you took damage. Conte and West, move the bodies to the vehicle, we'll evac from there. Form up, people." The platoon members began drifting back down the road, a few of them taking lingering looks at the remains of the enemy.

Rory tapped Heaton on the shoulder and said: "We better look after the injured raghead."

Heaton seemed to understand. He shouted: "Come on, all of you. Form up, now."

Rory limped over to the pair of warriors. He indicated the uppermost one and said: "He must have taken the force of a Stiletto when his shielding had gone."

Heaton grabbed the corpse's remaining leg and yanked it off the body underneath. "How the fuck is that one still alive?"

The warrior underneath also had blast damage and the lower half of his right leg was missing. Rory stared at Heaton. Satisfied that his fellow sergeant did understand, Rory opened a flap over a small pocket on his right thigh. He pulled out a thin, circular device the size of a large coin. Heaton did the same. Rory placed his right thumb in the central depression to confirm his identity, and holding the central part firmly, with his left thumb and forefinger he twisted the outer rim one-

247

hundred-and-eighty degrees, deactivating the Squitch. Heaton copied him.

At once, Rory slipped his fighting knife out from its sheath on his left calf, leaned forward and nicked the warrior's jugular. As he replaced the knife, he looked up at Heaton and murmured: "No prisoners taken."

Rory reactivated his Squitch at the same time as Heaton, and together they turned and made their way back to the abandoned vehicle in the road. Rory knew the break in the Squitches' records could be blamed on a glitch, or residual jamming, or peculiar atmospheric conditions, or some other bullshit if it had to be. But every one of them accepted that this war was lost, and any enemy life that could be taken, had to be.

Heaton said: "Twenty-five percent casualties from an eight-minute engagement with an enemy fireteam that was one-tenth of our strength. Fucking disaster."

Rory's Squitch said: "AATs will arrive in two minutes."

"Any sign of enemy ACAs?"

"Negative."

Rory turned to Heaton and said: "So they sent the advance fireteam into the town with minimal air cover and didn't back them up when they were in the shit."

Heaton nodded his head and said: "Aye, but we don't know the strategic issues yet."

"Well, I want to know now," Rory replied. He twitched his eye muscles and at the prompt said: "Moore, R. sergeant 102 Squadron, Royal Engineers." As he waited for access, he observed dots in the distance as the evac AATs flew in. "Squonk? Tactical summary of this morning's engagement along the line from sectors 113 to 121. In particular, speculate why the enemy fireteam at conurbation 293 was not sufficiently supported."

The British Army's super-artificial intelligence responded: "The probabilities are, in descending order of likelihood, that the tactical need to secure the town and valley lessened with the considerable gains made on other sectors of the front; that insufficient ACAs were in-theatre or were required to secure gains on other sectors of the front; or that this fireteam was abandoned by its commanding officer for reasons unknown."

"Wow," Rory said.

"Well?" Heaton asked.

Rory shrugged and said: "My money's on their CO dropping them in the shit, maybe because they didn't bathe often enough."

"What the actual fuck are you talking about?"

"It's not important." Rory nodded at the row of bodies lying on the ground and said: "They are."

The autonomous air transports landed in a column on the road. Rory strode forward to help the soldiers load their fallen comrades when the corps commander spoke: "Two platoon, two company. I gave express orders that preservation of the surviving enemy warrior's life was of paramount importance, and now it seems he's dead. What happened?"

Rory steeled himself and glanced at Heaton as he said: "Dunno, sir. He bled out before we could get a GenoFluid pack on him. Just bad luck, I s'pose."

Chapter 32

Dahra Napier opened the door to her office in Ten Downing Street. Terry Tidbury entered, the bags under his eyes looking heavier in the low light. Dahra nodded at the security guard who had accompanied the general on his journey from the War Rooms in the bowels of Whitehall, and closed the door.

"Can I get you a drink?" she asked.

"Brandy, please," he said.

"Won't you take a seat?" she said, indicating the cream-coloured couch. She watched as he lowered himself down with grace; a tired man still possessed of a sufficiently soldierly deportment. "I read somewhere, in one of those biographies of you that proliferated when the war began, that you enjoy a cigar with your brandy. Is that right?"

"At home, yes, but a cigar is not necessary to enjoy a good brandy."

"I'm sorry I don't have any in the place," she said, handing him his drink.

"Thank you," he said.

Dahra retrieved her glass of wine and sat in a soft armchair next to Terry. She deactivated the lens in her eye to help keep her attention undivided. She asked: "How chaotic are things in the War Rooms?"

"It's surprising how quickly one can get used to the drama. It's four weeks tomorrow since the enemy resumed his invasion. Sometimes it feels like four years; at others, like four hours."

Dahra scrutinised Terry as he gave a murmur of approval after sipping his drink. "Perhaps strange times can make time behave strangely?" she offered.

Terry gave a gentle shrug. "Perhaps."

There came a pause between them and Dahra sensed discomfort from the general. She needed to be careful not to alienate or antagonise him. She said: "I was wondering if your views on VIP evacuation had changed in the last few weeks."

Terry's eyebrows rose and he replied: "No, and they most assuredly will not."

"But you do have children, yes? Doesn't their future concern you?" Dahra worried that she'd gone too personal too soon, but Terry let out a loud laugh that surprised her.

"Yes," he said. "Yes, their future does concern me, but as they are both serving officers in the British Army, I believe they have their own opinions about using privilege to escape unfairly."

"I didn't realise they were so old," she said, choking back a compliment that Terry looked young which could easily backfire.

"There is a lot we don't know about each other, I expect. Your children are younger, yes?"

She nodded and sipped her wine, that vein of worry resurfacing.

"I think there may be justification for getting the young out to Canada, for example, so we will not be forgotten."

"Perhaps," she replied in a deliberate echo of his previous answer.

"Prime minister," he began, "if you don't mind me asking, why are we having this meeting?"

Dahra pinched the bridge of her nose and said: "Because I need your honesty, Terry. You are one of a very few people I trust completely, and you are not a politician."

Terry looked nonplussed at the declaration. "If I can help, of course—"

"Yes," she interrupted, "you can. How much longer have we got?"

"According to the latest reports, I believe we are looking at a fortnight, maybe three weeks at the maximum."

"And do you have any reason for not believing the latest reports?"

Terry shook his head and replied: "No."

"Aren't there any positives?

"No. To be honest, prime minister, I think the real picture is bleaker than is generally known."

Dahra felt a stab in her solar plexus. She tensed and said: "What do you mean?" before taking a large sip of wine.

"That young enemy warrior called Oveisi. The institute provides regular updates as they scan and refine his twenty-four years of memories."

"I see."

"You are on the distribution list, aren't you?"

"I have too many domestic issues to spend much time on military matters, Terry. It's one of the reasons I wanted to talk to you alone. Tell me the latest, please."

"One question that is being asked more often in the upper ranks is: why is it taking the enemy so long? According to that warrior's memories, we calculate that the enemy should—probably does—have anything from half a million to three million ACAs stockpiled, held in reserve."

"My God."

"And probably the same number of warriors, which is less relevant strategically because his ACAs do virtually all of the damage before his warriors get to the battlefield."

A wave of horror swept over her. She shook her head and asked, more of the room than Terry: "How did this happen? How could we let this happen?"

"It was hardly our choice," Terry answered.

"So that is a very good question: why are we still here?"

"I do have a theory, but I prefer to keep it to myself."

Dahra noticed the caution in Terry's voice. "We're alone," she said in the softest audible voice she could manage.

Terry paused and then explained: "We are the guinea pigs."

"What?" she asked, confused. "For what? Or whom? Or—"

Terry put out a placating hand. He said: "Militarily, Europe is, more or less, a training exercise for the enemy."

Dahra stared at Terry, appalled.

Terry continued: "When I analyse the new information, I believe that once he's finished with Europe, he'll turn his attention to India, or possibly Africa before India, I'm not sure."

"I hadn't thought of anything like that," Dahra gasped.

Terry sniffed the brandy and chuckled. He said: "But the damnedest thing I cannot work out is why he's taken so long. We thought the Tense Spring was all about—"

"I know why," Dahra murmured.

"Really?"

She nodded her head and said: "It's political. He doesn't need to rush, after all. He has been trying to show the world his benevolence. He's been doing all he can to convince the most important powers that he waited as long as possible to minimise the bloodshed, and NATO and the European governments have brought all this on their own heads by refusing to surrender."

"I'm no politician, but I can't accept anyone believes that line of—"

"Politics is a very nebulous business, Terry. Most people can't accept objective facts if they disagree with their own existing prejudices, so it's about moulding the facts to fit in with those prejudices, sort of like forcing a square peg into a round hole sufficiently so that most people will say: 'Oh, it fits'."

Terry smiled and said: "The fact that he began the aggression has no—"

"Don't judge him by our democratic standards or sense of justice, Terry," Dahra advised. "The Third Caliph's desire to right some kind of perceived historical wrong chimed well with autocratic rulers from Russia to Brazil, from Africa to China. How much of the world suffered under European dominion over the centuries? Politically, he did more than enough to get enough of the rest of the world on his side."

Terry shook his head. "It's probably for the best that you are the politician and I am the soldier."

Dahra smiled. And then she felt an overwhelming sadness. She glanced around the room, at the expensive, government-owned pictures on the walls, the rich materials in the curtains, the delicate fabrics of the furniture, and she perceived their time to be running out as though they were rotting pieces of fruit, with bruises and mould and little flies flitting around them. Their decay came rushing onwards far sooner than it should have.

"You know," she said, "a part of me was hoping that, somehow, there would be a miracle. I thought there might be a change or a chance. It is horrible to be the last prime minister of England."

"I do not hold out any hope, to be honest," Terry said. "My regret is that we are to be beaten by a quite merciless enemy... Prime minister, if there's nothing else, I would quite—"

"What? Oh, yes, of course."

Dahra stood at the same time as Terry.

She looked at him, not caring if he felt uncomfortable or embarrassed by the moistness in her eyes. "Thank you for talking," she said.

"Sorry I could not give you any better news."

She walked him to the door. "I don't know. The final confirmation that there is no hope feels somehow liberating. At least we shan't be around for history to judge us."

Terry appeared to consider her observation. He nodded and said: "I regard that as most improbable, although it won't stop the British Army doing its best in any case." He opened the door.

"Goodnight, Terry."

"Goodnight, prime minister."

The security guard stuck a hand out and Terry followed him. Dahra let the door close slowly under its own momentum. It clicked shut and her eyes roamed the void, her mind unable to dislodge images of fetid decay.

Chapter 33

22.57 Friday 30 June 2062

Trevor Jones loved Friday evenings. Every Friday evening at 11.00 pm for the last year, the secret group of which he was a member, called Cassandra30, met in the basement of his apartment block. Cassandra30 was led by Knight Lancelot, a chiselled mountain of a man who intimidated Trevor. But on this Friday evening even more excitement than usual ran through Trevor. Last week, Lancelot had promised them that tonight he would finally reveal their plans to join with all of the other underground groups in London and expose this sham war for what it really was: a plot by the super-rich to cull the innocent poor.

Trevor checked his appearance in the mirrored side of the lift as it approached the basement level. He licked the palm of his hand and pushed his hair back. He scratched the black stubble that made his jowls look larger than they actually were. He would have shaved but the stubble made him look tough.

The lift shuddered to a stop and the doors rattled open. He turned left and stomped in his Doc Martens past the pipework and ducts, anticipation growing. He arrived at a grey door. A hatch slid open and a voice said: "Passcode?"

Trevor followed Cassandra30's standard entry code and reversed the digits of that day's date. He said: "Two, six, zero, two, zero, six, three, zero."

The hatch snapped shut and the door opened. "Welcome, Squire Trent," said a voice.

Trevor's heartrate increased. Although he had been a 'squire'—the entry level for Cassandra30—for a year now, he knew he would be promoted soon, hopefully tonight. He descended ill-lit metal stairs, taking care not to slip. The excess flesh on his heavy legs wobbled and the base of his spine hurt, even though he did his best to keep in shape.

The foot of the stairs opened out into a dimly lit area with a raised lip of metal at one end. In front of this sat a row of chairs. In the dimness Trevor recognised the profiles of Squire Michelangelo, whose real name was Mike, and Squire Raphael, whose real name was Rodney. Both of them lived in the same apartment block as Trevor. They knew each other by sight but had vowed to Lancelot never to discuss Cassandra30 outside their weekly meetings.

Trevor sat with care on the small, metal chair, lest it buckle under his weight. The air in the basement chilled his exposed face, neck and hands. From the darkness at the edges came the gurgling and rumbling of water being pumped through pipes. It made him recall again how many times the local council had promised water replicators but had failed to deliver them, just one of the many things Lancelot had predicted. Beyond the pipework he could make out the narrow horizontal windows at the tops of the walls. These were not a security risk, for they opened onto an external concrete path that was itself still two metres below ground level.

Trevor's pulse quickened further when he heard the familiar light tap-tap of Lancelot coming down the stairs.

Behind hm followed Squire Alfred, better known as Ali, who had been guarding the door.

Lancelot's bodybuilder form strode up onto the lip of metal that acted as a stage. He held his arms out wide and declared: "Welcome, Squires," in that confident, gorgeous baritone Trevor adored.

Trevor sensed Ali's excitement equalling his own as Ali plumped down on the chair next to Trevor. Trevor joined the other three in intoning the customary greeting: "Welcome, oh Knight Lancelot, wise ruler of our humble band, speaker of truth, slayer of lies, guiding knowledge in this world of falsehood."

Lancelot put his fists on his hips and smiled at his band. Trevor wished he could be more like Lancelot, with such a trim beard and the embroidered, three-quarter length jacket. Trevor looked down at his Doc Martens, which denoted his lowly position. He hoped one day he would save enough from his Universal Basic Income to be able to afford something better, like the nice half-length jacket Squire Raphael had.

"My trusty Squires," Lancelot began, "there is little time before we must go and join our brothers in the other bands and, at long last, move on to confront—finally!—those who have blinkered us and our ancestors for far too long."

Trevor could hardly contain his excitement. At last, tonight they would begin to right the appalling wrongs.

"This 'war' is the greatest psychological operation of this century, and probably any other century. For so many decades the deep state has lied to all of the decent, ordinary, hard-working people of the world. And what lies they have been!" Lancelot cried.

Trevor felt familiar emotions rise inside him: indignation, anger, and a burning hatred for those who profited from all of the lies.

Lancelot continued: "This 'war' against an imaginary 'Caliphate'—which does not even exist, by the way—is being used to kill—no, *murder*—millions of innocent people in England, in Europe, and indeed in the world. It is only the latest of the many and vast injustices that those who pretend to rule us would us believe, oh yes."

Trevor recognised Lancelot's speech. It was the same one he gave most Friday nights, but now it meant more. Tonight, they would actually do something.

Lancelot said: "Remember the history they taught you in school? The meteor strike in Henan Province in China in 2053? A million dead and ten times that number injured? Seriously? And the Chinese, with all of their advanced tech did not see the meteor coming? Of course they didn't—because it wasn't a meteor, it was the Chinese government culling its own people. The poor, the downtrodden, the great ignored!

"And the floods all over Asia in the 2030s? Melting icecaps? How could those apocryphal icecaps melt when they were never even there to begin with? Lies! Lies upon lies! Go back further: the 'accidental' microwave burst in 2028 that brought down over ten thousand planes—just took them out of the sky and made them crash. An 'accident' by the US Air Force, they said. Never meant to happen, they said. But half a million unneeded and surplus people were wiped out in an afternoon; fewer mouths to feed, and more than a handful of the deep state's enemies conveniently 'dispatched' in an 'accident'. Easy if you know the right people, yes?"

"Yes, Knight Lancelot," Trevor intoned with the others.

Lancelot went on: "We can go back even earlier, to the real history they never taught you. The pandemic in 2020 didn't come from seafood but an experimental Chinese attempt at bio warfare that went wrong. But, hey, that's another half a million fewer people who might have helped limit or stop the deep state. In 2001, planes were crashed in the US which those perfidious Yanks used as an excuse to kill—no *murder*—half a million filthy Muslims. Further, in 1986, a nuclear reactor in Russian Ukraine, the old fission type, horribly unproductive but built in great numbers anyway, accidently-on-purpose blows up. And of course, back to the most obvious, the first and most egregious and most successful—until today—deep state action in history: the Holocaust of the second world war."

Lancelot paused as he always did at this point in his Friday night speech. He drew in a few heavy breaths and then continued: "The one historical 'event' they want you to believe most of all. And you know why? Because if you believe that the Nazis killed—no, *murdered*—six million Jews... Then you will believe absolutely anything the deep state tells you. Those Jews and everybody since were killed because the deep state needed them killed.

"But tonight? Tonight we can begin to right these wrongs. Tonight, my trusty Squires, we will go forth and take back that which the deep state has kept from us for too long. Us, the honest, the faithful, the—"

Trevor was surprised when Lancelot stopped abruptly. His eye twitched, so Trevor deduced the Knight must be using his lens to find out what had happened. A wave of consternation rippled inside Trevor, because Lancelot had said that none of them should ever wear lenses to their secret meetings due to the risk of discovery.

His sense of disquiet gave Trevor the courage to speak up: "Knight Lancelot, what has happened?"

There came more silence while Lancelot stared into the middle-distance, his right eye twitching. Then: "Trusty Squires, we must leave here now. The time to move on our enemies, the enemies of all honest people, is at hand. Let us go and gather our brothers and sis—"

261

The room shook under a sudden impact and the glass in the small, high windows shattered.

"It be 'dem," Squire Michelangelo said. "Deep state."

Trevor's concern rose. "Shouldn't we leave?" he asked, looking at his hero.

Lancelot dashed to the metal stairs and looked up. "Perhaps we'd better—"

A sudden crash from the wall made Trevor jump. His chest began to hurt. Something was seriously wrong. Weak orange light reflected off a thin line of metal as something entered from above. With surprising speed, more lines of black metal followed as broken glass tinkled on the pipework and down to the floor. On the ceiling above them, Trevor watched in growing fear and fascination as multi-jointed appendages grasped and split metal pipes. The thing positioned itself in the middle of the ceiling and stopped moving.

Mike asked: "What be it?"

Trevor answered: "Looks like what the media have been telling us all along." He looked down from the ceiling and back at Lancelot. He said: "But you told us, you said—"

Suddenly, Lancelot pushed past Trevor and leapt up the stairs three at time. Then the Spider detonated.

Chapter 34

23.59 Friday 30 June 2062

Harbour Master Felix Cartwright stared in terrified impotence at the scene from hell that confronted him. Across the entire Port of Dover, Caliphate Spiders had been raining down destruction and death, until now the view from his second-floor office overlooking the Eastern Docks was lit by flashing orange flames and bursts of glaring white light when something exploded. As he watched, he could feel the terror of the refugees in the boats and on the shore. This attack had come out of nowhere, and in just a few moments his overcrowded but functioning docks were now strewn with dead and injured.

He hated this war and hated the timing. For eleven years he'd been the harbour master. He'd overseen the reconstruction of both the Eastern and Western docks to combat the rising level of the sea, high tides that were always a little higher, low tides that never seemed to go as low as they used to. And now, after all that effort to meet the hitherto most challenging problem the human race faced, this war had come to his docks.

He called out to the port's super artificial intelligence: "Triton, what are you doing? I can't see you getting the people off the boats."

"Master Cartwright," a masculine voice replied, "I am making all efforts to inform refugees where and how to escape this situation. In the last minute, I have issued individual instructions to over seven thousand people, but they face material logistical problems evacuating to a safe distance given the increasing destruction."

"Jesus Christ," Felix profaned. He went over to the wall by the doorway and snatched a comms unit from a hook. He yanked open the door and flew down the flights of stairs, slotting the comms unit around his right ear as he did so.

"Where are you going?" Triton asked.

"I've got to do something," he said, fury burning as brightly as the fires outside.

"There is little you can achieve compared to my abilities to direct the situation."

"You are not directing shit. Those bastards in the sky are direct—" he broke off as he pushed the door open and suddenly the screams and the hissing and the creaking came to his ears. The flames made the harbour appear almost as though in daylight. Felix turned back and kicked a hatchway next to the door. The hatch sprang open. He reached in and grabbed two fire extinguishers. It might be no more than a futile gesture, but these were his docks and he was not prepared to stand by and watch all this destruction in impotence.

Felix unravelled the strap of one extinguisher and slung it over his shoulder. He unhooked the nozzle from the other and made his way towards the nearest conflagration close to the harbour wall.

"What are the navy doing?" he demanded.

"Attempting to draw enemy fire away from the port."

"They're not very fucking good at it, are they?" Felix hissed as he stomped towards the heat. People of all ages ran and staggered and limped and crawled away from the danger. A few screamed, some moaned, but most made no noise in the midst of such chaos. But the more distress Felix witnessed, the greater his resolve intensified. He tried to avert his eyes from the worst sights and then resisted that urge. He increased his pace as he crossed the area in front of the dock. A breeze from his right blew a wave of withering heat into him and he felt small hairs on the back of his neck and eyebrows shrivel.

Triton spoke: "Your wife is trying to contact you."

"Shit. Okay, put her through."

The nervous voice of Felix's wife, Anne, arrived in his ears and she spat: "You know I hate it when you route my calls through that fucking AI—"

"It's busy here, sweetheart. The port's under attack."

"Come home. Right now. It looks like an inferno down there. Leave it, Felix, now."

"I can't, love," he insisted. "It's my port—"

"You can't do anything to help those people," she shouted. "Leave while you still can, before you get blown up."

"I can't, love," he repeated. "I've got to—" He stopped when she broke the connection. He'd apologise later.

Myriad vessels packed the harbour, from the regular autonomous vehicle transporters to private charters and pleasure boats of many types and ages that had come up from Spain, Portugal and France. All of them carried people who had already suffered in their headlong flight in front of the advancing Caliphate forces, and more than anything Felix wanted to help them. He wanted them to be safe in England. The figures he passed looked gaunt and terrified. One young boy with southern-European features ran into him and hit his fire extinguisher. The teen reacted briefly before turning away and hurrying onwards. Felix had taken the time to chat to the evening's arrivals. One very old Turkish skipper had regaled him with tales from the days when ports like Dover had pilots to guide the ships in.

A vast explosion erupted behind him and he reeled forwards, feeling a searing wave of heat on the back of his cotton shirt. Another profanity began to escape his lips when he turned around to see the low offices in which he spent most of his time collapse. Flaming joist and breezeblock and chipboard fell in with sharp cracks that threw up clouds of embers and sparks.

"Christ," Felix breathed, "if I'd waited a few minutes longer."

He turned back to the fiasco on the water. Ships had been allowed in to stack abeam and let the refugees off by going port-to-starboard from one ship to another. He ran along the harbour wall, navigating around pieces of burning metal and bodies. A Spider must have come down more or less in the middle of six or seven vessels. The nearest one was a small RO-RO with its upper vehicle deck peeled open like a can of beans. Smoke poured from the passenger decks above and there came distant thumps which he assumed must be inflammable stores exploding.

In his ear, Triton advised him: "Another wave of enemy ACAs are approaching. You should seek cover."

"Bollocks." He hurried on, further along the harbour wall, further away from safety. High tide was in half an hour, so any injured people on ships that sank were certain to drown. "Going to be a right mess to clear up at low tide," he muttered. There came a sudden white flash from the other side of the dock and a small cruise ship rose stern-first into the air as though some hidden creature from the depths were pushing it out of the way. It came down on the deck of a smaller ferry.

The next row of vessels he reached were not burning so fiercely, although smoke billowed from several portholes.

People milled about, stunned and injured. "Get to land," he shouted at some refugees with a wave of his free arm as he passed them. But as he indicated to the low hills that encircled the port, there came another deadening explosion and he realised that the enemy ACAs must also be moving inland.

"Triton, any help coming in?"

"A squad of six aircraft will arrive in less than four minutes."

"Christ, what about our own fire-suppression vehicles?"

"All destroyed."

"Shit."

He approached a shattered barquentine, listing into the harbour wall, pinned there by three ferries and a small cruise ship abeam. Felix silently cursed Andy, who must have been on shift when the barquentine arrived, for putting her next to the wall and then piling the larger, heavier metal ships alongside her. People clambered from the larger ships but the barquentine's masts were on fire. As they burned, pieces of the sails unfurled and fell to the deck.

Felix pulled an older man on to the harbour wall and leapt onto the gangplank. He sprayed the fire extinguisher at the flames as more people climbed down from the larger ferry. He stopped to help people but could not take his eyes off the masts above them. More and larger pieces of burning sail came down. In the distance the wail of an airhorn split the air. He glance out to sea and caught his breath as one of the large RO-ROs turned on her side. He just made out a distant squirt of steam or water and she disappeared. The airhorn stopped.

"Help me, please?"

Felix came back abruptly to his surroundings, unsure from where the plea had come or if his ears had been playing tricks on him. He helped more men, women and kids clamber down from the lower deck of the ferry and hurried them off across the burning deck of the barquentine. A piece of burning sail came down on top of a young woman, who collapsed under the weight of the material. Felix doused the flames and the bottle emptied. He discarded it and brought the second fire extinguisher around from his back. Concern grew like an algae bloom that the fire must certainly consume the barquentine. He glanced back at the people on the ferries struggling to escape.

He waved his arms in urgency and shouted: "No, this way is not safe. Go back. Go back to those ships and get off that way," but he saw that the fear and panic were too great.

"Help, please," came to his ears again.

He looked around in confusion and perceived an arm grasping the edge of a smashed hatchway almost at the other end of the ship. He swore. Looking up at the burning masts as often as possible, he made his way along the deck. Felix decided to take a quick look and if he couldn't help, he had to get back onto the harbour wall. A few more stiff breezes and deflagration would be a certainty.

He used the extinguisher liberally as he made his way to the hatch. The terrified face of a woman peered up at him, her age impossible to estimate because of the blood and grease. Felix jumped back when a sudden, loud crack like a pistol shot rang out. Above them, the mizzen mast had split and Felix knew only seconds remained before it had to fall and the furled sails—now all burning briskly—came down on them.

He reached down, grabbed the woman's forearm, and pulled with all his strength. The woman came clear of the hatchway, scuffing her shins, and lay on the deck. At once a burning piece of sail fell and covered her like a fiery burial shroud. Felix sprayed the extinguisher over it and put the flames out with the last of the bottle's contents. He threw it along the deck, pulled the hot canvas off the woman, and grabbed her by her armpits.

"No," she pleaded, "my husband. Please."

Felix didn't speak: a quick glance into the darkness of the hatchway had indicated only sloshing water. If her husband had been able to, he would've emerged by now. The level of the water told Felix that the barquentine was sinking.

As if in confirmation, Triton spoke: "You are in extreme danger. You should move to a place of safety."

"My husband," the woman repeated.

"You need to walk. Can you walk?" Felix did not have time for this. If the woman could not get up and move by herself, he would leave her. He briefly entertained the idea of taking her over his shoulders in the emergency carry position, but felt certain his forty-plus-year-old knees would not support their joint weight when jumping from the barquentine to the harbour wall.

The woman seemed to realise the gravity of her situation. She lifted herself out from his arms and gripped his filthy white shirt.

"Can you move?" Felix asked.

She nodded and said through heavy breaths: "Yes. Can we get off?"

"This way, but don't stumble because there isn't time to stop." Keeping one arm over his head to ward off burning sail, he hurried back along the deck to the nearest gangplank. The heat had become intolerable. A silent figure covered from head to toe in crackling flames strolled past them, apparently in no rush, hit the rail, and toppled overboard.

Felix put one foot on the gangplank, slipped and fell, hitting his right shoulder. Abruptly, a slender yet powerful hand pulled on his left forearm and he got to his feet with relative ease. "Quid pro quo," the woman muttered, giving him a stern look before jumping onto the gangplank.

Felix followed her. He leapt back onto the harbour wall and his knee gave a painful creak. He turned to see the barquentine settle lower in the water. Waves coming in from the harbour made the ferries nudge the smaller ship with greater frequency. All of it above the water burned. Again, the woman pulled him away as a strong breeze blew the heat from the inferno into their faces. As he tensed his body against the hot pain, Felix had never considered how much hatred it was possible to feel for a simple breeze.

Another explosion in the middle of the harbour sent a vast plume of white sparks and orange flame into the sky. These flashed and passed, and a gout of ugly black smoke curled into a ball and rose into the air.

In his ear, Triton advised him: "You must withdraw inland. It is highly probable the entire harbour will be destroyed in the next few minutes."

He tried to run but the pain in his knee stabbed again and he began a ridiculous half-hopping, nonplussed as to why he suddenly couldn't put any weight on his right leg.

The woman came back and put his left arm over her shoulder, and together they struggled among the dead and injured and burning debris, heading back along the harbour wall and, Felix hoped, some semblance of safety.

"Now you must make the effort," she yelled over the sounds of water slapping against stone, hissing liquids, burning wood and the plaintive, metallic screeches of broken ships that were dying with their passengers.

Felix said nothing, for the pain had spread up his thigh and down into his calf. As he half-hopped and half-lurched along, leaning most of his mass on this poor woman, he gradually found he could put weight on his leg if he kept it straight and favoured the outer edge of his foot.

"We have not anywhere to go," she said, and for the first time Felix caught her accent, although he couldn't place it.

"Triton, what's going on?"

"You are still in material danger," the super AI replied.

"Shut up then, you little shit."

"Only the beach to the west remains free of attack—"

"It would be easier to get to fucking France than the west beach," Felix yelled.

An abrupt shriek rent the sky above and Felix ducked instinctively, as did every other figure that stood upright. In an instant, an ACA moving at a vast speed streaked down, over the harbour. Other smaller machines trailed in its wake. It smashed into the middle of the white-chalk cliff face that towered over the harbour. The smaller devices followed it in, travelling far too quickly to change course. Chunks of chalk tumbled down the cliff face and splashed into the sea a hundred metres below.

He resumed moving and kept his arm over the woman's shoulder. Now more used to the injury to his knee, he put his own arm around the woman's waist, grateful for an odd sense of intimacy that reminded him of the three-legged races he'd run when a child at school.

"Triton," he called, "tell us where to go. How about the overspill area?"

"Currently nowhere is safe. Military projections suggest the entire port and its surroundings will be destroyed. Everywhere inland from the main access trunk route has been subject to extensive attack."

"Contact my wife, now," Felix instructed.

"Master Cartwright, there is no response," Triton replied a moment later.

Felix swore and stopped walking. They had reached land. Felix's flattened offices were close by, still burning with ferocity. He let go of the woman and staggered. He stared at the chalk cliff face where the ACAs had hit it. At that moment, another vast chunk calved off, fell, and plunged into the sea, point-first.

271

He glanced at the woman. He had never seen her before and knew nothing about her, but her eyes conveyed an unmistakable message: she might just as well have said aloud: "There, Englishman, now you see what this enemy does to you."

"Come on," he said to those penetrating eyes. "We are not safe yet." He put his arm around her and she reciprocated. With other injured refugees, they hobbled away from the burning ships and headed inland.

Chapter 35

00.46 Saturday 1 July 2062

Mark Phillips ran as fast as he could along through the wheat field. Benefiting from surprise, he drew his short sword and raced at the Roman centurion who had only just heard him coming. The opposing centurion managed to draw his own sword. They traded a few thrusts and parries, and Mark plunged the blade into his opponent's stomach. Mark's victim grunted and fell, and Mark used the man's own weight against him to slice open his guts.

Now his way was clear to the expansive villa. He'd slain five other centurions to get this far and he'd relished every kill. He wiped the blood from his sword on the dead man's tunic and slid the weapon back in its jewel-encrusted scabbard. He turned and filled his lungs with the fresh warm air of the unspoilt Mediterranean countryside. He heard a rustle behind him. He spun around to see a young slave girl carrying a basketful of fat green grapes.

"Who are you and where are you going to?" he demanded.

The buxom girl opened her mouth—and then froze. A red warning triangle materialised in the top-left of Mark's vision, in the beautiful blue of the sky.

"Fuck," Mark cursed, "not again." He removed his helmet and threw it at the slave girl. It bounced off her head and rolled into the wheat. She did not react.

He struggled to control his anger. Who was it this time? His do-gooding brother Martin, 'doing his bit' in some hopeless regiment in the British Army, or his even more do-gooding sister Maria, a medical orderly presumably hoping to get killed before any of the rest of them? But it was most likely his parents, wanting to check yet again if he was all right. Christ, he wished his mother would stop worrying. How often did he have to tell her? He was slowly working his way towards qualifying for one of the famed Bounties, and then he'd show them. Then everything would change. But he couldn't win a Bounty if his family didn't leave him alone to play. This had been the fourth red triangle in the last hour, and he was sick of them.

"Activate Piccolo," he said. This told the gaming management system to allow contact with the super AI that ran the house in East Grinstead in which he lived, and where he currently reposed in his total immersion suit. He always blocked Piccolo to add an extra layer of difficulty for anyone outside the game who wanted to contact him. He'd ignored the previous red triangles because he had to get to the Roman villa, but once he located the coins in it, he would be too busy for several hours at least. And the waste sacks in his suit needed emptying.

The house's super AI spoke: "A general attack is under way by forces of the New Persian Caliphate and you are at risk."

"Seriously?" he queried in frustration.

The super AI did not respond. Suddenly, his view of the Mediterranean countryside warped at impossible angles. Mark had just enough time to catch his breath and realise what must have happened when—

Mark's consciousness rose up as though from a dream. The slave girl's lascivious smile turned into a grimace that became a sneer. She and the rest of the Mediterranean countryside then collapsed. He came to in darkness, unsure of how much time had elapsed. He tried to breathe and found that he could not. His physical body reacted to the demand for air and he choked. Very real dust blocked his nose and starved his throat of moisture. The coughing deepened and fear gripped Mark when he suddenly realised he might suffocate.

"There's one over here," he heard a gruff male voice call out.

Mark's primal fear of death receded a little when he managed to get some air into his lungs. He grimaced and tensed every muscle in his chest to stop the wracking cough, but to do so meant not breathing. His other senses alerted him to his surroundings: dust, filth, brick, wood splinters, wetness on his skin that remained inside the torn total immersion suit.

In the darkness above, something moved and he heard another voice call out: "Christ, what a stench here."

"Is it a body?"

"Smells like it fucking should be."

Mark's cough abated further. He drew in measured breaths and other impressions came to him. He recalled what he had been doing, contrasted that with his current situation, and extrapolated conclusions. He tensed and relaxed areas of his body and felt new pain.

"Fuck it," one of the voices said. "This one smells like it's dead. Let's leave it for the construction replicators."

Panic rose inside Mark when he thought he might be left in the wreckage and die after all. He tried to call out, but the act of forcing air through his vocal cords only made him cough deeply again.

"I heard something there—"

"So what? There must be a hundred buried on this street alone, and we've—"

"Just give us a lift here, will you?"

"Okay."

Dust and rubble cascaded onto Mark as debris above him moved. It stung his eyes and threatened to undo the recovery he had thus far managed to gain.

"Oh look," the first voice said. "We've got a gamer. He's still in his suit."

"So that's the stench, is it?"

"Yup."

"Then we should leave the little yellow fucker."

"Don't be like that. He's probably only a baby who finds the real world too much for his small mind."

The men's mocking laughter floated down to Mark, but he had not spent years gaming without learning when not to inflame a situation when one's antagonists had the advantage. Trying to sound as plaintive as possible, he said: "Sorry. Thanks for your help, really."

"How bad are you hurt? You need a Geno-pack?"

"No, I don't think so," Mark replied, unsure of the extent of his injuries.

"Good," the man spat back, "because there ain't none left."

"Come on," said the man's colleague, "Florence has just found another two live ones buried in the next street."

Rubble shifted and crunched as the men climbed off and moved away. Mark heard one of them complain: "Where are the construction replicators to sort this shit out?"

Mark shifted his body to the edge of his gaming bed. He unzipped the total immersion suit, wincing at the sticky mess he had to force his fingers through, which confirmed beyond doubt the waste sacks had split. He freed the clasps inside the suit. He shuddered in horror on realising he'd have to climb through the rubble naked when he left the suit. He craned his head and made out his regular clothes behind him, covered in dust. He grabbed the splintered roof truss the men had pulled from over him and used it to lever his body upwards and away from the mess of the split waste sacks. He strained an arm out and grasped his trousers and sweatshirt.

Mark coughed again but realised that the suit had cushioned him from potentially far worse injury. He pulled himself up and clear of the bulk of the debris. He turned around to where the rest of the house should've been and saw only a gaping hole in his view. He blinked, his mind unable to adjust to this fundamental change in his real-world surroundings. The weak artificial light revealed hunks of smashed walls. Irregular chunks of brickwork lay at random angles; broken door frames jutted upwards.

He looked in the sky above the street where emergency lights hung in the air, their AI observing and directing illumination. The stench of his confinement gave way to masonry dust that carried distant voices and the shifting of smashed bricks and tinkling of broken glass as debris settled. Mark temporarily forgot his nakedness as he stared at real-world destruction that he never imagined would visit such an anonymous English town. East Grinstead was not London, it contained no world-famous landmarks. He kept his trousers and sweatshirt in front of his groin as he scanned and noted the methodical damage. Of the fifteen houses in his terraced row, four had been obliterated and he'd only survived because his house had been on the periphery of the detonation.

Mark sat with care on some slate roof tiles and dressed. He worried about his bare feet with so much broken glass and other sharp points everywhere, but after searching carefully for some time, he improvised by tying torn curtains around his feet. At length, he hobbled to an ad-hoc triage point where his residential street met the main road. Despite the heat of the night, he began shivering. He stopped, sat on a wall, and waited for the trembling to pass. Before it did, he thought he might throw up, and then he felt as though he would void his bowels involuntarily.

"This shit never happens when I have a close fight in the games," he muttered.

He approached the triage point and joined others. He thought they looked dreadful, many with blood on their heads and bodies, until he realised he was in no better condition. Worse, he noticed people looking at him but couldn't work out why. Then he remembered the split waste sacks.

An older man standing in front of Mark, who held his arm close to his chest, turned to Mark and said: "You're one of the Phillips's kids, aren't you?"

Mark didn't recognise the man at all and wondered how he could've known who Mark was. Mark nodded and said: "Yes."

"You don't look that bad," the man said with a nod.

"I, er, I don't know," and suddenly Mark didn't know what he should do. He'd come to the triage point because he thought he might get some water and go somewhere to rest. But when he took in the people and the destruction around him, he began to understand that everything had changed. He said to the man: "I thought I should get myself checked over, you know?"

The man scoffed and said: "You're young, you'll mend easily." Then he sneered and said: "If you're looking for your parents, they're around the back."

"What?"

The man repeated: "Your parents are around the back, with all the other bodies."

The urge to throw up returned and Mark hurried away, half-limping as the knots holding the torn curtains on his feet loosened. He reached a wider area behind the houses that the previous day had been a small green for local dogwalkers. Rows of prone figures lay on the ground, unmoving and uncovered. He limped among them, staggered at the range of injures. He reflected how greatly real physical injuries differed from those he inflicted in his gaming.

"Who are you? What are you doing?" a female voice demanded.

Mark spun around to face an overweight but compact woman older than him. He stammered: "I, er, I'm looking for—"

"Is your lens working?"

"No, I didn't, er, don't have—"

"Name?" she barked.

"Mark Phillips."

Her eye twitched and she said: "Follow me."

He limped after her between two rows of contorted corpses. She stopped, pointed down and said: "Here is Anthony Phillips, and here is Jane Phillips."

Mark stared agape at the remains of his parents.

The woman said: "I have three immediate relatives listed; you, and your siblings Martin and Maria. Where are they?"

Mark shook his head. He could not accept that his parents were dead. There had to be a mistake.

"Well?" the woman demanded.

He replied: "They are serving in the British Army."

"Very well—"

"Wait," Mark said, suddenly finding his voice. "What happened to my parents? How did they di—how did they end up here?"

The woman shrugged her shoulders and answered: "Like most of these people, I assume, they came out of their houses to make their way to the emergency shelter on Grosvenor street when a Spider must have got them in the open. You're fortunate to have this much of them; with many of the others, it's going to take time to match up all the bits."

"Christ," Mark muttered, the tremors of shock coming on again. He imagined the alarm sounding, his parents hammering on his locked door, his father pulling his mother away, insisting they had to get to safety. Did his actions cause their deaths?

However, as the woman turned to go, the last thing she said chilled his blood: "You can have some time with them if you want, but you will have to deal with the formalities. I'll leave it to you to inform your siblings of your loss. And come and find me when you have."

Chapter 36

02.54 Saturday 1 July 2062

“Sir Terry? Sir Terry, wake up.”
    Terry came to with his adjutant Simms lightly but firmly shaking his arm. He felt the fatigue deep inside his joints. The sinews in his shoulders resisted all demands to return from rest. The discs in his neck creaked in protest at being denied a few more moments’ peace. Terry rubbed the growing stubble on his face and again wished he were thirty years younger, when snapping out of sleep and getting his body to full readiness in seconds was something in which he took pride. Now, he was old.
    His eyes stung as he tried to focus. “Yes, what is it?”
    Simms breathed in and replied: “Urgent contact from the navy.”
    “Okay.”
    “Tea?”
    “Yes, please.” Terry watched Simms leave his office in the War Rooms as his senses returned fully. He sat up in the chair and waved a hand in front of the screen in his desk.

The haggard face of Admiral William Rutherford appeared on the screen. His features were drawn and the shadows under his eyes evoked Terry's sympathy. "At last," he said, "Sorry to bother you TT, but I was hoping you could help with a problem."

"Everyone's having a bad night, Bill," Terry replied. "What's up?"

"I need to ask you to free some PeaceMakers to protect my ships."

Terry smothered his shock at the bluntness of the admiral's request. He said: "Bill, I don't have control over strategic deploy—"

"It's all getting rather boring, TT," the admiral interrupted with barely concealed frustration. "I am asking you, as a fellow serviceman of the greatest armed forces the world has ever seen, and, dare I offer, as a fellow professional fighter, to divert a fraction of your resources to protect the lives of the men under my command."

Terry repeated: "I do not have strat—"

"I've spoken to SACEUR but he insisted he could not help, that is why I am appeal—"

"Bill," Terry said, "I cannot countermand SACEUR, as you well know."

"Damn you, Tidbury," Rutherford spat, addressing Terry incorrectly. "Give me more PeaceMakers now or you will have to answer to history as to why four hundred years of tradition will end tonight with the sinking of the last of His Majesty's Royal Navy's ships."

Terry looked through the window, outside his small private office, to the screens above the stations in the War Rooms. "Look, Bill," he said, "this attack is following the same one four weeks ago. The enemy is prioritising terrorising civilian populations over military targ—"

"But without air cover my ships are sitting ducks."

Terry began to resent the edge of panic in Rutherford's voice along with the constant interruptions. Allowing his strained patience to come through his words, he said: "Coherence-length variation is giving your sailors much more time and that lets the computers calculate defensive measures with greater accuracy."

Rutherford repeated: "They need more air cover. We can't lose those ships."

Terry replied: "Sorry, admiral, there's nothing I can do. Good luck," and terminated the connection. He slapped a flat hand on the desk and silently damned Rutherford. Even if the surface ships were sunk, as seemed certain, he still had the submarines and his detachments of Royal Marines. The computers had been forecasting another attack like this for weeks, so the admiral had no excuse for displaying such emotion.

Terry stood, stretched his aching limbs, and left the office to check the state of the battle more closely. He exited his office as his adjutant approached.

"Here you are, Sir Terry," Simms said, handing Terry a mug of tea.

Terry took it, thanked him, and instructed: "Have a summary of the night's action sent to all corps commanders and tell them to expect stronger attacks at any point on the line."

"Yes, sir."

"Are all troops getting real-time notifications of family members killed in this attack?"

"If they are the only next of kin, sir, yes."

Terry sighed and said: "Pretty bad news to wake up to."

"Indeed."

"Thank you, Simms. Go and get some rest."

Simms nodded and replied: "I will insist you do the same soon, Sir Terry."

Terry smiled and strode to the Europe comms station. He spoke to the young man monitoring this aspect of the attack. "Summary?" Terry asked.

The young man spoke with confidence: "All cities not already under enemy occupation and with a population of over fifty thousand have been hit quite hard tonight, sir. Estimates show total civilian dead to be heading north of—"

"I can see that, son," Terry broke in. "What about munitions plants?"

"Second-tier targets. Enemy ACAs have preferred to hit cultural and historical monuments and only then have a go at militarily relevant targets."

"Can you give me a comparative analysis figure of the effectiveness of our defences against the attacks four weeks ago? And confer with the UK station as well. I want one overall figure for all territories that suffered attacks on both occasions."

"Yes, sir. Give me a moment."

Terry's eyes ranged over the large display that showed northern Europe. Hundreds of lines of different coloured lights streaked in every direction as NATO and enemy ACAs fought each other, all controlled by super artificial intelligence. Around the margins of the image, numbers continually cycled upwards; of NATO machines in the air and destroyed; of enemy machines emerging from the fog of jamming; of ground-based munitions expended; of casualties, both civilian and military. A small part of Terry marvelled at the enemy's ingenuity: he was destroying Europe piece by piece in a way unthinkable just a few years earlier. Any such attack would have had to involve the use of nuclear weapons. But today, by using overwhelming numbers of ACAs, a superpower could invade and subdue an entire continent without any irradiation.

"Sir," the young analyst at the station said, "NATO defences are showing an aggregated improved performance compared to the attack four weeks ago of twelve-point-one percent. Would you like to see the stats broken down by theatre and type of armament?"

"No, thank you," Terry replied. He drew the mug of tea towards his mouth. "Twelve percent is excellent, all things considered," he said in his normal voice, before whispering into his tea: "But it's not going to be anywhere near enough."

Chapter 37

21.09 Sunday 2 July 2062

Captain Pip Clarke heaved a sigh as the sitrep broke up. She said nothing and observed the soldiers meander out of the temporary field hut. She wanted to be alone; she needed silence. When the last khaki shirt had disappeared through the doorway, she rose, followed, and kicked one of the cheap, foldaway chairs on her way out.

She paused again outside in the heat. After the others had dissolved into the darkness, she checked her surroundings in her lens, and headed in exactly the opposite direction from the rest of the camp, through a dead hedgerow and into a patch of pine trees. She wanted very much to overcome her fear of going outside alone. The rustle of dry grass behind her gave away the presence of someone following. She choked down her flaring anger.

"Captain?" called a voice she recognised.

She stopped and turned, the display in her lens identifying the stalker. "Hello, Martin," she said.

"Look, if you need to be alone, that's fine, I can just go ba—"

"If you thought I needed to be alone, why the hell did you follow me?"

Martin put his hands on his hips and said with his easy charm: "Because you looked furious in that sitrep, and I thought maybe a chat might help."

"And what if I've come out here to kick the crap out of a tree?"

He raised his hands in mock defence and said: "Hey, that's fine with me, captain. I'll just be on my way."

There came a pause as she glanced at him in the dim, yellow light, the crescent moon hanging low in the night sky. Time passed and her eyes adjusted. She decided she did not want to be alone after all. "Let's go for a walk?" she offered.

Martin said nothing as he fell in beside her and the pair stomped off through dry grass, around mature pines and the occasional spindly oak, their feet sinking into the sandy earth.

"Yes, I am furious, so congratulations on your perception," she began. "I'm furious with this bullshit war. I'm furious that civilians are dying in these numbers and there is nothing we can do to help them because we even struggle to help ourselves."

"The fighting retreat is buying time for some of—"

"Bullshit," she spat with more venom than she'd intended. "We're all heading to the same destination, Martin."

"Did you lose someone important in the attacks on Friday night?"

She shook her head. "Not this time. You?"

"Not as far as I know," he answered.

"What I hate is that we are so completely outmatched. Look at these bloody sitreps. Every day," she exclaimed. "Every bloody day. Pull back. Retreat. Withdraw. All the fucking time." She stopped walking and looked into Martin's handsome face, now creased in concern. She said: "Leaving behind ruined homes, ruined lives. Letting the ill and handicapped and injured fall into enemy hands."

She saw Martin gulp. He said: "Captain—"

"Please call me 'Pip', for God's sake."

"Er, yeah, sure. Look, we all feel the same. We've all got families and friends who are suffer—"

Pip was shocked. She said: "I do know that, right?"

"No, I just meant—"

She shook her head in dismissal, "Yeah, I know what you meant. Maybe the people I've also lost just meant too m—" she broke off when an urgent comms request arrived in her lens. She caught her breath when she realised it was Rory. She looked at Martin, his face a mask of patience, and said: "Look, I'm sorry, I have to take this. I won't need long. Okay?"

Again, Martin gave her the easy-going shrug that suggested unlimited patience. He said: "Sure, go ahead. I'll go for a trot over there."

She felt an urge to tell him to stay, but she overrode it. She turned away from Martin, accepted the incoming signal, and said: "Hey mate, how you doing? Still enjoying the easy work while us over here do all the graft?"

"Yeah, kind of," Rory answered in her ear.

At once Pip knew something was wrong, thinking that perhaps he too had lost loved ones in the Friday night attacks. She said: "What's happened, mate?"

"Nightmares are getting worse. I should be dead. I should've been dead twenty times over."

She swallowed her surprise and tried to calm him: "That's okay, it's natural to feel like that—"

"Christ, Pip," Rory said, voice strained, "you know that contact I told you about a few days ago, with the team of ragheads my platoon squished, when we lost eight of the platoon?"

"Yeah."

"I checked the records. Turns out they were holding hundreds of ACAs back. Hundreds, mate. If they'd wanted to, they could've, just like—"

Her Squitch broke in with: "Muted. It is forbidden to reveal operational details."

Rory continued with: "Fucking Squitch. But Why? Why didn't they? We got out on transports less than ninety seconds before Lapwings turned up and le—"

Again, her Squitch interrupted: "It is forbidden to reveal operational details.

Pip said: "Don't worry, I heard enough of them."

Rory went on regardless: "You won't believe what my platoon is calling me now."

"What?"

"The lucky Jonah."

"That's a compliment, isn't—"

"I don't give a fuck if it is, the whole 'why me?' shit is driving me round the twist."

"It's nothing special, mate," she said, wishing she could end the conversation. "We've got this far because of our deployment, that's all."

"And your shit-hot resilience. That's what I tell people who ask me what it's like to take out a Spider: I tell them to contact you, since you've got the highest tally."

"They never do."

"Probably for the best."

Silence descended. An abrupt tiredness seeped into Pip's limbs. She wanted to relax, to be free of the relentless pressure. She allowed the pause to run on before she would end the conversation.

Rory said: "Look, Pip, I don't want to repeat myself, but pretty soon you and I aren't going to be so far apart."

"What do you mean?"

"If the raghead doesn't let up, only Blighty will be left to defend."

"I'm trying not to think so far ahead. Operation Certain Death will reach its endgame soon enough."

"It's coming, Pip, and I think—"

"Listen, sorry mate, but I need to call it a night."

"What? Oh, okay." She caught the deflation in his voice. "Yeah, sure. Be safe."

"You too." She ended the call, retraced her steps, and soon heard the rustle of others. "So how much did you accidently-on-purpose overhear?" she asked Martin with a smile, the energy returning to her body under Martin's intense gaze.

He replied: "Not a word, honest."

"I believe you," she said with irony. Warmth grew inside her along with another feeling, alien yet familiar.

"Would you like to walk some more? Or have you got rid of the negativity after that sitrep?"

Pip stepped closer to Martin and whispered: "I don't want to walk anymore. I would like to rest... somewhere safe."

From the look on Martin's face, she felt convinced he understood that the safe place was his arms. This was the escape she needed.

Martin moved towards her but then stopped suddenly. "Damn," he said.

"What is it?" she asked.

He shook his head and said: "My brother Mark is calling me."

Pip recalled that Martin had told her of his two siblings, whose names began with the same letter as his. "Is that strange?" she asked, before adding: "Go ahead and take the call. I can wait," thinking that extending the same courtesy to him that he had shown her was the least she could do.

He looked at her in the weak light and said: "Mark is a gamer. He spends days, sometimes weeks, in his total immersion suit. He never calls me or anyone else."

"All the more reason to accept the call," she said with a shrug, trying to keep the atmosphere light.

"Okay, thanks. I'm sure this won't take long."

Chapter 38

Terry Tidbury sat down at the breakfast bar in his kitchen and looked at the VR glasses via which he would attend the morning's briefing. He glanced over to see Maureen in the garden with an old-fashioned watering can, sprinkling droplets over the borders. The sense of time running out came to him again, and he wondered if this was how it felt to have a terminal disease: noting the last time for every trivial thing as it passed. He and Maureen would certainly not see another autumn or winter or spring.

Then his focus came into the room, and in the sink sat the dirty plates on which they had breakfasted on poached eggs. He smiled: he would have the pleasure of washing up at least one more time. He took a long, deep pull on his mug of malty brown tea and put it down on the work surface. He lifted up the VR glasses, gave his kitchen a long look, and put the glasses on.

"Thanks for turning up early, general," SACEUR said.

Terry glanced ahead, over rows of staggered seating, to see the hunched figure of General Joseph E. Jones, and

293

wondered if he saw more grey hair on the African-American's head. "Always a pleasure to talk with you, general."

Jones let out a mirthless chuckle and replied: "Bullshit, but the kind of bullshit I do not mind."

"Is there a reason you wanted to talk before the meeting?"

Jones heaved a long sigh before saying: "Yes, general. I never thought the United States' military would ever be on the losing side of any war in my lifetime."

"I sympathise, sir. The British Armed Forces are still the best in the world, and they always will be, but we have met a plague of locusts this time, and it seems that there are enough of them to overwhelm us."

Jones nodded and said: "I wanted you first of all to know that if Operation Foothold fails, Coll and the House will take America out of NATO and out of the war."

Terry smothered a curse, reconsidered, and nearly lost his temper: "But we bloody advised them that Foothold is not a good idea. We told them that we should not do it. They insisted. They decid—"

Jones raised his voice: "You think I don't know that? You think I didn't tell them? They are politicians, general, not soldiers. And they want NATO to be seen to make 'a stand'. And that stand is Operation Foothold."

"Christ sweet Jesus," Terry said.

"That times ten. The only silver lining we got is the SHF burner. You think it'll work?"

"Absolutely," Terry said at once. "I know those Porton Down types, and the embarrassment of it not working would be more lethal than a Lapwing's laser."

Jones scoffed and said: "Good. Listen, general, this is going to be a tough meeting. I have to announce something both of us know ain't a good idea, and I'm going to need your support to sell it."

"You've always got that, SACEUR."

Jones sat heavily back down on the chair. "I guess," he murmured.

Silence descended and Terry wondered with what dark thoughts Jones had to grapple on top of everything else. Terry himself endured moments of the most crushing despair and leaned on thirty years of military discipline and a fundamental, unshakable belief that he'd had the most outrageous good fortune to have been born British.

However, Jones had spent the last five months in impotent fury watching his command being taken away from him in the most brutal fashion by a merciless enemy. And now, as the situation grew progressively hopeless, his political masters had decreed that one more failure and they would abandon his charge altogether. Terry tried to imagine the anger and resentment that must surely burn inside the American general, but could not.

Nine o'clock arrived and people began materialising in the rows of chairs. Terry nodded in appreciation at the timeliness of the attendees. As people appeared, their names and ranks or positions materialised in the air close to them. The multinational audience included not only British and American ranks above major, but also equivalents from the remnants of the French, German, Polish, Spanish, Italian, Hungarian, Czech, Romanian, Greek and Albanian armies. In addition, attendees arrived from various related branches of governments who were struggling to survive, including military and scientific departments. In less than forty-five seconds, over sixty individuals arrived at the virtual meeting.

Despite being impressed by the range and authority of those present, a ripple of unease ran through Terry: what Jones would shortly reveal was top secret and any security breach would be certain to cost yet more lives and condemn to failure an objective that would require any advantage it could get.

Jones cleared his throat and began: "Thank you, everyone, for attending. As usual, we have a lot to get through and time is short, so I will start with the headline news: at just after five o'clock this morning, forces from Warrior Group West joined up with those from Warrior Groups Central and East, so the enemy now presents one united front in his continuing advance across the continent."

The air immediately to SACEUR's left resolved into a digital map of the European landmass with the territory lost by NATO denoted by the extent of enemy jamming.

Jones went on: "As far as possible, we are removing key personnel to a safe distance. As some of you know, the staffs at key research institutes, universities, and the R&D facilities at certain weapons manufacturers have been pulled back either to the British Isles or the American mainland. These include the *Institut Neuropsi* who are still working on the handful of injured enemy combatants to expand our knowledge of the enemy."

The VR image of Jones stopped speaking and remained motionless for a moment before continuing: "Since the major enemy attacks last Friday, our fronts have been consolidating more rapidly, which has led to some synergies in eastern France and southern Germany, as you can see on the map. This is allowing our forces to frustrate the enemy, but we expect only for a matter of days. Of greater concern are the remnants of the British Armoured Corps, which also includes units from several other countries' forces, that have now been cut off in the Cherbourg peninsula. This happened due to an unanticipated attack by the enemy's newest, larger ACA that caused so much damage to the Delta Works during the attacks on Friday night. The US Navy has released seven ships from the nearest carrier group to assist, although many non-combatant private individuals have taken it upon themselves to get involved.

"Elsewhere, the retreat continues with the inevitability we've had to get accustomed to since the enemy's invasion resumed nearly five weeks ago. Given his progress and apparent prioritisation of targets, we expect Paris and Prague to be overrun at around the same time, while Berlin and Warsaw will fall within the next couple of weeks. Indeed, current tactical data shows enemy units advancing to within ten kilometres of Paris."

Jones stopped speaking on a requested interruption from General Renouard, commander-in-chief of the French Army.

Jones, already looking wearied, asked: "What is it, general?"

"Forgive me," the upright Frenchman said in English that carried only the slightest lilt. "But the mayor of Paris would like to address this meeting. He is an old comrade-in-arms from our days in the Foreign Legion. We are about to lose Paris. He would like to say something."

SACEUR said: "Sure, go ahead."

The three-dimensional image of a thin, angular head with pointed chin and receding hairline resolved and dominated the area. The words 'Nicolas Favre, Mayor of Paris' materialised next to him. Favre squinted at the audience and spoke in heavily accented English: "Hello? My friends? Ah, thank you, my dear Augustin, and thanks to you, general Jones. I have not so much time. I want only to tell you all, dearest allies, Paris will never surrender to these filthy barbarians. We have, for weeks now, construction replicators tunnelling under the city to create spaces and caverns for those citizens who remain. The old and the children are of course gone abroad, but we have the young and strong. We have the last of the Second Armoured Brigade who have their weapons and ammunition. I tell you now, with the basic food and water replicators, we can have a siege of years. Do you hear me?

Years! We will keep up a campaign of relentless harassment. For as long as there is one of us alive under the streets of Paris, not one filthy barbarian will be able to walk in the daylight above in peace and comfort.

"My dearest allies, the only way the Caliphate will be able to stop us will be to destroy all Paris with a big and powerful nuclear weapon. If they do this, if they commit the ultimate despicable act, then the global disgust will draw other, more powerful states into this war to stop these filthy barbarians. And if that happens, then my dear Paris will not have died in vain. Thank you and goodbye. God bless you all."

The image dissolved and left a poignant silence. General Renouard looked stoic but his eyes glistened. It was one of the most inspiring yet saddest messages Terry had ever heard.

SACEUR coughed and said: "I am sure all of us here stand with the mayor and the remaining citizens of Paris. Godspeed." Jones paused again before moving on: "Now, we have an update on tech developments concerning the enemy's jamming of the territory it controls. I believe we have a person from the UK's Weapons Research Establishment. A Mr English?"

A new voice spoke. Terry glanced to his left and, a few rows down, a stocky man about his own age swept a pudgy hand across thinning hair. The man introduced himself: "Graham English, thank you, general."

"Please go ahead."

"Hello, everyone. I will be brief. The super-high frequency 'burner' is a device that burns through the enemy's white noise. In essence, we took the view that 'less is more' in that instead of trying to defeat it entirely, which would require a quite enormous projection, our devices will slice it up. Each device works in unison and should guarantee comms—both military and civilian—and reveal, initially at least, the enemy's own communications. These SHF burners have now been delivered to all military units and will be fitted to objective-specific SkyWatchers and other devices."

"Thank you," Jones said with impatience.

Terry sensed SACEUR wanted to prevent debate. If anyone had any questions, Jones wasn't letting them speak.

The American general went on: "I'm sure you are wondering why we haven't already started using these burners. And, yes, there is a good reason." The general glanced down and moved his hands while continuing: "I'm sending you the outline for Operation Foothold. It has been decided that NATO needs to show not only the enemy but also the whole world that we shall not cede the European mainland."

Terry glanced around him to see raised eyebrows and the occasional head shake. How long could it be before someone interrupted?

Jones went on: "Foothold calls for the insertion of two divisions of US Marines—which is almost half the total strength of the corps—one in Normandy and the other around Hamburg. The objectives are multiple and I hope at least a little obvious. At the tactical level, it will help ensure the evacuation of greater numbers of civilians. At the strategic level, apart from showing that NATO will not give up on the European mainland, these two locations will serve as bases for the future retaking of lost territory once superior munitions become available."

Terry heard someone behind him mutter, "Ambitious, I'll give them that."

"Ladies and gentlemen," Jones said in a harder voice, "I'm sure we have all had a bellyful of the Third Caliph demanding that NATO forces surrender. I'm also sure you all read the press and you understand the manipulation he is engaged in by not using weapons of mass destruction to ensure a swifter and more complete victory. And, to some degree, this is perhaps Foothold's most important objective: to deny our enemy that geographical success. The British Isles can never hope to survive once the enemy has overrun the rest of Europe. Now, as you will see in the high-level materials, this is where advances like the SHF burners can potentially make all the difference. In addition, the last three convoys have docked successfully and we have substantially more materiel to deploy. Operation Foothold is scheduled to kick off on Monday."

Terry had to admit that whoever had drafted the high-level outline had done their best to make the operation seem to have a chance of success: *if* the lead elements of Marines could be landed successfully and *if* the SHF burners worked and *if* the enemy forces languished long enough to allow the Marines' construction replicators to build defences and *if*...

The list of doubts in Terry's mind went on while the situation briefing continued. Jones introduced more speakers to describe how training and supplies were improving, how the contracting lines also led to benefits, how defences were being strengthened around the British Isles, and how the development of the next generation NATO ACAs was progressing. During this, news came in that contact had been lost with Prague. Through it all, SACEUR allowed no questions or debate.

Finally, the meeting concluded with Jones repeating his mantra of staying positive and keeping a healthy attitude no matter how bleak the future seemed. When Terry could at last remove the glasses and return to his kitchen, he felt as though hours must have passed. But his mug of tea still held a trace of warmth and he saw that the time was just approaching ten o'clock.

"Sir Terry?" Squonk asked.

"What?"

"The damage to England's transport network that affected your ability to travel to the War Rooms has now been repaired."

"Including all of the bridges over the M25?" Terry queried.

"Affirmative. Travel time to central London is back to normal."

Terry's gaze drifted to the garden, where Maureen sat under a sunshade reading a book. Terry said: "Normal will not last for very much longer."

Chapter 39

04.34 Saturday 8 July 2062

The Englishman sat on the toilet not entirely sure how bad he felt, only certain that resting on the porcelain bowl was probably the best thing given the drugs he had likely put in his body in the preceding twelve hours. Opposite him, high up on the wall, a frosted window let a light breeze in. He struggled to remember who he had been with and what they had taken. But that person snored gently in the bed outside the bathroom.

The Englishman sighed: nothing mattered anymore. Now he had been turned and the Chinese secret service had put bots in his body, they knew all that he said and did, everywhere he went, and could instruct the bots in his body to kill him at any time they chose. And Marshal Zhou had disappeared to God knew where.

Something gurgled inside his large intestine which reassured him that sitting on a toilet was the right place.

There were always opposites, he reflected. The GenoFluid bots that could save a person's life in the most extreme circumstances could just as easily be reprogrammed to take life away. The vastness and complexity of the human body had become quite the battleground: the Englishman might try to escape the effective range of the bots by fleeing China, or he might try to get other bots injected to destroy the government's bots. Then again, the government's bots were programmed with protocols to ensure a subject could never feel truly safe. He didn't care anymore. In his last contact with London a few weeks ago, he'd followed the prearranged script to let his handler know he'd been discovered, and thereafter anything that he reported should be considered unreliable. So, he didn't bother anymore.

Chinese security leaked so badly because the rollout of putting bots inside the bodies of all of their operatives had yet to receive Politburo approval. All the beautiful people could still have their fun. For now.

While still waiting for his intestines to do their job, a sudden memory surfaced. He caught his breath: had he really been with a woman? He pieced together bits of memories: the club, the bar, the hedonism, the inevitable sympathy. Christ, he hated it when Chinese people found out he was English and they told him they felt sorry for him; he had to control the urge to drag a broken glass across their slit-eyed faces.

But there had been something else, something that had provoked old urges and satiations. The woman. Fluorescent pink eyeliner. She'd broken through last night. She'd made him angry in the way he used to be angry, months ago, before the security services had caught him and turned him. What had little-bitch Pink Eyes told him?

He put his head in his hands while his intestines gargled again and something continued on its way through his body. But last night the music had been too loud. It was all shouting and yelling; in Mandarin, then in Spanish, then English. What had Pink Eyes been laughing about? That they knew everything the West did? Of course, this was still the diplomatic quarter in Beijing so any bar or club contained mostly those spoilt and entitled young Chinese who had grown up knowing they resided in the most powerful city of the most powerful country on Earth. The hedonism among Beijing's pretty young things was notorious globally.

Suddenly, his bowels emptied as the key memory rose up through the fog of his hangover. "Oh God, no," he said aloud over the noise of the diarrhoea hitting the water underneath him. He concentrated in desperation to ascertain its authenticity. Yes, it was accurate. Pink Eyes had really said it. He remembered how he'd joked his way to getting her confirmation—the requirement of his previous life, to be as sure as possible, and then how he'd gone down on her in a cubicle in the club's toilets not because he was grateful or wanted to pleasure her, but to disguise the hatred: for her as a person, for her as a woman, for her as a representative of a culture that was taking its place at the head of the whole world, but mostly to disguise his loathing of himself at failing England.

Relief spread from his bowels up his spine. It wrapped itself around his chest and warmed him. Clarity followed. Although he would not be believed, he had to tell London. He reactivated the lens in his eye, pointlessly encrypted the signal, and, just like the old days, spoke with authority and erudition: "The Englishman reporting from Beijing. Time of report: 04.37, Saturday 8 July 2062. Report begins: Code red, critical communication. According to a newly acquired contact, which I shall call PE, elements of the Chinese security services benefit from the presence of secret components inside NATO communications equipment supplied by Chinese companies. This allows their super AI to monitor all NATO comms and extract relevant and critical information. PE mentioned something called a 'software patch inhibitor', whatever that might be.

"Nevertheless, given the size of the departments and the ferocity of interdepartmental rivalry to gain favour with various government members, the contact was not able to specify how or to what extent this data was shared among other branches of the Chinese governmental machine. Therefore, it is critical for the governments of the NATO members to take immediate steps to limit and replace communications' equipment. Despite provocation, I was unfortunately unable to make PE reveal more details that would confirm this beyond any doubt. Additionally, when questioned under the influence of several narcotics, PE either did not know or would not reveal if the information were relayed to other nation states or political entities, for example the New Persian Caliphate. Message ends."

The Englishman twitched his eye to end the transmission and sighed, his hatred exhausted, his satisfaction tempered by the foreknowledge of futility. But at least he'd told London. From the other side of the bathroom door came shuffling noises. He reached for the toilet paper and decided to find out whose bed he'd ended up in, and if they could offer him some breakfast.

Chapter 40

Geneal Sir Terry Tidbury interlinked his fingers as he stood in front of the main display console in the War Rooms. A digital, topographical map of north-western Europe glowed from the surface, including part of England. In the space above the three-dimensional image, tiny indicators showed the locations of low-orbit SkyWatchers, poised to send the PeaceMakers in to attack.

Terry tensed his shoulders and felt the benefit of six hours' unbroken sleep. Opposite the console, the diminutive form of Air Chief Marshal Raymond Thomas squinted at the display, having accepted Terry's invitation to witness the night's events from the War Rooms in Whitehall rather than at his home base at Scampton. Terry's office had extended an invitation to Admiral Rutherford as protocol demanded, but since losing the last of the Royal Navy's surface ships, the admiral had officially been 'indisposed'. Terry knew the man had suffered some kind of breakdown and again sent a silent wish for his recovery.

A young lady called Evans stood on Terry's left, a deputy adjutant as Simms was recovering after he collapsed the previous day due, Terry believed, to exhaustion. A stern-faced woman from the Electronic Warfare Establishment, who requested authorisation to see how the SHF burners performed, stood on Terry's right.

An operator behind them called out: "Modified SkyWatchers in position. Advance Marine formations approaching the coast."

A geometric cluster of fifty SkyWatchers hung six kilometres above the North Sea, all fitted with SHF burners. Below them, three times as many PeaceMakers pitched and rolled and rotated to maintain the maximum level of effectiveness. Much lower down the image, two wings of four autonomous air transports that carried the Marines crossed the English Channel.

The operator called out: "Sixty seconds to SHF-burner activation."

Terry sensed the anticipation in the room. Finally, a chance—however misguided, in his opinion—to do something positive. A total of fifteen thousand US Marines would be inserted in the next two days, each with a division's supply of munitions. Operation Foothold called for each division to defend its designated area with resupply by air and sea. The enemy could not be allowed to gain full domination of the major European landmass.

"Thirty seconds."

The woman from the Electronic Warfare Establishment gulped and said: "I know this is going to work, I just hope it performs as well as it did during testing."

"If their own computers didn't see it coming and haven't taken countermeasures," Thomas observed, "then this will give us a useful advantage for a while at least."

The final seconds ticked down. Terry controlled his breathing. He desperately wanted Foothold to get off to the best start possible; indeed, it had to if it were to last. But the long-term goal of keeping troops on the mainland until a new generation of weapons could be tested and produced seemed fanciful at best.

"SHF burners lighting up now," the operator called.

In the image over the central console, the SkyWatchers above the battlespace emitted lines of light that broadened into conical streams as they entered areas over Caliphate-held territory. Suddenly, voluble background noise became audible in the War Rooms.

"Turn that down," Terry called.

"Yes, sir," came the reply.

The cacophony lessened to a hubbub. Terry called out: "Comms, what is it? It that the enemy?"

An operator from a different station answered: "Affirmative."

"Doesn't sound encrypted," the woman from the Electronic Warfare Establishment said.

"Why should it be?" Thomas asked with raised eyebrows. "Their computers have given them a probability of us being able to break their ja—"

"I'll be damned," Terry said suddenly as new data resolved in the image. "Squonk, get me SACEUR, now," he demanded.

General Jones's voice overtook the babble of intercepted enemy communications. "Yes, we see it too, general. The autonomous air transports have turned around. Operation Foothold is cancelled."

"Sir," Terry said, "it must go deeper than that. This information is not something that the enemy could have found out through conventional means—"

"That's for the autopsy, general," Jones broke in. "We got bigger things to worry about this morning."

Terry looked back at the display as wave after wave of enemy Blackswans emerged to attack the retreating NATO AATs carrying the Marines. Terry watched in horrified fascination as the PeaceMakers dived down to defend the flesh-and-blood troops.

After two minutes of frenetic activity in the sky and progressive losses on both sides, the remaining Blackswans defeated the last NATO PeaceMakers and chased down the AATs. All but one managed to reach English airspace and the added defence of surface-based missiles and battlefield support lasers. The last AAT was hit and broke up a few hundred metres short of the English coast and safety.

Terry shook his head and silently cursed the enemy yet again. Five months into this damnable war and still NATO lost highly trained and valuable troops while the enemy lost only chunks of metal. He glanced at the others around the control console and noted how the mood of cautious optimism had been crushed in the most brutal way possible: Operation Foothold had lasted mere seconds, and the reasons for its failure were many and varied.

As everyone's attention focused on further waves of enemy ACAs and the impromptu rescue mission to save the Marines on the downed AAT, Terry recalled the private conversation he'd had with Jones the previous Wednesday. Did the failure of Foothold now mean that the Americans would abandon NATO and pull out of the war?

Chapter 41

Crispin Webb stared at General Sir Terry Tidbury and the thought arose in his mind that he might have underestimated the crusty old soldier on the verge of retirement, who suddenly found himself thrust into the spotlight to fight England's last war. Crispin winced as he sipped his hot coffee and observed Sir Terry take a pull on a mug of tea which must have been nearly the same temperature. In addition, he knew Sir Terry had been at his post for fourteen hours straight, and had now come to Ten Downing Street to debrief the boss. Apart from a scouring of stubble around his jowls, he looked like his shift had only just begun.

Dahra Napier sat on an arm of the beige couch in the middle of the room, while the Defence and Foreign Secretaries reposed on the seat cushions. Sir Terry had just described the morning's events in emotionless, brief sentences, but the boss wanted clarification. She asked: "So knowledge of Operation Foothold leaked, yes? Someone spoke to the wrong person and it got back to the enemy. Is that right?"

Sir Terry shook his bald head and said: "No, PM. This is a completely different kind of conflict. The traditional ways your enemy discovers your plans to attack him are simply not available here. One: the enemy's society is completely cut off from the rest of the world, thus there can be no espionage in the historical sense; and two: betrayal is a near impossibility due to the extent of modern technology—our security forces would know if any civilian comms were directed at or went into enemy territory. Even with quantum encryption, an approximate origination point would be identifiable and we would be able to act.

"You see, this is not some finely balanced conflict where, for example, there might be some business of financial incentive in a citizen of one combatant nation to supply secret operational details to the enemy country for personal gain. We are not dealing here with a competing ideology that enjoys any great support in the Home Countries."

Foreign Secretary Charles Blackwood brushed the crease of his immaculately pressed trousers and said: "And I assume you've no reason whatsoever to doubt anyone in the chain of command?"

"None whatsoever."

The defence secretary, Liam Burton, said to Blackwood and the boss: "I spent twelve years in the Royal Corps of Signals. And I can assure you both that all NATO armies have always been united in their antipathy towards the Caliphate. I would not doubt Sir Terry's appraisal."

Crispin watched the boss consider what the men around her had said. Then she asked Sir Terry: "So what went wrong?"

"Squonk?" Terry said, calling the British Army's super AI.

"Yes, Sir Terry?" came the response, seemingly from somewhere above the picture rail.

"Relate and summarise my inquiry based on the complete record of events surrounding the failure and cancellation of Operation Foothold."

"Of course, Sir—"

"And only include the most likely reasons, and don't bother with percentage probability figures," Terry added.

There came a pause and Crispin wondered if it were possible for super artificial intelligence to be offended.

Squonk continued: "Based on intercepted and unencrypted communications gained at the start of Operation Foothold earlier this morning, it is certain that enemy forces knew of its imminent commencement in advance. The deployment of its substantial ACA fleets were at the optimum to destroy the incoming NATO transports, had the operation been allowed to proceed. A complete diagnostic survey of NATO's communications systems was instigated, which took over four hours. This survey has identified a flaw. An SPI in the quantum encryption core allows key, high-level data to be extracted and bypasses the substantial levels of security and cross-checking outside the liquid nitrogen—"

"Wait a minute," Burton interrupted, his face a mask of shock that turned to fury. "You're telling us that NATO's quantum encryption core is unsecure, and you've just happened to notice it, now, today?"

Terry put out a calming hand and said: "It's not as straightforward as Squonk makes it sound."

Burton turned to Napier and said: "Would you like my resignation now, PM, or in ten minutes?"

Crispin watched the boss give the red-faced Burton a kind smile and say: "I don't want your resignation at all because, one: these are not normal times, and two: I'm sure this flaw's been in its position longer than you've been in yours. And there's a thought: how long has this 'flaw' been there?"

"Squonk?" Terry said.

"The liquid-nitrogen core at the centre of NATO's quantum-encryption communications network requires periodic restructuring every twelve to fifteen months. Each core overhaul is put out for tender and is open to all international software providers who have proven track records of delivering super-chilled quantum-encryption software. This SPI was inserted during the quantum programming restructuring and operational update on 16 February 2055."

"'Put out for tender'?" Burton aped, aghast. "We're talking about the communications systems for our militaries, and Squonk makes it sound like we're considering bids to build a fucking primary school. Oh, sorry, PM."

Squonk said: "It is standard practice to seek the most cost-effective solu—"

"Including in matters of national security? I thought that mentality went out with manned aircraft," Burton said.

Charles Blackwood stood abruptly, cast a sympathetic glance at the defence secretary while pulling down a jacket cuff, and said: "I do not appreciate your use of the passive voice, 'was inserted'. By whom was the SPI inserted, eh?"

The British Army's super AI answered: "The Chinese company Norinco Super-Chilled Software Limited."

"Well, that's just perfect," Burton said with a slap of his hand on the couch.

The boss shook her head and seemed to ask no one in particular: "How could they have inserted it without anyone knowing, and how could it have worked for so long?"

Crispin observed the men in the room glance at each other. Only Sir Terry remained immobile, fingers interlinked as he sat forward in his chair.

Sir Terry instructed: "Squonk, speculate answer to PM's last question."

"The genesis of the issue most probably lies in the SPI's ability to remain invisible through repeated, unlimited re-encryption cycles while simultaneously copying, assessing the relevance of, and then passing sensitive data to the parent company."

"So how did you find it today, then?" Burton said with a note of belligerence in his voice.

"Because the complete diagnostic survey involved checking three-point-two trillion Yottabytes of communications data sent since 16 February 2055, and then cross-referencing this comms traffic with all military deployments and actions during the same period, and then running a logical process of elimination until the offending SPI could be established from among a total of forty-two octillion such SPIs."

"Oh, right," Burton said, sounding somewhat mollified.

"But does this issue affect the military forces of all NATO allies?" the boss asked.

"Affirmative," Squonk answered.

A shiver ran down Crispin's spine at the atrocious implications of this security breach.

Burton looked up at Napier and asked in a plaintive tone: "Who's going to tell the Yanks?"

The boss replied: "I'd imagine their Ample Annie super AI is probably telling President Coll a similar thing to what our computers are telling us." Dahra stood, tucked a strand of auburn hair behind an ear, and said: "It doesn't matter, really. We can probably agree that the Chinese have been supplying knowledge of our defences to our enemy even though it was not really necessary given how much more powerful than us they are. What's important is what happens next. Terry?"

Sir Terry said: "With Foothold cancelled and that minor interference removed from the battlefield, the enemy's progress across the European mainland will likely be complete in a few days. Our target now, both militarily and, dare I say, morally, is to try and save as many troops and civilians as possible. Then, only the British Isles and the Scandinavian countries will remain."

Crispin noted how the others seemed to defer to the old soldier's superior knowledge. Even the boss looked at him as an acolyte might gaze on her Svengali. But instead of jealousy, Crispin also stared at Sir Terry with a deeper respect. Pity he was so old.

Chapter 42

Maria Phillips stared at the construction replicator which worked at the vast mountains of rubble that used to be the street on which she lived in East Grinstead. She'd been allowed forty-eight hours' compassionate leave, but any notion of a decent, proper burial for her parents had been quickly dashed. What had her friend Nabou said when they parted the previous afternoon? Something about acceptance being the only option.

The sky shone a bright, early morning blue and the air tasted clean despite the puffs of dust the replicator's work threw up from time to time. The road between the rows of terraced houses was flat and clear of debris. Dotted along it sat containers for body parts and personal belongings that the replicators found while clearing the mess up and beginning reconstruction. The street had two replicators, one at either end. They looked like massive scorpions, only with multiple tails. Each multi-sectioned body gurgled and processed, while its jointed appendages pitched and dipped and scooped and dropped. Dust shifted among the ruins, wood split, and

317

broken glass clattered along masonry and fell into hidden voids. The machines crawled over the destruction like scorpions, too. Eventually, when they finished their work, they would leave reconstructed buildings.

Her friend Nabou had offered to come with her for moral support, but Maria knew this visit would involve more than one painful meeting, and friends were friends, not family. A numbness suffused her limbs. To stand in this place, the street she'd grown up on and played on, brought back so many memories of better times which at once were swamped by feelings of guilt: why should she not suffer when so many others already had?

Her military training fought against the little girl's maudlin despondency that invaded her spirit. She focused and understood that she wished she'd been able to say goodbye to her parents. She recalled the last time, the smile on her mother's face but the sadness in her eyes—

"Hello, sister."

Maria spun around to see Mark, the middle child. She recalled the last time they'd been together, when she pulled him out of his stupid game. Now, he stood with his head tilted to one side and a half-sneer on his pretty face. "Hello, brother," she answered. With a nod at the pile of rubble, she asked: "Did you get your Bounty before the Spider demolished the house?"

"The cremation isn't until nine o'clock. Why are you here so early?"

She ignored his question, walked towards him, and asked: "Tell me what happened?"

His thin chest shrugged and he replied: "I told you when I called you. Do you not believe me?"

She reached him, tried to see beyond his blue eyes, and said: "We are both very upset. I will never stop missing them. Could you tell me once more?"

318

He seemed to consider this and relax. He said: "Come on, have you eaten?"

"Not for a while."

He turned to go and she followed. He said: "There is a café close to the high street where the food isn't completely vile."

Fifteen minutes later, Maria stared into the dirty white porcelain mug at the remaining tea, listening to the brother with whom she'd usually fought and who, she now realised, she barely knew at all.

He picked at the crumbs on his plate left over from the bacon sandwich and alternated his glance from his plate to the wrecked street outside, where a Spider had almost flattened the council offices opposite the café. He concluded: "Whether or not I'd heard them and left the Universe sooner makes no difference, except to me, of course. I can imagine Mum probably had to drag Dad away from the door and out of the house. If I close my eyes and concentrate, it's easy to picture them worrying about me. They thought I would be killed. They didn't for a minute think it would be the other way around."

Maria had also turned her gaze to the street. Memories flooded her mind, but these were joined by a sense of inevitability: the black humour of her basic training in the Army and the injuries and bodies she'd already come into contact with on the battlefield made those memories feel as though they belonged to someone else.

However much of it was left to them, the future remained. She asked her brother: "What happens next?"

He looked confused and answered: "The cremation. Although there won't be many mourners there. Some of Mum and Dad's friends were also killed, but Auntie Tasha said she'd be there. Pity Martin couldn't get compassionate leave, bloody Army."

Maria sighed and said: "I meant with you. I'm going back to my regiment this afternoon. What about you?"

Mark hesitated and Maria felt anger rise inside her. She didn't blame Mark for their parents' deaths; she believed his story because records of the attacks that night backed him up. She readied herself to hold on to her temper when the inevitable answer came.

He looked her in the eye for the first time since they'd entered the café and said: "I've joined up."

Her anger evaporated, replaced with shock. "The British Army?" she asked in disbelief.

Mark's face creased in uncertainty, a look Maria had never seen on her older brother before. "Yeah, that's right," he mumbled.

"How?" she asked, struggling to keep the incredulity from her voice.

"I dunno. Well, you know, afterwards. After I told Martin and you and the family and friends, and they told me how many of them had been killed as well that night... I dunno."

"Mark, I did not expect to hear th—"

"I was walking around, you know? Sort of lost, I suppose. And this guy comes up to me; about Martin's age, more or less. Says his name is Simon. And we chat. I tell him about the Universes and how I was going to get a nice Bounty before the Spider came along. And he says something like that happened to him. He lost his family in the attacks four weeks earlier. And then he says the Army is looking for guys like me. So, I went with him to help. We helped local people, getting possessions back to those that owned them, doing what we could, you know. Me and Simon talked a lot—"

"Sounds all right," Maria said.

"And I mean a lot. For hours and hours. And helping other people helped me get over losing Mum and Dad, somehow. I don't know if that makes sense. You know, I told him about the problems you and I had and everything. Hope you don't mind."

Maria said: "That's okay."

"Oh, thanks," he replied.

Another wave of shock went through Maria: her brother had never sought her approval for anything. Whatever he and Simon had done, it had changed Mark. Her shock gradually gave way to a different emotion.

Her brother said: "Anyway, time's getting on and we have to go and say our goodbyes to Mum and Dad." He stood.

"Yes, yes we do," Maria said, her face becoming heavy with a sudden need to weep. She also rose.

"Oh, I forgot," Mark said, fumbling in the pocket of his jeans. He took a lump of grey, weathered wood, a few centimetres long and burned on one side, in the shape of a toe or a claw. He stuck out his hand to give it to his sister.

"What's that?" she asked.

"Billy," he answered. "Well, one of his toes the construction replicator found. I know you loved that daft wooden rabbit sitting on the chimneystack. And if a rabbit's foot is supposed to be lucky, I reckon maybe a toe will help you while you're out there helping the soldiers."

Maria took the piece of wood and stared at it for a moment. She looked at Mark but couldn't speak.

Mark gave her a sheepish look and said: "Actually it was Simon's idea, you know. Sorry."

Maria grasped Billy's singed toe so tightly she thought she might crush it. She looked down and blinked back the tears in her eyes.

Chapter 43

Dahra Napier slapped the top of the marble mantle above the fireplace in the living room in the spacious Ten Downing Street flat. She turned to face David Perkins, head of MI5, and hissed: "You told the COBRA meeting our contact in Beijing had been turned and their information was unreliable. And now you tell me they warned us about that flaw in the Chinese software that left all of our communications exposed?"

Perkins sniffed in disdain and replied: "With respect, PM, the contact followed the pre-agreed protocol with which we train all of our operatives in the event the host state turns them. Thereafter, I made discreet inquiries at the ambassador's residency to confirm the contact's unreliability and, by the way, attempted to find a replacement."

"I don't care about your efforts to find a replacement. I want to know about this contact that was supposedly turned."

"There's no 'supposedly' about it."

"Does he or she have a name?"

323

"Several, I should expect."

Dahra stepped closer to the man, liking him a little less, and said: "Don't be facetious with me, Mr Perkins."

His shoulders sagged and he replied: "I am not, PM. This is subterfuge. We turn one of theirs, they turn one of ours. We try to get an edge by supplying as much false information while trying to gain as much genuine information that we can. We win some, we lose some."

A pain began in the bone next to Dahra's right eye. She said: "Very well. Clearly I am not being plain enough. Please tell me whatever else this contact has reported, reports, and will report. Do you understand, Mr Perkins?"

"Yes, PM."

"Thank you. Now, just to clarify: the only reason you did not disseminate this information, which transpired to be vital to our defence, was solely because you deemed it unreliable, and you were mistaken, yes?"

With some satisfaction, Dahra observed the man's face drop as he realised the trouble he was in. He said: "It was standard protocol, PM. If my department briefed you on every titbit of information we get, you'd have time to consider nothing else."

"I want to know everything that contact reports, understood?"

"Perfectly."

"Good. You are excused."

Perkins tilted his head in acknowledgement of the dismissal. Dahra watched him slink to the door, but when he reached it, he turned and said: "I would just like to point out that to be turned like that, the contact would have had to endure substantial torture, and will almost certainly be killed when this war is over."

Before she could answer, he opened the door and left. At once, her aide Crispin Webb appeared and held the door to show in Aiden Hicks, Liam Burton and Charles Blackwood. Monica followed and steered around the others with her usual grace. Dahra glanced at her and mouthed 'Thank you' as she proceeded to organise drinks.

Dahra said: "Welcome, everyone, take a seat. I assume no one's changed their minds about the meeting this morning and we should in fact not declare war on China, correct?"

Nervous smiles creased the faces of the ministers whom she'd invited to the call that would shortly take place. Foreign Secretary Charles Blackwood replied: "With the greatest respect, PM, I do believe our Armed Forces might be irredeemably insulted if you were to give them such an easy objective."

"I'll second that," Liam added.

Dahra wished she could have Terry with her, but he was needed at the War Rooms as the situation on the mainland became more critical. She pushed the thought aside as Monica arrived on her right with a glass of chilled white wine.

A few minutes later, with the men attended to with scotch, brandy and red wine, she said: "This is going to be a difficult conversation, gentlemen. If you think at any time that I have gone too far, I would like you to signal this by coughing loudly enough to break into it. All right?"

The plump home secretary, Aiden Hicks, said: "As you wish, PM. The way things are, I don't think there's much to be gained making it harder than it has to be."

Dahra looked at him with an eyebrow raised.

He backtracked: "Of course, totally up to you."

She glanced at Crispin and nodded.

Crispin said: "Going through now... Waiting for a response."

The large screen above the fireplace came to life with an image of a portcullis.

The pause lengthened.

Dahra looked back over her shoulder to Crispin and asked: "Is she actually available?"

"Yes, boss," her aide replied. "She does not have any other comms business going on right now."

Dahra mused, "Do you think she does this deliberately?"

Before anyone could speak, an image of the US president flashed onto the screen, sitting behind—and seemingly dwarfed by—the Resolute desk. "Hi Dahra. How are you doing?"

"As well as can be expected in the circumstances, thank—"

"Sure, sure."

Dahra drew in a careful breath. "Madelyn, I need to ask you for your assurance that the United States will not withdraw from NATO and its current military operations. The support your exemplary armed forces have provided to date, and indeed the sacrifices they have made, have—"

"Been a total waste of time, money and lives, Dahra," Coll interrupted.

"Hardly," Dahra responded, shocked that her counterpart could be so impolite. "I would like to remind you that we are not quite finished yet."

"Yes, you are," Coll said with a shake of her head. "Listen, Dahra, I'm real sorry to be the one to break it to you, but NATO and Europe have reached the endgame. And I—and, by the way, most of Congress—don't see the sense in sending more troops to support a war whose outcome is clear. If Operation Foothold could've secured some kind of base from which we might have launched counterattacks at some point when we—"

"And you know why Foothold failed, don't you?"

"Yes, Ample Annie found the same problem your people found."

"How could you let that happen?" Dahra asked in disgust, determined to put Coll on the backfoot.

"What?"

"How could the US allow such a devastating problem to go undetected for so many years?" Dahra disregarded the objective unfairness of the question; anger boiled inside her and now she'd release it.

Coll shook her head but fell into the trap anyway. She said: "Because, duh, Chinese companies are cheaper. Because they've always been cheaper—"

"And because of that, they knew every step we planned and sent that information to our enemies."

"I don't recall puny, little England offering to put up more money so NATO could have sourced this software in a member country."

"But because of this, you Americans are now going to abandon Europe—"

"Because the war is over," Coll yelled. "We can fix this problem, but what's the point? Europe is still finished. And I'm bringing those Marines and all other troops home as soon as Congress approves it."

Dahra spat: "You and all those in Congress are cowards—" one of the men behind her coughed loudly but she ignored it. "And I sincerely hope that once the Third Caliph has finished with us, he does not turn his attention to you. After all, it looks as though his weapons can reach as far as continental America."

Coll leaned forward and sneered: "All the more reason for us to consolidate and get our people back ASAP. If I were you, I'd seriously consider his latest offer to surrender—"

Dahra spun around and drew a thumb across her throat in indication. Crispin's eye twitched, he nodded, and she turned back to see the portcullis placeholder image. She heaved in a deep breath and muttered: "That could've gone better."

"I did cough, you know," Charles offered.

Dahra glanced at Monica, in conversation with Crispin. Eventually, Crispin gave Monica a withering look and went to the drinks' cabinet. Dahra addressed her other colleagues: "Can you all use diplomatic channels to bring the temperature down on this?"

Charles nodded at Liam and said: "We'll start at once, PM."

Liam frowned and said: "She sounded pretty sure of what she wants."

Aiden's jacket stretched over his plump arms when he leaned forward and said: "I think the priority for now is that we keep the convoys that have already left America on track."

Crispin handed Dahra a glass that held a strong gin and tonic.

Charles said: "I'm not sure she could turn them around mid-Atlantic even if she wanted to, could she?"

Dahra sipped her drink and said: "She probably thinks the war will be over before they arrive."

Aiden shivered and said: "My God, is the situation really that bad? My PPS said that the failure of Foothold would increase pressure on us to surrender and 'save any unnecessary loss of life', and I told her to dismiss any notion of us taking that route. But I thought we still have at least some time, don't we?"

"Perhaps," Dahra said. "You know how this blasted super artificial intelligence—which doesn't seem to be all that super to me—changes its mind whenever you ask it for a forecast. Sometimes it says a couple of days if this or that happens, other times it can give us longer if we stop defending that French town or German city a little sooner."

Aiden said: "I don't think we could be doing more. Southern England has filled up with refugees from the whole continent. Thank God for the water and food replicators; I've no idea how we'd keep them fed otherwise."

Liam said: "Not to mention what's left of their militaries. We've got so many leftovers from all of them we're having to requisition commercial premises and reactivate bases that have been shut for decades."

Charles frowned and asked: "They didn't make the ultimate sacrifice, then?"

The defence secretary scoffed and said: "Specialists who were behind the lines by some way... A lot of them not very fit, either." He paused, stared into the bronze scotch in his glass and added: "All the frontline troops have been blasted to pieces or burnt to a crisp, that's for sure."

"Gentlemen," Dahra decided to conclude, "thank you for coming along. At least you have had a glimpse of the situation at the head of the governments. I will leave it to your substantial abilities to see what can be done behind the scenes to keep the US in NATO until the conclusion is beyond any doubt. Once Europe is finished, I don't think any of us will begrudge the Americans doing all they can to look after themselves."

She sipped her drink. The kick from the gin opened a door to an escape, a place where numbness made everything easier to cope with. Exhaustion followed the kick. She steeled herself and said: "We will speak soon, I'm sure. Good luck for now."

Chapter 44

23.46 Thursday 13 July 2062

General Sir Terry Tidbury squeezed his eyes shut and then opened them and tried to take in the wealth of information above the main display console in the War Rooms. "This is turning into a rout," he muttered.

"Sir," called a flaxen-haired operator with a light but nervous voice, "SACEUR is requesting."

"Put him through," Terry urged in exasperation.

"Good evening, general," came Jones's laid-back American accent. "I guess you can see what is happening here."

"Yes, sir," Terry replied. "Recommend you evac SHAPE at your earliest convenience."

"Negative on that, general," came the response. "That would be premature right now—"

"Negative on that, general," Terry broke in, aping SACEUR's idiom. "The SHF burners are revealing an overwhelming superiority of enemy arms. You must commence evacuation. I think I may be able to offer you a bench in the corner of my office, sir."

Terry breathed in relief when he heard a chuckle. But Jones insisted: "Let's see how the next half an hour pans out. I will let my non-essential staff go now, general. I will be in touch in due course. SACEUR out."

"Christ alive, Simms," Terry said to his adjutant next to him.

"Sir Terry, some of the US Marines stood down from Foothold are standing by at RAF Fairford. I imagine they are champing at the bit to get SACEUR out about now."

"Indeed, but I can hardly countermand a five-star American general."

"Might I suggest getting them in the air purely as a defensive response to a potential enemy incursion?"

Terry nodded in appreciation of Simms's subtlety. "Yes, you may. Please do so."

"Very good."

"Squonk?" Terry called. "Are there any further reserves we can activate to defend SHAPE?"

"Negative. Existing resources are being continually reassigned as new data becomes available."

"For example?" Terry asked.

"Repair-material transports at the Delta Works have been reassigned south to evacuate civilians from points central and east of Ghent. The remaining twenty-three wings of laser-armed PeaceMakers have been redeployed to various altitudes over the Cherbourg Peninsula to defend retreating elements of Army Group West..."

Terry stared at the display as the British Army's super AI carried on. When it finished listing the reassignments, Terry asked: "What's the weather forecast for the Channel and North Sea?"

"The current low-pressure area is deepening. Wind strength and precipitation are increasing," Squonk answered.

Terry gave Simms a worried look and said: "If the weather deteriorates much further over the next few hours, it will be the worse for us than for the enemy."

Suddenly, a red oblong materialised and flashed high up in the display. The operative at the NATO comms station announced: "Detecting more flights of enemy ACAs emerging from jammed areas into the SHF burner corridors."

Terry said: "Squonk, how many?"

"Over one thousand ACAs and increasing. Attack patterns indicate the enemy is beginning its final assault."

"Final?" Terry queried.

"To expel the remaining NATO forces from mainland Europe."

Terry folded his arms to hide his mounting frustration. In the holographic display in front of him, hundreds more Blackswans and Lapwings swarmed down from higher altitudes into the battlespace, pirouetting and spinning and diving through space that represented thousands of metres to attack the defending PeaceMakers.

"Squonk, formulate a plan to evacuate SACEUR as expeditiously as possible."

A second later, Squonk answered: "Formulated."

"Comms," Terry instructed, "get me General Jones, now."

"Aye, sir."

Terry scrutinised the display as the enemy's Blackswans and Lapwings destroyed NATO's PeaceMakers and then the SkyWatchers.

The operator said: "You're through, Sir Terry."

"SACEUR?"

"Yes, general?" came Jones's laconic voice.

"Our front is collapsing, sir. The computers show that the enemy will be at your position in less than an hour."

333

"Yes, I can see that. Well, that bench in your office is starting to sound like it might not be too uncomfortable."

Terry smiled for the first time that evening. He said: "Thank you, sir. See you soon."

"Jones out," SACEUR said.

"Squonk? Activate the Marine transports to recover SACEUR and his remaining staff."

"Affirmative," Squonk replied.

Terry glanced at Simms with a satisfied smile.

Simms's thin eyebrows came together in a frown and he said: "Sir Terry, SACEUR appears to have ordered the super AI to prioritise the recovery of subordinate units over his own evacuation."

"No," Terry said, "he can't do that."

Simms said: "He has."

"Squonk, give recovery priority to SACEUR."

"Sir Terry," Simms said: "General Jones is relying on the Marines. He's directed the super AIs to devote the defences to allowing the evacuation of frontline troops."

Terry shook his head and instructed: "Enlarge and show me the Marines."

The image zoomed and Simms said: "They have their own small and very fast extraction autonomous air transports—"

"Yes," Terry broke in, "I was given a ride in one last year. Six-man flying coffins if you ask me."

"We're losing them," Simms said as part of the display flickered.

"Christ, what's the forecast? I didn't think the air pressure could drop so low over the North Sea."

Simms shook his head and said: "They are not going to outrun Blackswans."

"Well, if we can't see them inside that low pressure, then presumably neither can the enemy."

Simms answered: "With respect, Sir Terry, it is not difficult for the enemy's super AI to work out where the extraction AATs are heading."

Terry looked up at his adjutant, said: "Fair comment," and wondered if Simms pointing out such an obvious conclusion did not evidence his own exhaustion. He added: "The enemy can extrapolate the most likely courses once inside the bad weather. Law of averages says they'll be bound to get some of the Marines."

"It will," Simms agreed. "And the bad weather might allow us to get a few more troops off."

"Pity the refugee boats trying to get across."

Squonk said: "The enemy is constantly introducing further ACAs into the battlespace. Do you wish to authorise the release of the twenty emergency reserve wings of PeaceMakers in northern England?"

Terry caught Simms's look and knew that his adjutant didn't envy him. Terry did not want to decide who lived and who died inside the cauldron of metal, missile and laser in the inclement weather above France and the English Channel. He said: "Squonk, speculate: how many lives will releasing the emergency reserves save?"

"The battlespace is currently too dynamic to sustain a resp—"

"Not good enough," Terry shouted. "I repeat: speculate."

"Between eleven and two hundred."

"And then the British Isles will be defenceless, correct?"

"Apart from land-based assets, affirmative."

"When and how can those PeaceMakers be replenished?"

"Materials are available for ten wings that can be assembled in eight hours after unloading. Convoy SE–21 is carrying two hundred units and sufficient Pulsar Mark Three offensive laser—"

"Speculate," Terry hissed, furious at the computer's pedantry at such a time. "If I commit the last of our PeaceMakers now, will the enemy press his tactical advantage knowing that the British Isles have no aircover?"

"Unlikely."

Terry said: "Assume the enemy knows that we will have committed the last of our aircover. What then?"

"Slightly probable."

Simms said: "Sir Terry, the enemy cannot know that we will have deployed the last of our PeaceMakers."

Terry recalled the debacle with the Chinese software buried inside NATO's comms equipment like a tiny, relentless parasite. He gave Simms a hard stare and replied: "The enemy knows everything, trust me. Squonk? Do not deploy the emergency reserve wings of PeaceMakers."

"Confirmed."

"Sir," called the operator at the NATO comms station, "SAC—"

"Put him on," Terry barked.

Jones's voice spoke throughout the room: "General? We've got Marines inbound, but there's an awful lot of civilians who are going to be left behind."

Terry wanted to sympathise but he could see time running out in the numbers in the display in front of him. He just said: "Safe travels, SACEUR, we're waiting for you here."

"SACEUR out."

"Squonk? I want to know the progress of those Marines; every step, got that?"

"Affirmative."

Terry stared at the vast complexity of the holographic image that confronted him. From low Earth orbit to ground level; from Amsterdam to Brest and all across the English

Channel, a million life-and-death dramas played out in the innumerable lines of light that danced and twirled in front of him.

Simms asked: "Tea, Sir Terry?"

Terry shook his head and said: "Better make it a brandy."

Chapter 45

00.21 Friday 14 July 2062

Rory Moore ran across the uneven ground as fast as he could towards the autonomous air transports. The night vision his Squitch provided seemed to be playing up; he'd already fallen down once, and he was not alone: among the hundred or more troops around him, all legging it in the same direction, he noticed the occasional one fall down, and no one was shooting at them—yet.

"Get a fucking move on, lad!" yelled Sergeant Heaton from the safety of one of the AATs waiting to fly them back to Blighty. "This front's got more holes than a fucking cheese grater."

Rory staggered again when his foot landed in a depression his night vision hadn't shown. "Just keep my seat warm, you muppet," he hissed. The time didn't worry him, for the AAT sat squat and ugly a mere twenty metres away, and the base commander had declared the evacuation of the transit base only when the outcome was beyond any doubt.

In front of him, a running figure stumbled and fell headlong. Rory silently thanked his good fortune because but for that soldier, Rory would have surely tumbled over instead. He ran past and then stopped, guilt getting the better of him. He trotted back to the depression in the sandy earth.

"That's one of my corporals. Give her a kick, will you?" Heaton said in Rory's ear.

The display in Rory's vision told him the corporal's name. He reached down and said: "Come on, Sara."

She grasped his forearm and he pulled. "Thanks, sarge—ah, fuck," she cursed before falling back to the ground.

"What's up?"

"Ankle's all bent up, sarge. Sorry, sarge."

"Are you getting this, Heaton?"

"Yeah, she's normally a tough little cookie."

"Piss off, sarge," Sara said. Then: "I meant my sarge, sarge. Not you, sarge, obviously."

Rory smiled.

Then his Squitch announced: "Danger: Caliphate Lapwings approaching from the east. Board the AAT as soon as possible."

"What the f—"

Heaton shouted in his ear: "A wing of the bastards just peeled off the main body heading towards Calais and Dunkirk. Step on it."

Rory looked down at Sara. "You are going to owe me a serious beer for this. Drop your weapon and kit." Without ceremony, he crouched, pulled her up, and threw her over his shoulders. He cursed; she weighed more than he'd appreciated when seeing her on the ground in night-vision green light.

"Sorry, sarge," she said.

"Fuck," Rory muttered as he began stomping back to the AAT. Relief that the door was just a few metres away aided his effort. Flashes of bright light suddenly flashed from the roof of the AAT as it fired its missiles. In a few more steps, Rory collapsed into the doorway as other hands took the weight of the corporal off him.

His Squitch adjusted the night-vision levels to compensate for the ambient light, and as he climbed into the lit interior his vision returned to normal.

His Squitch instructed: "Please secure yourself. The journey will involve mild turbulence."

He scrabbled on the metal floor to clear the entrance. He could hear shouts and curses near and far, but the gentle hum of the engines told him those outside had run out of time. A last soldier threw himself in as the metal door slid up smartly. There came a desperate thump outside—an unlucky squaddie—and he felt the AAT rise.

Two hands grabbed his armpits and pulled him to the side of the fuselage. "Come on, shit for brains," Heaton said.

Rory found himself in a seat wondering what had happened to his Pickup. Heaton pulled the straps over his shoulders and clipped him in before seating in his own seat and securing himself. The AAT climbed and accelerated, and Rory's stomach fell. The changing air pressure hurt his ears and he told himself it should not take long to get across the Channel.

His Squitch announced: "This autonomous air transport has been targeted by enemy ACAs. Stand by for turbulence."

"Oh joy," Rory said, before clenching his entire body from his teeth to his buttocks as the AAT first climbed and dropped like a brick while rolling. He looked up when he heard a terrified shriek and saw the corporal called Sara fall from her seat. She dangled in space for a moment, one hand entwined with one of her straps, before another sudden jolt freed her. She fell the length of the fuselage past all of them and smashed head first into the aft bulkhead.

Over the next few minutes, Rory stared as the acrobatics required to prevent the enemy destroying the AAT meant Sara's body flopped and flailed among all of the other passengers, doing further physical damage to the surviving soldiers and untold psychological damage.

When out of danger, the AAT levelled and flew on a straight heading. For the rest of the journey back to England, Rory stared at Sara's body as it lay crumpled and twisted against the forward bulkhead. She'd seemed nice. She'd been quite pretty. He'd liked the lightness in her voice. And now she was gone forever. Just laying there, a carcass like so many other NATO soldiers.

At length, his ears popped again as the aircraft descended. It bumped when it landed. The door slid upwards to reveal darkness outside. As those who were physically able alighted, he stole one last glance at Sara's body and asked himself for the thousandth time when it would be his turn.

"Goodbye, Sara," he whispered as he heaved his tired and aching body off the AAT and breathed in the air at RAF Fairford. Rory hated the war.

"Hold up, there, Sergeant Moore," Sergeant Heaton called from the AAT.

Rory ignored him and strode on and away from the aircraft, towards the building his Squitch indicated. "At least Europe is finally finished," he muttered to himself, staring at the ground. "If any of those idiots in charge have a brain in their fucking heads, we'll surrender and that will be that... Christ, I am so fucking tired."

Chapter 46

Pip stepped out of the autonomous air transport and onto English soil for the first time in six weeks that had, against her furthest expectations, been harder than the months since February. The night air at RAF Odiham clung humid and close to her dirty skin. She followed the other troops disembarking as they made their way to the hangar that promised fresh food and tea. Martin was somewhere on the same transport, in the other ranks' section, not the officers', but exhaustion drove her on and set her priorities as food and tea above a handsome smile.

She recalled asking for her commission as an officer decades ago in February. She closed her eyes and could smell the aroma of Colonel Doyle's elegant office and see him again stroking his full moustache with a thumb and forefinger as he told her and Rory that the entire regiment were proud of what the two Royal Engineers had achieved in battling the enemy and escaping from behind the lines on *HMS Spiteful*.

Then he awarded her the commission and she'd had twenty-four hours' leave followed by three weeks' officer

343

training.   Before the war, officer training had lasted eight weeks, but they told her there wasn't so much time anymore.

And now that felt so very long ago.   Images of all the places she'd seen since what they called the Tense Spring had ended so abruptly at the beginning of June fell through her mind's eye like a pack of playing cards sprung from the shuffler's fingers.   At the start, she'd made brief digital notes on the towns in southern France through which NATO forces retreated.   She wanted to remember them.   But that allure waned soon enough.   Wrecked buildings and vehicles littered the endless streets and highways that linked one town to another.   Modern civilian infrastructure that allowed the people to move and the towns to function lay broken in innumerable places.   Even the castles, perched high and overlooking valleys and rivers they'd guarded for centuries, seemed to know, and appeared not majestic but forlorn and dilapidated.

The indelible images, those that stayed in her mind and which jumped out at unexpected moments, were the eyes.   She had looked into so many different eyes in those weeks, yet it seemed she could recall and place each individual owner.   Old women pulled net curtains aside and stared out in misery and teens stole glances from skylights at the retreating soldiers, not thinking at least one of those soldiers might be looking up.

Civilians' reasons for not moving were as varied as humanity itself.   Families chose to remain together because elderly relatives could not move; parents stayed behind having given their children all of their wealth to buy passage on God-knows-what transport, making some vague promise to follow on later, before it was too late; yet others, mostly women with small children, had been abandoned to face the future alone. Still more observed the near-total chaos of civilian evacuation and the overwhelmed 'transit centres', and elected to stay put, deeming fleeing to be the greater danger.

And now, because of her uniform, she trod on England's barren soil once again, having left all of those poor souls behind. And not only the civilians. Of course, the old argument that anyone who joined their country's armed forces should be prepared for the worst still had a kernel of validity, but Pip's militaristic acceptance of fate and gallows humour was tempered for those who'd volunteered. More eyes invaded her memory: Mia, the small, young girl with long lashes and slightly crooked teeth; always talking about her boyfriend, until one contact when shrapnel from an exploding Spider sliced her head off as cleanly as a guillotine. Or Dave, the line manager from a 3-D ultra-graphene moulding firm; a lumbering brute with gentle eyes that never quite hid his fear of battle. And with some justification as only twenty-four hours earlier, Pip had to hold him and watch the life bleed from his eyes as the blood bled from more than fifty separate lacerations to his body that the GenoFluid pack could not manage. The images of other brothers- and sisters-in-arms came to her in the darkness of the airfield. She asked herself how she would ever sleep peacefully again.

At last she smiled when the faces of her old squad came to her mind. She used to enjoy joking about Operation Certain Death. Now the joke had lost its humour—if it even had any to begin with—after she'd looked into so many eyes whose owners knew that certain death had been precisely their fate. Perhaps she would call Rory and talk to a friend. But only when she had eaten something and rested. She finally reached the hangar and the noise of other people and the smell of good food.

Chapter 47

11.07 Sunday 16 July 2062

Serena Rizzi stole a glance down at her only friend, Liliana, who looked numb. At least she only had to hold herself together for half an hour or so. Serena concentrated and reminded herself that today was the one hundred and forty-second day since she and Liliana had been taken from Italy on the Caliphate transport. In a dim and distant past, she recalled a life working as a trainee nurse in a hospital in her native Italy. Then, so long ago, her only desire had been to help people and save lives. Now, most of her waking hours focused on a single objective: to stay alive long enough to kill.

She and Liliana stood at the back of the family. As the women were *'Abd*, servants of the house, they at least had the benefit of invisibility during important occasions like this. The men of the family stood in the front; the women behind them. The Third Caliph was about to address the entire Caliphate with an important announcement. This would be made in the traditional manner, via loudspeakers in millions of local mosques throughout his domain. Serena kept the sardonic look from her face as she wondered why the exalted Caliph did not simply speak into their heads, which the implants she and Liliana—and certainly every other *'Abd*—had, allowed.

She looked at the backs of the rest of the family. The father was Badr Shakir al-Sayyab, a heavy-set, bald, middle-aged man whom she and Liliana only saw from time to time, and whom they were not allowed to address, unless he gave them permission. However, when they had been introduced to him, Serena felt at once that Badr was not a mischievous man; he did not seek or gain pleasure from the discomfort and pain of others.

Ahmad, however, certainly did. A stiff, whitehaired and thin man with a gravelly voice, Ahmad had bought them during a 'spoils of war' auction at a market in a desert town whose name she never found out. If Ahmad only could, Serena felt certain he would rape both her and Liliana. So far, the worst he had done was to keep them both hungry by ensuring there was little food left at the end of each day. On the other hand, Serena appreciated that Ahmad had purchased both of them together, instead of separating them, so Serena could take some care of Liliana.

The Third Caliph should have begun at the beginning of the hour, but he was late. Serena didn't care. Her view over the heads in front of her led out to the spacious courtyard. Shaded colonnades ran around three of the four sides, and the columns themselves featured detailed lattices of many shapes that repeated over and over. In the open space of the courtyard, orange trees reached skywards with gnarled branches. Little brown birds hopped about and chattered, and cool stone benches surrounded a fountain from which water trickled. Compared to that which Serena and Liliana had endured, the courtyard represented a place of calm safety, and the murderous Third Caliph could take as long as he wanted.

As far as Serena had been able to ascertain, the family had some standing in the city. The house seemed large although comparable to others along the broad boulevard outside. Serena had taken in every detail since she and Liliana arrived nine days earlier. Many of the ornaments dotted on the whitewashed stone ledges and elegant mahogany sideboards could have had personal or religious significance, but for both of them the priority was not to break the rules.

Ahmed warned them daily that any infraction meant punishment, and that he had the power of life and death over them. Both women did not need to be reminded that the implants in their bodies could be directed to kill them on the whim of whoever controlled the implant. In the early hours and despite exhaustion, Serena and Liliana had discussed the risk and arrived at the conclusion that nothing mattered. Someone could listen to their talks, and, who knew, perhaps even read their minds with these implants? Thus, nothing held any significance. Serena herself felt immeasurably relieved their privacy had been so completely invaded, for it meant she kept her true feelings to herself. She could never tell Liliana of what she had resolved to try to do, if only she could live long enough.

There came a mechanical hiss in the air and Serena's attention returned to the sheer bright sunlight that bathed the courtyard. Ahead, one of the robed men of the family wagged a finger at a child standing next to him. This made Serena glance down at Liliana. Her round eyes stared ahead, her expression still numb. Good.

A fanfare sounded. Serena wondered if the Third Caliph's voice would be transmitted directly into her head, as had been the case when she was abducted in Italy. The fanfare whined to a close. Silence. A wasp darted over the heads of those waiting patiently. A voice announced something through distant metallic speakers. Relief flooded Serena when she did not hear the English translation in her head, but Italian words materialised in her line of sight, just above the walls of the courtyard: "Citizens of the New Persian Caliphate! Stand for our illustrious leader, the merciful Third Caliph!"

Silence.

A new voice came through the speakers. While he spoke, Serena read the words as they resolved in her vision, even if she closed her eyes. But she listened to the fountain and stared longingly at the ripening oranges.

"Citizens of our great Caliphate! I speak to you from the Palace of the Prophets in Tehran. I address you today to give you wonderful and uplifting news. For today, the fighting in Europe is at an end."

Cheers rose up and carried on the hot air. Serena heard distant applause ripple across the sky like an impotent rumble of thunder.

The Third Caliph went on: "The Christian infidel is crushed. The historical wrongs of the Crusades have been corrected. The heinous injustice that took place in the year of Mohammed 1062 has been avenged. Our glorious warriors have subdued the entire European landmass. And the territory gained and now controlled by our honourable and faithful warriors is from this moment subservient to the needs of our glorious Caliphate.

"To mark this momentous achievement that hundreds of future generations will rejoice for millennia hence, there shall be a celebration. Four days from now falls the Prophet's birthday. On that day, let every house, every street, every village, every town and every city exult in the success of our brave warriors, who with Allah's mercy have shown the infidel the error of his ways. And Allah's mercy is truly limitless. As the Qur'an says: 'Limitless is the Lord in His mercy'.

"Therefore, in observance of Allah's mercy and in magnanimity and gratitude for this historic victory, I make these promises to every citizen of our blessed Caliphate and to show the world that Allah is indeed merciful. First: despite their perfidious aid to the infidel, all attacks on the Nordic countries shall cease at once. Second: those little islands are once again urged to surrender. Their situation is clearly now beyond salvation. They must accept the benevolence of Allah's mercy. Third: those countries who afforded assistance to the infidel must now question the wisdom of their actions. It may be that Allah will deem a punishment to be necessary.

"But today, citizens of our glorious Caliphate, today you may consider that a great victory has been achieved, the greatest since Allah in his wisdom brought all Muslims together and forged our solidarity."

Silence.

Serena wondered if the archfiend had finished or if it was merely another pause for dramatic effect. Suddenly, the fanfare began again. In front of her, the family members turned and spoke to each other, heads nodding while faces smiled. Serena looked for the wasp but could not see it. She stole a glance at Liliana. Yes, Liliana knew it was time to return to the house, to the chores and labour and performing the most menial tasks until late into the evening with barely a promise of watered-down, leftover *Shorba* lentil soup to ease the hunger.

Serena did not mind. Every pang only added to the hatred, a condensed ball of fire that burned inside her as fierce as any sun. Her only concern was to live long enough so that she would be able to direct and use her hatred. One of these men would pay, perhaps not one of the five who had so far raped her, but one day, one man would suffer a similar pain.

Chapter 48

Terry turned away from the panoramic window overlooking the English Channel and said: "Accept."

The face of Lieutenant-General Studs Stevens of the USAF appeared on the screen and said: "I guess I should congratulate you on your promotion, field marshal."

Terry gave a mirthless chuckle and replied: "It's meaningless and we both know it, Suds." He walked to the highbacked leather chair and collected his snifter of brandy from the occasional table next to it. He lifted the glass and said: "I bet you're glad you're not here. Cheers."

Stevens smiled and held up his coffee cup. He said: "It's still a little early here, but cheers."

"Although I was surprised I was asked. I expected another general from the US Army to be appointed SACEUR. I'm sorry we lost Jones."

"Me too," Stevens said. "Damn Marines screwed it up real good."

"The weather worsened. It wasn't their fault," Terry countered.

"Maybe," Stevens conceded.

"Did you hear the announcement?"

"Uh-huh," Stevens replied. "Goddamn son of a bitch knows how to play to the gallery."

Terry shrugged and said: "I don't really care what the rest of the world thinks about him or what he's done."

"They're glad the fighting is almost over."

"They think he's going to stop with Europe?"

Stevens frowned, the scar above his right eye deepening. "You don't?"

"NATO was just the live-fire exercise, Suds. Once he's finished with Europe, he's got three million battle-hardened and bloodthirsty warriors, and a few million lethal ACAs, looking for something—or someone—to beat up. You think they're just going to go home? Mark my words: the little shit has got his eye on global domination."

"No way," Stevens said in dismissiveness. "India alone would lead to a massive nuclear exchange."

"He'll take them all on: India, Russia, and then China. Those fools have no idea of the monster they've unleashed."

"I don't think that's gonna happen, Earl."

Terry sighed and said: "I don't care. Not for a future I won't see."

"How is it over there? There's a ton of diplomatic pressure—"

"Not going to happen, no way. Don't even ask."

"Okay, okay," Stevens said in placation.

"You need to remember his announcement was just another steaming pile of bullshit. Firstly, it's not over. Paris, Berlin and Warsaw are underground and in contact. There's a big, fat area around Hamburg that's still open. Secondly, the British Isles are not 'little islands'. What I wish is that your Flake-in-Chief would not withdraw your military's support."

"You've still got the support."

"Really? What's the latest?"

"The convoys already at sea will not be turned back."

Terry breathed out in relief. "Thank God for that," he said.

Stevens shrugged and said: "But that is of course because she thinks the war will be over before those convoys reach you and will have to turn back anyway."

"She's a real sweetheart, isn't she?"

Stevens said: "There's a reason I called, Earl."

"It wasn't because you were missing me?" Terry asked with a smile.

"Not only," Stevens replied. He paused and then said: "Look, I don't wanna tell you what to do—"

"So don't," Terry broke in.

There came a moment's silence as the two old friends stared at each other, and Terry felt that he and Suds held an entire conversation in that space of quietness. They required no secret code to converse when the subject of their concerns was so absolute.

Finally, Terry said: "I appreciate it, Suds, I really do. I'm glad we understand each other."

"You're not through yet, Earl. Good luck."

Terry nodded in acknowledgment of his American friend's sensitivity. Stevens' face vanished.

The British Army's super artificial intelligence, Squonk, spoke: "Updated reports from the SHF listening stations indicate that the enemy is building up ACA forces in and around Normandy. Shall I prepare your vehicle to take you to Whitehall?"

"Yes," Terry answered. "I will leave in fifteen minutes."

"Confirmed."

Terry sipped his brandy. He walked to the panoramic window and looked out at the English Channel. Under the deep blue sky, puffs of white spray lifted from the cresting waves to be blown to invisibility by the wind. But the Channel would not—could not—save England as it had for centuries. Not now, in 2062. Technology had at the last advanced too far: flight propulsion systems and super artificial intelligence combined to render the choppy, often bleak, stretch of water no more insurmountable than a river or even a puddle.

Terry's spirit recoiled in a manner he expected that a rat trapped in maze might recognise. For five months he had been obliged to orchestrate a rear-guard action which, despite the cleverness of the computers, had seen hundreds of thousands killed. NATO had lost more troops from all of its member nations than at any time in its one-hundred-and-fifteen-year history. And now England lay finally at the enemy's mercy, waiting only for the executioner's axe to fall.

He drained the final drops of whiskey from the snifter and cleared his throat. If the battle for Europe were truly over, he had little to fear from whatever the enemy could bring to bear on the NATO forces that remained. Field Marshal Sir Terry Tidbury strode from his smoking room with a renewed determination to find a way to delay the inevitable.

THE END

Coming from Chris James in 2021

The Repulse Chronicles
Book Four

The Endgame

For the latest news and releases, follow Chris James on
Amazon

In the US, at:
https://www.amazon.com/Chris-James/e/B005ATW34C/

In the UK, at:
https://www.amazon.co.uk/Chris-James/e/B005ATW34C/

You can also follow his blog, at:
https://chrisjamesauthor.wordpress.com/

Printed in Great Britain
by Amazon

85429478R00212